A TREE, MISTLETOE & A SUNSET

A SMALL TOWN HOLIDAY MYSTERY ROMANCE

HOPE & HEARTS FROM SWAN HARBOR
BOOK 5

SOPHIE BARTOW

CONTENTS

My street team;
The Wall-Giennie Wicks-Delaney,
Connector Inspector- Linda Hagerty
Reactor Inspector- Jami Fenton
Plot Catcher- Barbara Berry
Sign Crew- Kate Semenyuk

*The Clean-up crew: Cindy, Laura, Kim, Maggie, and Sylvia, whose feedback
was valuable.*
And my family, who are still waiting for me to clean the house.

**Inspiration began
when a lost girl fell for a lost boy**

Two Hearts Press
An imprint of LLIPSS, INC.
Copyright © 2020 by *Sophie Bartow*

This book was updated and completed editing in August 2025.
Cover Design by Kate Semenyuk

Without hope there would be no happy endings.

FROM DARKNESS INTO LOVE

KITTENS, PUPPIES & LOVE

BROTHERS, HOPE & HEARTS

KISSES, FAMILY & HOPE

A TREE, MISTLETOE & A SUNSET

HOPE, HEARTS & FOREVER

THE MEMORY OF LOVE

THE INNOCENCE OF LOVE

THE FORGIVENESS OF LOVE

THE POWER OF LOVE

THE CHRISTMAS LOVE SONG

THE KISS OF LOVE

THE LESSONS OF LOVE

THE HEART OF LOVE

THE JOURNEY TO LOVE

Bonus Hope & Hearts

CYGNETS & DREAMS

Hope & Hearts Historical Novellas

GUIDED BY LIGHT - 1952

GUIDED BY HEART - 1964

GUIDED BY LOVE - 1969

WELCOME TO SWAN HARBOR- 1979

FINDING HER LOST HEART- 1983/1990

GUIDED BY A KISS - 1995

SOME RESIDENTS OF SWAN HARBOR

Harper Taylor: She is a professor at Swan Harbor University in the Education Department. Her parents are **Beverly** and **Greg Taylor,** and sibling to **Rod** and **MacKenzie**.

Aiden Jones: He is an English professor at Swan Harbor University and the cousin of **Killian** and **Liam**.

Quinn Jones: He is an investigative journalist who travels the globe chasing stories that catch his fancy. He is the brother of Aiden and the cousin of **Killian** and **Liam**. His story is told in **The Forgiveness of Love.**

Sarah Jones: Sarah is in town for the holidays and interested in Swan Harbor's history, especially the ruby heart. She is the sister of **Aiden** and **Quinn**. Her story will be told in **The Heart of Love.**

Rachel Adams: She teaches music classes at Siren's Song and is Tyler's singing partner. She is best friends with **Harper** and **Eden** and the mother to ten-month-old **Riley.** Her story is told in **The Christmas Love Song.**

Eden Fowler: She is a second-grade teacher at Swan Harbor Elementary. She's best friends with **Harper** and **Rachel.**

Killian Reade: Investigator for the Swan Harbor Sheriff's Department. Brother to **Liam Reade** and son of **Finley Reade**. Engaged to **Emma Foster**. Their story is told in **Kittens, Puppies & Love.**

Emma Foster: The Veterinarian and owner of Swan Harbor Veterinary

Hospital. Daughter of **Ava King** and **Peter Foster** and engaged to **Killian Reade**.

Liam Reade: Firefighter/Paramedic in Swan Harbor. Is the Chief Paramedic for the Swan Harbor Fire Department. He's married to **Elsa Winters**. Their story is told in **<u>Brothers, Hope & Hearts.</u>**

Elsa Winters: She has a private pediatric practice in Swan Harbor and is married to **Liam Reade.**

Finley Reade: Owns a real estate business in New York City. Father of **Liam** and **Killian**. He is married to **Ava King.** Their story is told in **<u>Kisses Family & Hope.</u>**

Ava King: Philanthropist and businesswoman for King Industries. Mother of **Emma Foster**. Married to **Finley Reade.**

Beverly Taylor: She is an Economics professor at Swan Harbor University, married to **Greg,** and mother to **Harper**, **Rod**, and **MacKenzie.**

Greg Taylor: He is the Captain of the Swan Harbor Police, married to **Beverly,** and father to **Harper**, **Rod**, and **MacKenzie.**

Rod Taylor: He is an E.M.T. for the Swan Harbor Fire Department.

Laura Hall: She is the director of Harbor Cross Nursing Home, married to **Joshua,** and mother to **Devin**, **Jenna, Leah,** and **Zoey.**

Joshua Hall: He is a History professor at Swan Harbor University, married to Laura, and father to **Devin**, **Jenna, Leah,** and **Zoey.**

Terri Patterson: She is the matriarch of Swan Harbor, mother to Danny, Beverly, Laura, Troy, and Rhonda, and grandmother to many. Terri is also a mother figure to **Captain Jack.** Her story is told in **<u>Guided by Light.</u>**

Rusty Langley: He is an investigator for the Swan Harbor Sheriff's Department and partner to **Killian Reade.** He is married to **Rene Langley** and father to **Roland.** Their story is told in **<u>The Power of Love.</u>**

Rene Langley: She is the mayor of Swan Harbor, married to **Rusty,** and mother to **Roland.**

Dylan Prince: The Sheriff of Swan Harbor, married to **Molly Barnes Prince.** He is the brother of Jessie and the late James and son of the late Ruth and Robert. Their story is told in **<u>The Innocence of Love.</u>**

Molly Barnes Prince: She teaches first grade at Swan Harbor Elementary School and is married to **Dylan Prince.**

Rupert Duncan: He is best friends with **Jimmie**, married to **Lois**, father to **Lanie,** father-in-law to **Wyatt,** and grandfather to **Roman** and **Lucy.** He is also an ex-agent for The Agency and occasionally helps the Sheriff's Department. Their story is told in **<u>Guided by Love, set in 1969.</u>**

Jimmie Tanner: He is best friends with **Rupert,** married to **Madge,** father to **Wyatt**, father-in-law to **Lanie,** and grandfather to **Roman** and **Lucy.** He is also an ex-agent for The Agency and periodically helps the Sheriff's Department. Their story is told in **<u>Guided by Heart, set in 1964.</u>**

Captain Jack: Retired Naval officer and local legend of Swan Harbor who gives out sage advice to the town's locals. Owner of Captain Jack's Fine Dining, located at the newly renovated pier in an old Spanish galleon. His story is told in **The Journey to Love**.

Christy Hopkins – She is the theater teacher at Swan Harbor High School, married to **Jason**, mother to **Amanda,** and grandmother to **Ethan**. Christy is best friends with Desiree, Donna, and Marisa.

Welcome to Swan Harbor

A Haven of Hope for Lost Hearts.

ONE

QUICK NOTE: *If you enjoy A Tree, Mistletoe & A Sunset, be sure to check out my offer for more Aiden and Harper at the end.*
With that, enjoy!

Swan Harbor Town Square
December 1
9:00 p.m.

"That's my bra!"

It took effort, but Harper Taylor pulled her attention from the giant Christmas tree to her grandmother.

"What did you say?"

"That bra is mine." Terri Patterson pointed to the bright red bra, size 40DD, hanging from one of the branches.

"Grandma," Harper tried again. "There are several bras up there. How can you be so sure?"

Her grandmother gave her a disgruntled look. "I may be 90, but I'm not senile. I need to talk to the sheriff!"

Harper exchanged looks with her best friends, Rachel, and Eden.

"I never said you were senile, just ..." Except it was too late. Her grandmother had taken off, apparently in search of the sheriff. "Now what?"

Rachel giggled. "You either help her get her bra back or—"

"—Stay here and wait for her to return," Eden sighed.

Harper shook her head in annoyance. "How did this happen?"

"The answer depends on the question," Rachel laughed. "Are you asking how your grandmother's bra ended up on the town's Christmas tree? Or are you asking how bras in general ended up on it?"

"Does it matter?" Harper asked. "And we were having so much fun, too."

"I'm still having fun," Eden assured her. "This is our first tree lighting in ages."

Harper immediately felt bad because her friend was right.

"I'm sorry, Eden. I should look on the bright side instead of being such a downer."

"Come on, Harper." Eden linked their arms as they started walking. "You're not being a downer. Things happen, and that's okay. You look at what happened, and if it was your fault, step back and try again. That's life."

Harper exchanged looks with Rachel before stopping to give her attention to Eden.

"That's very pragmatic of you, but you lost me."

Eden sighed. "No, *I'm* sorry. I just ..."

"Saw Cameron and his wife Jessie," Harper guessed, knowing her friend was still embarrassed about her past behavior with Cameron Hunter.

"Yes." Eden blew out a breath. "It's just ..."

"Some things are harder to push aside than others," Harper suggested, knowing she'd brought the conversation back to herself.

"Aren't we a fun group?" Rachel offered. "I fell for Austin, who left me pregnant before running off to join the Army. Eden fell for a man who wasn't available."

"And I fell for Joel," Harper continued the pity party. "Who was sleeping with my roommate."

"Do you think we need therapy?" Eden's laugh sounded strained.

Harper looked back at the Christmas tree. The seventy-five-foot Balsam fir stood proudly in the center of the town square, decorated with lights and large, colorful balls. Except, when the mayor had yelled, 'Flip the switch,' the citizens had gotten an eyeful.

"You must admit." She pressed her lips closed to keep from laughing. "Whoever did the 'decorating' was quite creative."

"Because they hung bras on the tree?" a confused Rachel asked.

"No," Harper exclaimed. "Because of the colors. How many drawers did they have to go through to find bras that matched the balls already hanging?"

Eden glanced at the tree before turning back, and her lips twitched. "There are no drawers up there."

It took Harper an extra minute before Eden's joke clicked, and all three women began laughing.

"That was bad, Eden," Harper chuckled.

"What's so funny?"

Harper's gaze bounced over a fellow professor before landing on the one who'd spoken.

"Nothing important."

"Are you sure?" Logan Clark's sexy smirk was firmly in place. "That was some laughter for it to be nothing."

She had to fight to keep the annoyance off her face, and her gaze went to her friends before landing on Aiden Jones. *Help*! But since he was so quiet, she assumed her silent plea had fallen on deaf ears.

"I—"

"Leave her alone, Logan," Aiden responded, almost as if he'd understood her silent plea. "Have a good evening, Doctor Taylor." Then he pushed his friend up the path.

"Who was that?" Eden whispered.

"Which one?" Harper watched the men as they disappeared into the crowd.

"Both."

"They work at Swan Harbor University with me," Harper explained. "And I'm afraid Logan, the blond, is my secret match."

Rachel frowned. "What makes you say that?"

"My latest message." Harper took out her phone and opened the app. "See."

Dear Rosalind,

Thank you for your message. I won't say I'm the man you're looking for because I want you to listen to your heart. And perhaps on New Year's Eve, you can let me know.

When asked what kind of woman I'm attracted to, I've been hard-pressed to put it into words. Every woman has their own 'something' special. But I can share what I admire with you.

I admire a woman who is comfortable in her own skin. One who is loyal, not only to her family, but also to her friends. One who is alright with silence and is just as interested in what I have to say as she wants me to be in what she says.

I hope to hear from you soon.

Your Secret Match,

Clark

"Sounds romantic," Eden sighed. "But why do you think it's from Logan—?"

"—And not the dreamy dark-headed one with the accent?" Rachel finished.

Harper pointed to the name. "Hello, Clark … as in Logan Clark. How unoriginal can you get?"

"But he's gorgeous, Harper. What's not to like?"

Harper once again glanced in the direction the men had gone and tried to put her thoughts into words.

"You're right. He's nice to look at, but he knows it. Mostly, though, he reminds me too much of Joel."

"That would do it," Eden hummed.

"What about Aiden?" Rachel asked. "He's easy on the eyes and seems very sweet. In fact, I just found out he lives in my apartment complex."

"He's quite awkward and unsure of himself," Harper offered, thinking of his behavior the few times she'd been around him. "He makes me feel … like I need to fill the empty spaces."

"But he says those few words in an oo la la voice," Rachel murmured. "And he makes you *feel*. That's no small feat after what Joel put you through."

"Maybe." Harper shrugged. "But there are my matches. While I have no interest in Logan, there was something ... sweet about Orlando and Rhett."

"Wouldn't it be romantic if—?" Rachel began.

"Harper, come with me," Terri interrupted. "I think one of your bras was on the tree too. They need you to identify it!"

Harper sent a panicked look to her friends. "Could this night get any worse?"

Swan Harbor Town Square
December 1
10:00 p.m.

"You want me to do what?" Aiden gave his cousin, Killian, an annoyed look.

"Man the box," Killian, who was a detective with the sheriff's department, repeated.

"And why does this box need to be '*manned*' again?" huffed Aiden.

"Because we want to find out who appropriated these." Killian fingered one of the bra straps hanging over the edge of the box. "And I can't do it all."

The innocent look on his cousin's face had Aiden taking a step back.

"And there's no one else to take on this task?"

"Come on, Aiden," Killian prodded. "It's no big deal. You act like you've never handled ladies and their lingerie before. All you need to do is write their name and phone number with the item they claim on a piece of paper. We'll do the rest."

Aiden humphed. "All I have to do is take names and numbers?"

"Don't forget the item's information." Killian picked up a bra and separated the tag. "For this one, you would write the owner's name and number, pink bra, size 34C."

"Well, alright."

"Thanks." Killian tossed the bra back into the box and turned to go. "You know, it might be easier if you separated them all. That way, the women can just look for their size."

Aiden watched Killian leave and wondered where he'd gone wrong. His brother, Quinn, was off chasing some new story. Sarah, his sister, was back in Cornwall, researching their pirate relative. Whereas he was, "Complaining," he muttered, pulling out a handful of bras to sort.

It took several tries before Aiden developed a system that seemed to work. He'd just started sorting the last handful when a new pile of bras landed on the table.

"Bloody hell, Liam." Aiden met the laughing eyes of his cousin. "What are you doing?"

Liam gave him a look that said, *Are you daft*?

"I'm bringing you more of the colorful clothing."

"Then ask where to put them," Aiden grumbled. "I'm trying to sort."

"Excuse me." Liam moved his pile into the box. "I didn't mean to interfere with your system."

"Good," Aiden grunted. "Your bloody brother asked me to help, so here I am."

"Liam!" A petite, gray-headed woman rushed into the tent. "Killian sent me to claim my brassiere."

"Lois, meet my cousin, Aiden Jones. Killian put him in charge of sorting everything."

"Cousin, you say?" Lois turned her dark eyes in Aiden's direction. "I know you."

Aiden exchanged confused looks with Liam. "No, Madam, I don't believe we've met before."

"I'm sorry." She laughed. "I meant ... I know *about* you."

"You do?"

"Oh, yes," she exclaimed. "Been in Swan Harbor since August. Teach in the English department at Swan Harbor U. Live in the Camelot Arms Apartments, and you're currently not dating anyone." Then she turned a smile on him as if to say, '*How did I do?*'

"Bloody hell."

Liam snickered. "Swan Harbor gossip line, right, Lois?"

"That's right," she confirmed. "So what do I need to do?"

"Aiden will explain everything. I'll see you later."

Lois looked at Aiden expectantly, and for a second, he wished he had a bit of his cousin's confidence.

"You're here to reclaim your missing garment?"

"Oh, yes," she giggled. "Rupert, he's my husband of fifty years, said he saw my pretty green bra hanging up there on that tree and well ..."

"Just put your name and phone number right here." He handed her a pen. "Then choose which of these green ones is yours."

While she was writing her name, he continued sorting the new bras, surprised by the variety of colors.

"There are quite a few green ones," Lois murmured. "How do I know which one is mine?"

He wanted to ask how it was possible she didn't recognize her own unmentionable. But when another woman arrived, he left Lois looking at the green ones and went to help the newcomer.

"Write your name here," Aiden repeated. "Then we'll find your garment."

"Thank you, son." She wrote her name with a flourish. "And now?"

"You find—" he began, only to be interrupted when she reached for the same green bra Lois was holding.

"That's mine!" she shrieked.

Lois's startled eyes met Aiden's before she turned her ire back on the woman who was trying to tug the bra from her hands. "Stop it, Madge. It's not yours. It's mine."

Aiden glanced around for someone to help, but with only him and the two older women in the room, he was out of luck.

"Ladies," he exclaimed. "Please, let's talk about this."

"What's to talk about?" Lois cried. "It took me forever to find my bra, and she's trying to steal it."

"Me!" Madge screamed. "That's my brand-new Christmas bra from Jimmie. He bought it for me from *Rebecca's Fantasy*."

The questions, *Where's Jimmie?* and *What's Rebecca's Fantasy?* flashed through his mind. He didn't need either answer to solve the current predicament, so he searched for a match to the bra.

"Rupert bought this for me," Lois shouted. "I've worn it several times."

"Then I bet it's old and faded," Madge snickered, pulling the straps taut. "You can tell this one hasn't been worn."

"Baloney," Lois retorted. "It's mine. Let it go."

Aiden stepped around the table. "Ladies, please. Let's discuss this calmly."

"There's nothing to talk about," Madge cried.

"Let it go, Madge," Lois demanded.

"Fine!"

There was something in her voice that should have acted as a warning, but Aiden was too far gone. Madge let go, and the strap kicked back, hitting him in the face. "Bloody hell," he exclaimed.

"Now, look at what you've done," Lois shouted.

"Me?"

Aiden worked his jaw up and down several times, the place where the strap had snapped still stinging.

"What's all the ruckus?" another voice entered the tent.

Aiden turned to tell the newcomer he had everything under control, and his gaze met the brown eyes of his colleague. Heat climbed, and he wished ....

Bloody hell!

"Are you okay, young man?" the older woman asked.

"I'm ..." He shook his head and attempted to push away the embarrassment. "I'm fine. There seems to be a bit of a misunderstanding."

She humphed. "There's always a misunderstanding between these two. Let me see if I can be of some help."

"Thank you." Aiden slipped back around the table.

"It's not a problem." Her smile grew. "I'm Terri Patterson, and this is my granddaughter, Harper." She nudged the younger woman closer to the table. "My *single* granddaughter, Harper. Maybe you can help her find her bra."

Harper winced, her grandmother's introduction making her wish there were a hole to crawl into.

"Grandma!" She gave an exasperated sigh. "I've got this."

Are you sure about that?

Their gazes met briefly before Aiden's flitted away, obviously just as embarrassed as she.

"I'm uh, I'm sorry about that."

He dismissed it with a casual wave of his hand. But then, instead of moving on, he rubbed his fingers over the red welt slashed across his cheekbone.

"Are you really okay?" Harper asked.

"It's nothing."

Harper took a deep breath and glanced at the assortment of bras spread out in front of her. Cotton and satin, old and new, plain and flowered.

"How did this happen?" she muttered the same rhetorical question as earlier.

"I'm sure I don't know," Aiden responded. "But why don't you ...?"

Her gaze bounced to his, curious if he was serious. He glanced up, and behind his tortoiseshell lenses, there was a twinkle in his eyes. It had her breath catching, and her heart ticking up a few beats.

"What do I do?"

"Which, uhm, which ..." He cleared his throat and tried again. "Which garment is yours?"

Harper glanced at the rows of bras on the table and picked up a royal-blue satin bra. "Here it is. Now I know why I couldn't find it when I put on the matching panties today."

Aiden's gulp was her first sign she'd vocalized that last comment. "Oh, gosh," she clamped her hand over her mouth, "I'm sorry."

"It's quite alright," Aiden assured her. "I'm happy you once again have a matching set."

His quip was so unlike him, Harper was taken aback for a second. Since he refused to look at her, she grabbed the paper and jotted her name. Then she stuffed the bra into her pocket.

"Grandma, did you find what you were looking for?"

"Don't be so impatient." Terri plucked a green bra off the table. I'm solving a problem. "Now, Madge." She held out the green item to the redhead who'd been fighting with Lois. "This has to be yours. Your cup would runneth over if you tried to wear that other one."

Harper thought she heard Aiden groan and noted his face had turned even redder. Before she could comment, Madge took the green bra from her grandmother.

"Seems you're right, Terri." She quickly filled out the piece of paper. "I'll see you all later."

"That woman," Terri tsked. "Sometimes she doesn't use the brains the good Lord gave her. There's no way she didn't know her ta-tas wouldn't fit in that little thing Lois was holding."

Harper looked around for a hole to sink into, and her eyes accidentally met Aiden's. *I'm sorry* she tried to telegraph.

He gave her a look that seemed to say *I understand.*

Had they just exchanged silent communication?

"What did you say your name was again?" Terri pinned her steely, dark-eyed gaze on Aiden.

"Aiden Jones, Mrs. Patterson," he replied. "It's a pleasure to make your acquaintance.

"That's right," Terri went on. "We met at Ava and Finn's the other day, didn't we?"

"Yes, ma'am."

"Such manners." Her grin had Harper preparing for an embarrassing comment. "The Christmas Gala is coming up soon. If you need a date—"

"Grandma!" Harper exclaimed. "Just stop!"

"What?" Terri gave Harper a look that said *I'm old and can say what I want.*

Aiden cleared his throat. "Uhh, I'll remember that."

Almost against her better judgment, Harper once again looked up. Their eyes met, and he winked, causing all the spit in her mouth to dry.

"Aiden." Suddenly, several more people filled the tent at once.

"Come on, grandma." Harper cupped Terri's elbow. "Let's go."

"Okay, dear."

They'd just about reached the exit when she heard. "Have a pleasant night, Doctor Taylor."

Harper tossed a grin over her shoulder, all the while trying to figure out why his wink had affected her so. After all, it was just a simple eye reflex. Right?

The look on Aiden's face had Liam glancing toward the door.

"Did you see that?"

"Did I see what?" Killian mumbled, his attention on his notebook.

"The way Aiden was looking at Harper."

"Bloody hell, Liam," Killian grumbled. "Don't tell me you're at it again.

"What?"

Killian raised his brows. "You know what! Aiden's a nice guy. Leave him alone."

"I know he's nice," Liam agreed. "But he needs some help getting ... put together."

"You don't like the tweed, plaid, and glasses?"

"I don't mind the tweed, plaid, and glasses," Liam retorted. "But ... he always makes me feel he just grabbed from a laundry basket."

"Don't tell me you don't do the same," Killian argued. "In fact .... Bloody hell ..."

Liam glanced toward the door to see what the exclamation was about. He was just in time to see Morgan Ross sashay into their makeshift headquarters.

"Hi boys," she chirped in a low and seductive voice. "I'm here to reclaim my bra."

"Morgan," Liam greeted her. "Aiden can help you."

"Yes, he can." She sauntered toward the table, and something about her movements reminded Liam of a barracuda.

"Doctor Ross." Aiden's face was redder than before. "Do you, uhh, do you see your garment?"

Morgan leaned over and skimmed her fingers lightly over the items. "Here it is." She held up a shimmery gold bra.

"Good, good." Aiden pushed the paper forward. "Just put the description right here."

"Description?"

"The, the color and size," Aiden explained.

Her smile turned predatory. "Okay. Will gold, 36D work?"

"That's fine."

Liam took pity on his cousin and stepped closer. "Is that all, Morgan?"

Morgan's blue eyes flashed. "For now." She turned her attention back to Aiden. "I'll see *you* at work."

"Right," Aiden murmured. "Have a good evening, Doctor Ross."

"Is she always like that around you?" Liam asked Aiden as soon as she'd left.

"Like what?" Aiden frowned.

"Flirty, giving you the come-hither eyes, showing off her assets." Liam listed a few of her behaviors.

Aiden shrugged. "I guess."

"Boy, cuz," Liam replied. "We really do have work to do."

"We do." Aiden pulled out his phone. "I heard from Rosalind. What should I say?"

Liam looked over Aiden's shoulder at the message from his secret match.

> Dear Clark,

> In all the years Swan Harbor has been holding the Christmas tree lighting ceremony, I've never seen such a sight. Imagine the thought processes that had to go through someone's mind to plan and implement such a feat. I heard last year that someone decorated the snowman family in front of Sally's. But this year, someone went above and beyond. What about you? Did anything stand out to you tonight?

> Your Secret Match,

> Rosalind

"What should I say?" Aiden asked.

"She's digging." Liam read through a couple of lines again. "Plus, she's telling you a few things about her."

Aiden took the phone back and reread the message. "What's she telling me?"

"That she looked beyond the fact the tree lighting had numerous undergarments on it," Liam patiently explained. "And she's impressed by the ingenuity behind the act."

"I guess," Aiden muttered. "But what should I say?"

"Just answer her question," Liam encouraged. "She gave you a simple one."

"Answer her question, you say?" Aiden murmured. "Alright, how's this?"

> Dear Rosalind ....

TWO

Swan Harbor University
December 2
9:00 a.m.

AFTER A RESTLESS NIGHT, HARPER ARRIVED EARLY AT HER OFFICE and began grading exams. Her subconscious, though, had other ideas. It was busy breaking down her latest '*secret match*' message. The words written by her '*Clark*' wouldn't connect with the man she knew as Logan Clark.

> Dear Rosalind,
>
> Thank you for your message. What stands out in
> my memory from last night is the look on the
> children's faces as they gazed at the tall tree.
> There was something about that scene that
> reminded me of holidays long ago.

He noticed the families. That hadn't been what she'd expected. And later in his message,

> Perhaps, like last year, there will be no more
> incidents. But I must say the coordination to pull
> off such an event makes me quite envious.

That someone had taken so many bras without being noticed impressed her as well. Not only had they taken them, but hung them on the tree in a very specific manner. Something that would have taken stealth. It was also a detail that didn't fit her image of Logan.

By the time she'd finished grading, Harper had mentally reworked the words multiple times. They still didn't connect, though. Which had her feeling as if she'd put together a jigsaw puzzle that had extra pieces. Almost as if she were being led to a new puzzle and being fed the parts a little at a time.

Her thought processes died when Logan sauntered into her office, his patented smirk firmly in place.

"Good morning, Doctor Taylor. You're looking quite lovely today."

Harper glanced down at the outfit she'd tugged from her closet while half asleep. A gray skirt, a pink sweater, and knee-high black boots. She'd pulled her brown hair into a low bun, and because she hadn't slept well, put on her glasses. Lovely wasn't an adjective that fit … cute, maybe.

"Thank you," she replied with a tight smile.

"Did you have a good time last night?" He planted himself in a chair in front of her desk.

"It was," she hesitated, "typical Swan Harbor. What about you?"

Logan laughed. "I thought the mayor was going to faint when she flipped the switch, and those bras were on display for everyone to see. Just glad it wasn't jocks. The tree wouldn't have been so colorful."

And there it was, she thought. The answers she'd expected from him.

"Makes you wonder if the thieves are males," she quipped.

He reared back in surprise. "Why would you say that?"

Harper shrugged, hoping he'd take the hint and leave. "Just makes sense." Her attention wavered just enough for her focus to move to the study guides she'd picked up earlier. "Oh no, these aren't mine."

Logan uncrossed his legs and sat forward.

"What are you talking about?"

"I need to go." Harper hurriedly stacked the tests she'd graded and grabbed the box. "They gave me the wrong study guides."

"But," Logan sputtered, obviously not used to being thrown out of someone's office. "I wanted to ask …"

"I'll see you later." She rushed from the office, pulled the door shut, and ran down the stairs to the copy center.

"Hi Harper," Jami greeted her when she entered. "I didn't expect you back so quickly."

"I picked up the wrong study guides." Harper pushed the box across the counter. "This is *Intro to Diversity*. I need *Intro to Teaching*. And I have a meeting that starts in fifteen minutes."

"Let me get the right one for you." Jami took the box, and in what seemed like no time, located the right one. "Here you go. The copies of your exams are in there too."

"Thanks, Jami. You're a lifesaver." Harper grabbed the box, and on her way out, crashed into the person entering. "Watch it!" she cried as the box fell from her arms.

"Bloody hell!"

The curse uttered with a smooth British accent slithered up her spine, and she had to admit there was merit to Rachel's comment. Up close and personal, ooh la la definitely described his voice. An attribute she hadn't considered every other time she'd spoken to him.

"Uh, sorry, Doctor Taylor." Aiden haphazardly shoved the papers back into the box. "I shouldn't have just barreled through the door like that."

"It wasn't your fault," Harper insisted. "I wasn't paying attention, and well ..."

He looked up from where he was still shoving her papers back into the box, and she had the strangest desire to straighten his crooked glasses. *I'm sorry*, she read in his eyes.

"It wasn't your fault," she reiterated.

Aiden ducked his head and stood holding her box. "Are you really alright?"

"I'm fine," she told him breathlessly. "You?"

"Fine." He bobbed his head twice and finally pushed his glasses back into place.

He was back to his awkward self, and Harper couldn't help but wonder where the man who'd winked at her last night had gone. The man in front of her reminded her of ... just who exactly, though, eluded her.

"Glad you're okay." She started out the door. "I'm off to a meeting."

But as she slid into a chair in the back of the auditorium, her encounter with Aiden was still on her mind. There'd been something different, almost as if ....

"Isn't this exciting?" a woman on her right asked, scattering her thoughts. "Are you enjoying your matches?"

"I have," Harper responded quietly, unsure if she wanted to say more.

"You know," the woman went on. "I really liked my first match, but there's something about this one ..."

Harper thought back on her three matches. Could she separate Orlando, Rhett, and Clark in her head? Orlando and Rhett's messages had been short but sweet, as if they were shy. Clark's messages just confused her. But she didn't know if it was because of what he said or because she was trying to push the words into the wrong person's mouth.

"Is this seat taken?" Aiden whispered.

"Aiden! Doctor Jones," Harper immediately corrected. "No, uhh, no, go ahead."

He slipped into the chair with a sigh, and she couldn't help but note he was more disheveled than usual. Something she hadn't noticed earlier. His wavy hair was sticking up at odd angles, his dark beard heavier, and there was a wet spot on his tie as if he'd spilled something and tried to wash it off. Was he having one of those days too?

Aiden took a deep breath, and the light floral scent of Harper's perfume settled around him. He'd been experiencing one of those days. His toe still ached from where the box holding her exams had landed on it. The mark on his cheek had prevented him from shaving. And he'd had to wash jelly off his tie. Suddenly, those things didn't seem to matter, though.

"Good morning," Beau Johnson, a computer science professor, greeted them. "Thank you for coming. Let me go over the guidelines for this research project once again."

The project was a joint venture by the computer science, psychology, and sociology departments. They were researching the formation of emotional connections. Participants answered survey questions, chose an alias, and then a computer program matched them with a partner. Once their correspondence with one partner was complete, a second survey was done. They were currently on the third and final pairing.

"I can't believe I need to say this," Beau went on. "But please don't share your '*match name*' or the '*name*' of your match. If you know personally with whom you're corresponding, it invalidates your data."

"Bloody idiots," Aiden murmured.

A snicker from his right had him glancing in that direction. When his eyes met Harper's, there was a teasing glint in hers that had him catching his breath.

I agree, they seemed to say.

His heart raced as the thought of what just happened filtered through his mind. He'd seen silent communication in action before. In fact, recently between his newfound family members and their significant others. It was something he'd even achieved a time or two between him and his siblings. But that silent communication was possible between him and someone of a different sex ... had never occurred to him. Suddenly, though, it had happened several times ... and with the same person.

"Unfortunately," Beau was saying when Aiden tuned back in. "There was a glitch in the processing program during the last match. I'm going to let Hayden Patterson, the student in charge, explain."

Aiden glanced at Harper, as the young man who was speaking shared a last name with her grandmother.

"My cousin," she whispered as if she'd heard his unspoken question.

"As Professor Johnson mentioned," Hayden began. "There was a glitch in the program. Instead of using the '*character name*' some matches used real names. We're going to give you options. You can continue as you are without knowing. Or you can find out if it happened and get a new match."

Since Aiden didn't feel the need to find out, he decided to leave, jostling Harper just as she was standing. Her laughing eyes met his.

"Two times in one day, Doctor Jones. That must be a record."

His tongue stuck to the roof of his mouth, and once again, he wished for some of Liam's self-confidence.

"I'm, I'm sorry, Har ... Doctor Taylor. I'm such a klutz."

Her tinkling laughter whispered across his skin, stealing the embarrassment he'd typically feel.

"It was an accident. If you'll excuse me." She waved goodbye and headed toward the front of the room.

Aiden watched Harper walk forward, greeting those she knew along the way. Not for the first time, he wished for some of that comfort around strangers. If so, he would be much more prepared to handle certain situations. Like this one, he couldn't help but think when the overpowering scent of perfume surrounded him, and it was too late to run.

"Doctor Jones." Morgan Ross plastered her well-endowed body against his side. "Were all the bras claimed?"

His thoughts scattered as he worked to come up with a way to put some distance between them.

"There were a few left behind," he said, dropping the calendar he was holding. "Uhh, sorry. I've been a bit out of sorts today."

She gave him an indulgent smile. "Anything I can do?"

"No, no." Aiden cleared his throat and dug inside, to pull out the manners his mum had established. "I'll be fine as soon as I get a cup of coffee."

"Oh?" Morgan's brows arched playfully. "I can help with that."

"I'll be fine." Aiden tipped his chin toward the door. "Now, if you'll excuse me?"

Morgan gave him a toothy smile, reminding him a little of Curley's predatory wife in *Of Mice and Men*. "What's your hurry, Aiden?"

"Class," he lied. "I need to prepare."

"Now, Aiden," Morgan practically purred. "I've heard you're always prepared for class. Besides ..."

She let that hang in the air for several heartbeats, and Aiden found himself searching for help.

"I was thinking," Morgan went on. "Since you're new in town and all ..."

Aiden spotted Harper heading back toward him and sent her a silent plea. But she was staring at her phone, making him think, more than likely, it flew over her head.

"... That I'd allow you to take me to the Christmas Gala," Morgan finally got to the point.

"The Christmas Gala?"

"Yes," Morgan gushed. "It's *the* event of the season. The place to see and be seen."

"I thought that was Sally's," Aiden responded, knowing the diner was a hotbed of gossip.

"Oh, well." Morgan hesitated as if she weren't sure what to say next.

"Sally's is the place for everyday happenings, but for something special, it's the Christmas Gala."

Aiden hadn't even considered attending the Gala, as large events like that made him uncomfortable. Especially when he was the odd man out, as he'd told Liam when he'd mentioned it. And yet, last night, Mrs. Patterson had mentioned his asking Harper, and now Morgan was ....

"Doctor Ross—"

"Morgan," she interrupted.

He cleared his throat and tried again. "Morgan, while I—"

"I won't let you tell me no," she gushed. "I even bought this divine green satin dress that fits me like a second skin."

"Uhh, well." Aiden could feel the heat climbing up his neck and had to fight not to loosen his tie. "I'm sure you'll look very nice in your dress, but ..."

"Okay, I'm ready." Harper looped her arm through his, causing his breath to catch. "Are you?"

"Wait," Morgan exclaimed. "What's going on?"

Aiden side-eyed Harper, just as confused as Morgan, "We ..."

I've got this, Harper's eyes seemed to say.

"You were talking about the Gala, right?" Harper raised a brow in question.

"Well—" Aiden began.

"Not that it's any of your business," Morgan jumped in. "But yes. He was telling me what time he'd pick me up."

Aiden glanced at Harper, sending her a panicked message. *That's not true.*

I know, she smiled, and for a moment, he got lost in the warmth of her eyes.

"Aiden's taking me to the Gala," Harper continued. "Three might be a crowd."

Morgan turned her frosty blue eyes on him, and Aiden had to fight to meet her gaze head-on.

"Why didn't you say something?"

"I—"

"That's my fault, I'm afraid," Harper offered. "I just told him I'd go with him this morning, and well," she shrugged delicately as if it was a nonissue.

"I'm sorry, Morgan," Aiden apologized. "As I mentioned, it's been one of those days."

"Yes, well," Morgan sighed. "Save me a dance, will you?" Then, with a wink, she flounced off.

As they walked from the auditorium, Aiden thanked Harper for coming to his rescue. "But please don't feel obligated to ..."

"Harper, there you are."

Aiden looked around to see Logan Clark rushing in their direction. When he glanced back at Harper, she appeared just as ill at ease as she had the previous night.

"I'm right here," Harper retorted, but something in her voice had Aiden wanting to rescue her. "What did you need, Logan?"

Logan glanced at Aiden before effectively dismissing him, and once again, turned back to Harper.

"I wanted to ask you to the Gala."

I helped you, Aiden could have sworn he read in her eyes.

Something had him winking at her as if to say, *I'm here for you*.

"Harper was gracious enough to accept my invitation to the Gala," Aiden broke in, sounding more confident than he was feeling.

"You?" Logan laughed. "You didn't tell me you were dating her last night."

"I didn't? Well." Aiden searched for what to say. "I've admired Doctor Taylor for a while and—"

"—Our families set us up." Harper sent him a look that said, *play along*.

"Your families?" Logan mumbled.

"Yes," Aiden agreed, even though he had no clue where to take the story.

"My grandmother is friends with Ava, who is—"

"—My uncle's wife," Aiden completed the circle, as where Harper was going finally clicked.

"Oh," Logan murmured. "I see."

"I need to go," Harper broke in. "Class."

She walked away, and something about the territorial way Logan followed her movements set Aiden's teeth on edge.

"If you're looking for a date, I heard Morgan Ross was available."

"Morgan?" Logan sent him a '*What did you just say?*' look.

"Yes, Morgan," Aiden repeated, thinking she was more Logan's type. "See you later. I've got a meeting."

Sheriff's Department

December 2

2:00 p.m.

Killian glanced up from his notes when the Sheriff, Dylan Prince, entered his office and tossed two folders on his desk.

"Tell me again why the sheriff's department is handling this and not Chief Fowler and his men in blue."

Dylan winced. "Politics passed down through time."

"What the bloody hell does that mean?"

"It means we have a bigger budget," Dylan explained. "What's wrong, Killian? Don't think you're up to the task?"

"You know what you can do with that task." Killian flipped the folders around. "What are these?"

"Remember last year when Sally's underwear ended up on the snowman," Dylan began. "And I told you I thought it had happened before?"

"Aye."

"Amy's been searching the archives and ..."

"She found a connection," Killian replied, thinking it was lucky they had such an organized office clerk.

"Not exactly," Dylan hedged.

Killian studied his boss for several minutes before opening the first file to read.

On December 1st, 1980, multiple colorful bras were discovered on the Christmas tree in the town square. Officials removed the brassieres, and as they began questioning, they discovered....

"That's it?" Killian glanced at Dylan with a frown.

"Yeah." Dylan flipped the folder around and pointed to the date. "My grandfather, James Prince, was the sheriff then. Maybe Walt will have an idea, as he would have been new on the job."

Killian jotted a few notes to speak to the night dispatcher and reached for the second file.

"Is this any better?"

"Not much," Dylan admitted. "But the second time occurred after my dad became sheriff."

"Indoctrinating the new sheriff?" Killian tossed out.

"But who?"

"Fowler?" Killian offered, even though he couldn't give a specific reason.

"Makes no sense," Dylan argued. "He would have been new on the force in 1980."

"What does your gut say?"

Dylan shook his head. "I know you don't like Fowler, but I don't see his prints on this one."

"Why?"

"It's too blatant," Dylan shrugged.

"So, we're back to what I thought last year," Killian sighed. "It's kids."

"Maybe," Dylan hummed. "But the whole thing seems quite coordinated for it to be kids."

The second folder offered little information.

December 1, 2000
When the Christmas tree in the town square was lit up, there were multiple bras dangling from the branches. The bras ranged from size 34B to 44DD and included a variety of colors. Only 5 of the thirty garments on the tree are unclaimed.

"That's interesting."

"What?"

Killian sorted through the notes he'd made and reached for the box on the floor next to his desk. "There were over thirty garments hanging on the tree, and all but 5 were claimed."

Dylan whistled. "That is weird. Does it say any more regarding the old case?"

"Ernie Luka was the investigator in charge." Killian flipped through the rest of the file before turning it around and pointing at the pages. "Tell me your thoughts."

"I looked at it already," Dylan pushed back. "What are you asking specifically?"

"Check the page numbers."

Dylan glanced through the chart once and then repeated the process. "I'll be damned. Much of the chart is missing ..."

"And," Killian added. "If the bits and pieces in there are to be believed. There are more briefs to be dug into."

"That was bad," Dylan laughed.

"I work with what I have," Killian smirked. "Do you know Luka?"

"Luka lives at a retirement center. Check with Amy."

Killian heard Dylan greet his partner as Rusty entered their office.

"Check with Amy about what?"

"Luka's contact information," Killian told him. "He was the investigator during the last bra raid."

"Did he find out who the thief was?"

"That part of the file is missing." Killian looked through the pages once again. "In fact, most of the notes are missing."

Rusty frowned, then spread the notes in front of him. "Bras on the tree on December 1. Something on December 4 as it says - dozens were seen hanging ..."

"But what '*were hanging*' and where?"

"And on December 12," Rusty read on, "skivvies were flying ..."

"Skivvies were flying?" Killian repeated. "Flying off, flying on .... What the bloody hell does that mean?"

"No idea," Rusty murmured. "But then it says, 'December 26, the culprits were discovered when—' and that's it."

"December 1 happened just as it did in 1980 and in 2000. What's happening on December 4th? Anything?"

Rusty shrugged. "I don't know the dates, but the annual festivities include the gingerbread house making at Sally's, a cookie exchange at our home, and the Gala at the Lighthouse Inn."

Killian gave his partner a disgruntled look. "Which means all are fair game."

"Keeps us on our toes," grinned Rusty.

"As long as they stay away from my house," murmured Killian, adding Rusty's notes to his.

"Well, considering someone took thirty bras, hung them on the Christmas tree in the middle of town, and no one has caught them," sighed Rusty. "I think we have our work cut out for us."

"So, what you're saying is to slow down and not get ants in my pants," Killian quipped.

"That's right," Rusty snickered. "Best not to be caught with your pants down in this situation. We wouldn't want to let anything slip through our fingers."

THREE

Swan Harbor University
December 3
11:00 a.m.

Harper watched the clock tick down, reminding her students the test was almost over. Then, her forty students would put down their pens and look up. Many resigned, others elated, but most unsure. Once she posted the scores, students would inundate her office with questions about their grades. Final exams followed, and in January, everything started all over again. Such was the life of a professor, and she loved it.

"Time," she called. "Please turn your papers over and pass them to your left." Harper moved down the aisle collecting the tests, and as the pile grew heavy, wondered whose idea it was to give an essay exam so late in the semester.

Yours, you idiot.

"Remember," Harper said after she'd gathered all the papers. "Your final is next Wednesday at 11:00 a.m. If you have any questions, come by my office or send me an email. I'll see you then."

Some students waved, others smiled, and she wondered which ones would stick with education. But her job wasn't to worry about the students who dropped the major. Her job was to make sure those who stayed got what they paid for - or what their parents paid for, anyway. Except that sounded cynical, which wasn't like her at all. *Thanks, Joel.*

"Doctor Taylor." Mia Spruce, one of the quieter students in the class, approached. "This was attached to my exam. I'm not sure if it's important or not ..."

Harper spared the page a brief glance before giving her attention back to Mia.

"Thanks for this. How do you feel about the exam?"

Mia's face turned red, just as it did every time she was called on. That the student was uncomfortable had Harper wondering how she would handle student teaching.

"I, I think I did okay."

"That's good to hear. Any questions regarding the final?"

Mia shook her head. "I'm good. I'll see you later, Doctor Taylor."

Harper watched the younger girl for a few more minutes before turning back to the errant page. It was a test question for a literature class that were studying the play, *As You Like It*.

Where had it come from?

But then she remembered how she'd run into Aiden in the copy center—literally. While she'd stood there like an idiot, he'd shoved all the papers back into the box.

Rachel had been right in saying he made her feel. And while she certainly hadn't been looking for him ... or anyone, the way they could read each other's thoughts was something she'd hoped for her entire life.

Except, did he feel pressured to take her to the Gala? Had he saved her from needing to make excuses to Logan only because she'd saved him from Morgan? She'd heard his *Help me* plea clearly. But should she offer him an out? After all, as they were leaving the auditorium, he'd almost said *Don't feel obligated.*

Harper took the stairs to her office on the fourth floor and sat down to grade the exams. She made it through three of them before her attention wandered to the paper Mia had given her. Should she drop by his office and offer him an out?

Before she could second-guess her decision, she crammed the exams into her briefcase to deal with later. Aiden's office was on the second floor, and as she approached his door, her steps slowed.

Why was that? Was there a part of her that *wanted* to go to the Gala with him?

He makes me feel ... like I need to fill the empty spaces.

And then, a notification appeared on her match app, telling her she had a message from Clark.

First though, she had to talk to Aiden. Harper took a deep breath and started to knock. His phone rang before she actually did.

"Sarah," Aiden exclaimed, his voice sounding more animated than she'd ever heard. "I'm so glad you called me back. What took so long?"

Sarah?

"You what?"

Aiden chuckled, and the husky tenor of his voice had a ... dare she say ... a shiver racing up her spine.

"Are you going to make it for Christmas?"

At his question, Harper backed up slowly and, almost as if in a fog, looked around for the stairs.

Since he'd winked at her at the tree lighting, her thoughts and feelings had been all over the place. What was going on?

Captain Jack's Home
December 3
5:00 p.m.

"Aiden, my boy!" Captain Jack exclaimed when he opened his front door. "Come in, come in. It's quite blustery out there."

"I hope I'm not keeping you from anything," Aiden began. "But I spoke to Sarah—"

"—And she's learned some more about our Ian Jones," Captain Jack guessed.

"My sister's like a dog with a bone when she's on the hunt."

"Is that your way of saying she's stubborn?"

"Just a wee bit."

Jack led him into the back room, where a roaring fire and soft music greeted them.

"Would you like something to drink? Coffee, tea, or a hot toddy?"

"A spot of tea would be lovely."

While Jack was making their refreshments, Aiden took out his notebook and glanced through his notes.

Sarah had learned that their ancestor, the pirate Ian Jones, wasn't as well-known as Edward Teach or Bartholomew Roberts. However, he'd sailed the seas around the same time.

Since learning that Ian had landed—and loved—in Swan Harbor over three-hundred years ago, a spark had burst to life inside Aiden. It was guiding him in a new, but exciting way. One that he hadn't expected. Had it been there when he'd first learned about the ship? Or had it begun when they'd discovered Ian and Hope's journals? Or could it have been his conversation with Jack right after Thanksgiving?

Ava & Finn's Cottage
Saturday after Thanksgiving
1:30 p.m.

Jack crossed the room and stopped next to him. "I think Ian and Hope have a story that needs to be told."

"Think so?" Aiden glanced at the older man. "If you were writing it, where would you start?"

"Where every good romance begins," Jack hesitated, "with the first meeting."

"Have you read the journals?" Aiden asked, turning to the first page.

Jack hesitated for several seconds. "I looked through a few pages, but then pushed them away."

"Why? You searched for it for years. Why not continue learning everything you can about the man, the woman, and the ship?"

Jack's expression turned contemplative. "I don't believe Ian and Hope's story is for me to tell."

"You think it's Killian and Emma's," Aiden said regarding what he'd heard at Thanksgiving.

"Perhaps." Jack inclined his head. "But this is Swan Harbor, son. Something tells me that, as a Jones, you'll have a part in the end of their story too."

"Isn't their story over?" Aiden asked.

"Great love stories are never over." Captain Jack winked. "If they were, there would be no happily-ever-after, now would there?"

"Like Rosalind and Orlando, Jane and Rochester, Catherine and Heathcliff, or Elizabeth and Darcy?" Aiden rattled off great pairings from the literature he so dearly loved.

"Yes," Jack smiled, as if his point had gotten across. "Lovers that continue to live between the pages years later. Someday that will be Ian and Hope."

"Except their ending was more Romeo and Juliet," Aiden muttered.

"I prefer to believe they'll be reunited like Vega and Altair," Jack confessed.

"Reunited one day in the stars?" Aiden questioned, referring to the myth.

"But I'm hopeful they'll be together more than just one day a year."

Was that conversation what was driving him? Or was it his love of a good story and the need to see Ian and Hope reunited in the stars? Or was it something else?

"Here you are." Jack set a tray with cups and a plate of cookies on the table in front of him. "While you're at it, have one of Terri's peanut butter cookies. They hit the spot."

The mention of Harper's grandmother reminded him of the story they'd spun for Logan. The one about her family being intricately woven with Jack's family—which also included his family.

"Now, tell me what your sister's tenacity has uncovered," Jack continued once seated. "Do we know anything more than we did?"

Aiden set his cup aside and opened his notebook. "Before I tell you what Sarah found, I want you to know I decided not to read any more of Ian's journal."

"Really?" Jack sent him a surprised look. "I would have thought you would have read both journals from cover to cover already."

He wasn't sure how to explain the feelings that had washed over him when he'd tried.

"I'd planned to," Aiden admitted. "But when I opened to the first page, it felt ... well, wrong."

"Like you were reading a letter that was meant for another," Jack offered.

Aiden searched for a better explanation. "It's as you said. Ian and Hope have a story that needs to be told, and I've been guided to help, but ..."

"Reading Ian and Hope's words didn't feel right."

"No." Aiden took a sip of tea and watched the flames dance around for several minutes before continuing. "But it makes no sense why I feel this way."

Captain Jack chuckled. "I've thought the same thing for years when I tried to explain the connection between Jonesy and Swan Harbor's hope."

"Do you really believe that?" Aiden asked, watching Jack's expressions for any sign he was speaking an untruth.

"I believe there's a connection between Swan Harbor and Jonesy," Jack offered, without really answering the question. "Now, tell me about Sarah's discovery."

"She found an old family Bible," Aiden responded, the excitement he'd felt upon learning the news still bubbling inside. "Ian was born in May 1690 and died in July 1722."

"He went back to England and died of a broken heart," Jack murmured.

"You think?" Aiden hummed. "Maybe. But he was close to the average life expectancy for men of that time."

Jack looked over his cup of tea, his dark eyes serious as if to say, '*You doubt me?*' "True, but whatever Ian was doing in the year after Hope's death had to have taken a toll on him. He left his son and his home behind. Why? We don't know. It must have broken his heart."

His voice cracked, and suddenly, he pushed up and walked across the room to stare off into the distance.

Aiden studied the older man and had to wonder at his story, but the conviction in his voice said he was speaking from experience.

"Have you been to the library yet?" asked Jack.

"I thought I would go in the next few days."

"Good, good." Jack nodded. "Amanda Kane's our new librarian. Lovely girl."

"Do you really believe there's information about Ian in the Swan Harbor library?"

"Why do you ask?" Jack frowned. "What are you thinking?"

Aiden wasn't even sure why he'd asked that specific question, but he had to agree with his subconscious once it was out there. Ian and Hope's story has remained hidden for centuries.

"Why is it—?

"—Coming out now?" Jack hazarded a guess as to where he was going.

"Yes."

Jack grinned. "This is Swan Harbor, where things happen when they're meant to happen. I'm assuming it's time."

Goosebumps worked their way along Aiden's limbs, but whether they were ones of anticipation or dread, he couldn't be sure.

Ava and Finn's Cottage
December 3
6:00 p.m.

Knowing she was running late, Ava rushed into their house. "I'm sorry." She bypassed Finn to go change. "I—"

"—Lost track of time," her husband of almost two weeks completed indulgently.

She finished unbuttoning her blouse and tossed it in his direction, knowing his penchant for organization would have him taking it to the hamper.

"I'm only a little late." Ava added an extra layer before tugging a thick sweater over her head. "But Terri started telling me about the time Grandmother Rose first met my Grandfather Ray and, well …"

Finn stalked toward her, and just like every other time she looked at him, her heart raced, and her breath stuttered. He wrapped his hands around her waist and pulled her against his firm body.

"Do you really want to go searching for a Christmas tree tonight, love?"

Ava kissed him, even knowing it would make it much harder to leave the warmth of their home.

"As much as I love our time together, walking through a tree farm is another—"

"—One of those teen moments?"

"Yes."

He whispered a kiss across her mouth. "Your heart's desire," he kissed her once more, "it's what I want to give you."

"Oh, Finn." Ava stared into his dark eyes, full of so much love, sometimes it took her breath away. "You do. Every day and in every way."

"Good. Before we meet the kids, though, I have a surprise for you."

"A surprise?"

"Yes," he winked. "Jack called."

"Did you invite him to go along?"

"I did." He started the car and drove a few doors away to her uncle's home. "But he declined."

"Looks like he has company," she murmured.

"I think that's Aiden's car," Finn said, helping her out of the car.

"Aiden," she hummed. "Ian and Hope talk?"

"That's my guess."

As soon as they stepped onto the porch, Finn kissed her. It scattered her thoughts and made her knees weak.

"Not, not ..." She ran her tongue across her bottom lip, still feeling the imprint of Finn's mouth. "Not that I'm complaining, but what was that for?"

He pointed up. "Mistletoe."

The door opened while she was still staring at the plant, and she heard Jack chuckle.

"Don't tell me that's the first time you've stepped under it this holiday."

"It's not hung all over the cottage." Finn winked. "But I'm pretty sure I saw some in one of our trees."

"You don't need mistletoe to kiss me," Ava told him.

"Just watch yourself when walking through town," Jack warned. "It's plentiful."

"Stay away from Heidi," Ava murmured, tongue-in-cheek, referring to an incident in October.

"I'll do my best," Finn assured her. "Jack, are you sure you don't want to go tree hunting with us?"

"Positive." Jack led them into the back room. "But I can't believe you haven't found a tree yet."

Finn scoffed. "Obviously, you haven't gone tree hunting with my wife." He pitched his voice higher. "It's not tall enough. No, Finn, it's not full enough. There's a hole. It doesn't have the perfect shape."

"You're just like your mama," Jack laughed. "She would drag Ray and me all over town until eventually—"

"—He'd take her to the tree farm," Finn retorted with a long-suffering sigh.

"Yes. Now look at these." Jack opened several boxes and spread them across the floor. "I found some old Christmas ornaments. I thought maybe …"

Ava had a hard time keeping her mouth from dropping open. "Christmas ornaments?"

Jack gave her a crocheted angel. "I remember when Rose made this. I think I was six, and she was halfway through it, and your mother started crying. I decided I could do it just as easily as she could."

"Oh, no," Ava exclaimed. "What happened?"

"I unraveled most of it," Jack admitted sheepishly. "When Rose returned, I was trying to put it back together."

"Did she get mad?"

His voice softened. "No. Rose put her hands over mine and tried to show me what to do. I grew bored and, after a few stitches, went to find something else to do. Later that day, after she had put it back together, I helped her hang it on our Christmas tree."

Ava pointed her finger at him. "You need a tree, even if it's a small one."

He picked up another crochet ornament, this one a bell, and Ava's eyes met Finn's. *We're bringing him a tree.*

His subtle nod told her he'd received the message.

Jack picked up an ornament made of plaster. "Grace painted this. She said it reminded her of our dog, Betty."

Even with the old, faded paint, Ava could tell her mother had lovingly decorated the dog.

"Was Betty one of the dogs my mother used to drag home?"

Jack laughed. "You've been reading your grandmother Rose's journals, haven't you?"

Ava smiled, thinking of all the wonderful memories Rose had left that were now waiting for her to enjoy. "I've read a few of them."

"More than a few, Jack," Finn corrected. "She's read and reread those books."

"And Rose was very meticulous about keeping track of her journals, too."

A shadow crossed Jack's face, and Ava was once again reminded of his loss. But this year, he had a family.

He put the ornament back in the box and handed it to Ava. "I want you to have these ornaments."

She blinked back the tears that threatened. "I'll make a deal with you. When we get our tree, we'll get one for you too, and we'll decorate them together."

"I had a feeling that's what you were going to say." Jack walked them to the door. "And ..."

"Face it, Jack," Finn replied. "You know you won't get a better deal."

"Is it a deal?" Ava held her breath, waiting for an answer.

"Oh, okay," Jack laughed. "It's a deal. But not a big one."

"Good." Ava kissed Jack's cheek and waved goodbye to Aiden. "Thanks for backing me up," she told Finn as they drove away.

Finn flashed her a grin. "You know I'm always on your side, don't you?"

"I do." She laced their fingers. "Now what about that other thing we discussed? Did you contact Sanders?"

"Did anyone ever tell you how bossy you are?"

"Yes," she giggled. "You said you didn't mind."

"Oh, it doesn't bother me," he sent her a sexy wink, "as long as I'm compensated."

"What did you have in mind?"

"I saw a new *Rebecca's Fantasy* catalog ..."

FOUR

Sally's Diner
December 3
7:00 p.m.

Harper glanced up as Eden and Rachel slid into the booth across from her.

"We're here." Eden crossed her arms on the table and pinned Harper with an intense look. "What's the emergency?"

Harper sighed. "What makes you think there's an emergency?"

"Please," Rachel retorted. "You used to call and leave one-word messages. Now it's a text."

"Technically, ice cream is two words," Harper pointed out, wondering if she truly wanted to get into everything.

"Potato, potatah," Eden muttered.

"And we aren't at Two Scoops." Harper tossed out the name of the ice cream shop that belonged to one of her aunts.

"Pfft." Rachel wiped away the excuse. "That just means you don't want your family to overhear what we're talking about."

"But Hayden works here."

"Quit making excuses, Harper." Eden picked up a spoon and dug into the colossal banana split in the center of the table. "You're busted."

"Oh, alright." Harper hesitated long enough to take another bite and lick off the spoon, hoping it would give her courage. "It's about Aiden ... and Clark, Rhett, and Orlando."

"Aiden?" Eden frowned. "And *all* your secret matches?"

"Yes." Harper huffed. "You know my first two matches were Rhett and Orlando, right?"

"Go on," encouraged Rachel.

"I thought my last match was Logan and was ready to write that one off."

"You were worried about that at the tree lighting," Eden pointed out. "So, what happened?"

"I found out Logan isn't my match."

Rachel exchanged looks with Eden before turning back to Harper. "You've lost me."

"Me too," Eden agreed. "I thought the idea behind the matches was to see if you had a connection with one or more of them."

"It is."

"So?" Eden pushed.

"That's just it," Harper huffed. "What if I want to meet Rhett, Orlando, and Clark, but ..."

"But?" Eden grinned. "I'm assuming this is where Aiden comes into the picture?"

"Yes."

"Keep going," Rachel prodded. "What has Aiden done?"

Harper quickly explained what had happened with the dance, Morgan and Logan. "I thought I'd give him an out. You know, just in case he was being nice."

"Commendable," Eden acknowledged.

"So, I stopped by his office, and he was on the phone and ..." But she let that hang, still not understanding her feelings.

"And?"

"I'm getting there, Eden," Harper grumbled. "Don't be so pushy."

Eden snickered. "Come on, Harper. We both know you should have gone into creative writing ..."

"Because no one stretches out a story like you," Rachel added. "Just spill."

"Aiden was talking to someone named Sarah, and what felt suspiciously like jealousy flew through me," Harper spit out in a rush. "What's with that?"

Eden glanced at Rachel and rolled her eyes.

"What?" Harper huffed.

"Come on, Harper," Eden sighed. "You're neither dumb nor blind. Not only does it mean you are well and truly over Joel—"

"Good riddance," Rachel interjected.

"—But your heart is talking once again," Eden continued, as if Rachel hadn't interrupted her.

"And more importantly," Rachel added. "You're listening."

"What if I go with Aiden, and we have fun?" Harper asked. "But I'm also enjoying my talks with Clark, and want to meet Rhett and Orlando as well?"

"Harper," Eden grumbled. "You're creating problems before there are problems."

"But—"

"Look," Rachel interrupted. "Just stop. What if you go with Aiden and decide he's too quiet? What if none of your matches want to meet you because they had better connections with their other matches? Take it one day at a time and keep listening to your heart."

Could she do that? Take every day as it came and stop looking for problems.

"I'll try," Harper finally mumbled.

"But it's going to be hard because you're Harper, and you're trying to find what your parents have," Rachel repeated the handy excuse used before.

"Do you blame me?" Harper asked. "Everything with them has always seemed so ... perfect. They even ..." She let that thought drop because ....

"They even, what?" Eden wondered before tossing out, "Communicate silently?"

Harper gasped. "How?"

"Come on, Harper." Rachel rolled her eyes. "You've been looking for what your parents have since you were sixteen and started mooning over Ben."

"Yes, well, considering Aiden and I've exchanged several of these 'silent communications,'" fell from Harper's mouth. "Is it any wonder I'm freaked?"

"Sounds romantic," Eden sighed. "Maybe you can hand Clark off to me."

"I couldn't do that," Harper declined. "It would mess up the data for the research project."

"I was afraid you were going to say that," Eden mumbled. "Now, I wish I had signed up for that project."

Harper shrugged as if to say, *I told you so*, because she'd tried to get her friends involved.

"You know why I didn't sign up," Rachel reminded her. "Riley. What man wants to get involved with a woman with an infant?"

"Oh, Rach." Harper reached across the table and squeezed her friend's hand. "I'm sorry. Here I am complaining about my woes, and I haven't even asked about yours. Plus, how's Riley?"

Rachel had met and fallen in love with Austin the summer his family had spent in Swan Harbor. Several months later, she'd discovered he was working at the Portland Jetport and moved there. But the future she'd wanted hadn't been written in the stars. It wasn't long before Austin joined the Army, leaving her pregnant and alone.

"He's good." Rachel grinned. "Sleeps more, but not through the night, and is smiling now."

"Are you still hoping to get money for your music school?" asked Eden.

"I am." Rachel's voice grew more animated. "Ava's help has been invaluable in completing the forms. Now I just wait."

"So, a new business," Harper posed. "Then we can work on finding your replacement for Austin."

"One thing at a time," Rachel warned her. "Since your heart seems to be talking first, let's work on you."

"I do need a dress," Harper decided. "Will you go shopping with me?"

"Well, duh!" Eden snickered. "We'll pick a dress that will knock Aiden speechless."

Harper laughed. "He's quiet as it is. I'm not sure that's a good thing."

"Maybe his talents lie in other directions," Eden teased. "Singing, teaching, writing ..."

Aiden's Apartment
December 3
9:30 p.m.

Aiden glanced at his research notes once more, then stuck the notebook into his briefcase. He'd done all that was possible without spending time in the library, and that couldn't happen at 9:30 p.m. But he was restless for reasons he didn't quite understand.

Since he owed Rosalind a message, he opened the app and reread her last question.

Clark,

As a child, what was your favorite gift and why?

Rosalind

Earlier in the day, he'd sent her a quick, *Good question. I'll reply later tonight.* Not only because he didn't want her to feel ignored, but also because he wasn't sure what to say.

Tell her you received a book.

Except that could give hints about what he taught, which was against the rules.

How about a game?

But his favorite game involved searching for answers, which was too close to what he was doing regarding Ian Jones.

Then ....

Aiden glanced around the sparsely decorated apartment he shared with Quinn. When his gaze landed on the keyboard set up in the corner and an idea began to form.

Rosalind,

I received my favorite gift when I was ten—a
keyboard. Now, I play when I have time. How
about you? Do you enjoy music?

Yours,

Clark

As soon as he'd sent the message, Aiden tossed his phone on the table and sat down to play. He worked his way through the simple finger exercises his instructor had drilled into him. Then, he transitioned to a few pieces he remembered from past recitals. Ones he'd played, yet never enjoyed.

But his love of music hadn't changed, and he was halfway through the theme from the 1970s version of *Superman* when his phone dinged.

Determined not to leave the music hanging, he completed the piece before checking his phone. *It's Rosalind,* he thought with a smile, and quickly opened the app.

Clark,

A keyboard is a wonderful gift. I played the flute in high school, but I wasn't very good. Music, though, is something I'm passionate about. Jazz, classical, pop, rock—it all depends on my mood.

Rosalind

Aiden read and then reread the message, and something had him recording himself playing the Superman theme. Would she know the music?

Rosalind,

Enjoy.

Clark

Then he attached the recording to her message.

When she didn't immediately respond, he wanted to kick his own arse, as maybe he'd pushed too fast. Then—his phone buzzed, and his heart did a little flip.

Clark,

That was beautiful. Now I understand where Clark came from. Superman has always been my favorite superhero. Was there a reason you chose his alter ego as your 'match' name?

Rosalind

"Bloody hell," he muttered, wondering what he could say that wouldn't give away too much information regarding his identity.

How could he tell her he admired Clark Kent's transformation into Superman? That as soon as Clark removed his glasses, he became Kal-el. He stood taller, appeared more confident, his voice was lower pitched ... and what he wanted, he went after.

Aiden left his phone next to his keyboard and ended up in the bathroom. Just like Clark, he took off his tortoiseshell glasses, and yet all he saw was the same person. Even dropping his tie and mussing his hair didn't change the man looking back at him. Had that been because Superman was the '*real*' man, and Clark was just the '*mask*'?

What would it take for him to have some of Liam's confidence, Killian's way with words, or his brother's ability to flirt?

Wasn't that what you were doing when you winked at Harper?

No ... maybe.

Isn't that what you're doing with Rosalind?

He hadn't planned that. It had just happened.

Isn't that the kind of woman you want? Someone you can behave naturally around and not feel the need to pretend.

Yes, but ... being a secret match is different.

How?

As for Rhett and Orlando, while he'd not known the person he was corresponding with, it was different. Those characters weren't in disguise. But Clark was, and once he'd gotten used to the idea, there had been something freeing about the situation.

The anonymity helped, making it easier not to worry that every word he said was the wrong thing. By pretending to be Clark, he could think through what he wrote. The awkwardness he usually felt around women wasn't as noticeable.

Aiden opened the app and started typing. For every word he wrote, he deleted two. It took him several tries to get the right tone, the right words. But finally, he hit send.

> Rosalind,
>
> Just as the character whose name you borrowed
> behaved differently because she was 'in disguise,'
> so did Clark. He was just a normal, average guy
> who was a touch awkward.
>
> Clark.

Once he sent the message, his heart fluttered, and his nerves rushed around inside. Had he said too much?

Less than two minutes later, the phone buzzed, and Aiden practically jumped out of his chair.

> Clark,

> Is that your way of telling me you're just an average guy who's a touch awkward?

> Rosalind

"That was bloody brilliant, Jones," Aiden grumbled, realizing while trying not to describe himself … he'd done just that.

Emma and Killian's Apartment
December 3
11:00 p.m.

Emma ran ahead of Killian, opening doors and moving things out of the way, as he carried their six-foot Christmas tree up the stairs. While she knew it was going to be a tight squeeze in their small apartment, there'd been no way she'd resisted the tree's pull. And the way it made the room smell had her heart beating a little faster with anticipation.

"Just a little to the right," she instructed Killian on which way to move the tree's trunk.

When the trunk slid into the stand, Emma tightened the screws.

"Bloody hell, Doc, hurry," Killian grumbled.

"Just hold it," she returned.

He mumbled something under his breath, but she ignored him and worked her way around the tree.

"Okay, let it go." She held her breath so that it wouldn't fall. "I need to check to see if it's straight."

"Check away," he responded, and she had to bite her lip to keep from smiling. While he was doing quite a bit of grumbling, she'd watched him while they'd been at the tree farm. His eyes had glowed with happiness.

Emma scrambled backward to determine if their tree was straight and noticed the attentive looks of their cats, Millicent, Trudi, and Nina.

"Ah, oh."

"Is that ah oh the tree isn't straight?" Killian asked. "Or something else?"

"It's ah oh, I forgot about the cats."

He peered around the tree branches. "What about them?"

"Cats and trees," she winced. "Now, I'm not sure."

"Come on, Doc," he grinned. "Our *Felis catus* are perfectly behaved. We'll just tell them to leave it alone."

"Right," she laughed. "And what if they climb it?"

He shrugged. "My brother's a firefighter/paramedic. I'm sure Liam would rescue his nieces if needed."

"Rescue them, maybe," she muttered, not acknowledging the niece label. "But what about the tree?"

"Is the bloody tree straight?"

Emma tilted her head in each direction a few times. It surprised her to discover it was relatively straight.

"The tree is straight, but—"

"Don't tell me," Killian interrupted before she could finish her thought.

"Don't tell you what?" she asked him innocently.

"That you were wrong, and it's not really straight."

"Okay." Emma grinned and followed up with, "It's straight enough, but we can't leave it in that corner."

"What do you mean we can't leave it in this corner?"

"Because that corner is too close to the kitchen and—"

"Alright, alright," he huffed. "Where do you want the tree?"

Emma hurried to move a chair and a few boxes from another corner on the other side of the small room.

"There." She pointed to the new spot. "That should work."

Killian dutifully picked up the tree and carried it to the new corner. "Satisfied?"

"No."

"No? Why the bloody hell not?"

"Because of the beam." She pointed to the structure. "I'm sorry."

His blue eyes met hers across the room. "You can make it up to me later."

"I'll think about it."

"Doc."

"I'm working on it," Emma explained, already busy clearing another area for the tree. "How's this?"

Killian picked up the tree but had only taken a few steps before setting it back down. "It won't work."

"It won't work," Emma echoed. "Why?"

"Because Doc." He pointed at the fireplace. "It's too close. If a spark pops out ..."

"The tree will catch on fire," she realized.

"Right." Killian crossed the room and tugged her into his arms. "Which is why we put it in the first spot we tried. Remember?"

Emma leaned her head against his chest. "I know."

"Next Christmas, we'll be in our own home and will have more options." He kissed the top of her head.

She grinned. "I already know where it's going to go. In front of the picture window. That way, everyone can enjoy it."

"Just don't make me string lights all over the house." Killian moved the tree back to its spot next to the kitchen.

"We'll see."

He gave her a disgruntled look, but something told her he wouldn't complain too loudly if she wanted lights.

"Now what?"

"We decorate."

"With?"

"You know the answer to that as well as I do."

There were several boxes of new lights on the kitchen table. Next to the lights, there were two old boxes—one from Emma's mother and another from Killian's father.

"Lights first."

He sent her another disgruntled look, but he helped wrap the lights around the tree for the next few minutes. Once they finished, he turned them on, and her heart melted.

"It's perfect."

Killian waved toward the tree. "Doc, aren't you going to complain about the imbalance? About too many lights on the right side and not enough on the left. Or too many on top and not enough on the bottom."

"Nope." She opened the box Ava had given them. "Now, the ornaments."

"Is that you?" Killian nodded toward the first item she removed.

Emma turned over the construction paper tree she was holding. "It says Emma, 1995. The teacher took our photos, and we glued them onto the tree. When I took it home, I wanted so badly to show it off, except my mom was at work, and who knows where my dad was. But Johanna was there, and she made a big deal about it and hung it on the tree." She hesitated, and *that* feeling in the pit of her stomach twisted.

"And then what?"

"The next morning when I came downstairs, it was gone. Grandfather Leo said it didn't belong on his professionally decorated tree."

"Bastard."

Killian's succinct response jumpstarted her heart again because those days were behind her.

"He was." Emma smiled. "But Johanna put it on the small tree she had in her room. The next year, when I made something, I didn't even try to put it on the main tree. Sometimes my ornaments ended up on the staff's tree ..."

"And other times?"

"They disappeared."

"Disappeared?"

Emma grinned and hung the ornament on the tree. "It wasn't until my mom gave me this box, that I found out why."

"Your mom had them?"

"Yeah. It seems she found a few and put them on a small tree in her office."

"Why didn't she tell you?"

Emma shrugged. "Mom said she didn't tell anyone except her assistant. I guess she was afraid grandfather would mess with that tree, as well."

Killian's smile was tender and full of love. "I'm surprised Ava didn't want these on her tree this year."

"I think she kept a few. But she also found the box with ornaments she'd made as a child, plus the ones Jack found. Which reminds me. I'll be right back."

"Doc?"

"I'll be back."

Emma had run into Patti's Pampered Pets the week before and made a spontaneous purchase. She'd bought clear ornaments with instructions on how to take a picture of your pets and insert it into the ball to hang on the tree.

When she stepped into their bedroom, she saw one of her bras lying on top of the dresser. And the drawer with Killian's underwear wasn't completely shut.

"Killian, what were you doing with my bra?"

He poked his head around the door frame. "Did you just ask what I did with your bra?"

"I did." Emma pointed to the dresser where a pale pink bra lay. "Did you put that there?"

He stepped around her to get closer. "Why the bloody hell was someone in our drawers, Doc?"

The memory of the bras hanging on the tree was still present in her mind. She'd been thankful one of hers hadn't been included, but had her luck ran out?

"Wait," she frowned. "I thought you said no one knew when or who took their bras."

"They didn't."

"Then why would the *'underwear thief'* have been so blatant?"

Killian pulled out his phone. "Because they've issued a challenge."

"A challenge?"

"Think of it like this, Doc," he explained. "They're throwing down the gauntlet."

"So, they threw down my bra?"

"Aye. Except I'll not allow them to give me the slip again," he smirked.

Emma left the room while he talked to his partner, Rusty. Otherwise, she might have been tempted to check for other missing items.

FIVE

Terri Patterson's Home
December 5
10:00 a.m.

HARPER HAD BEEN STANDING IN HER GRANDMOTHER'S KITCHEN
for over an hour. Her job was to fill a Christmas-themed baggie with cookies, add a twist tie, and place it in a basket. Once she finished, she would deliver them to the residents and staff of the Harbor Cross Nursing Home and the Harbor Rehabilitation Center.

While she worked, her grandmother was scrolling through her phone, holding it close.

"Oh, my," Terri chuckled. "Will you look at that?"

Harper glanced up and realized her grandmother was still scrolling.

"How in the world did that happen?" Terri exclaimed again.

How in the world did her ninety-year-old grandmother get so adept at using a smartphone?

"Why, look at that!" Terri uttered.

Why did her grandmother need a smartphone? A question she'd asked her mother upon returning home.

"Because your grandmother wants to keep up with Swan Harbor's gossip line," Beverly explained.

"Will you look at that?" Terri circled back to her first comment.

"Will I look at what?" Harper finally asked, even though she wasn't sure she wanted to know what had captured Terri's attention.

"Oh, I'm sorry, dear," Terri apologized. "I forgot you weren't tapped into the gossip line yet. Look at that!"

She handed her phone to Harper, and the glint in her grandmother's eye should have warned her.

"Why are boxers flying from a flagpole?"

"That, I can't tell you," Terri snickered. "But it's not just one flagpole either. Apparently, they're all over town."

"Really?"

"See," Terri slid her thumb across the screen, "these have kittens on them. Here's a pair with stars. Another with stripes. I can go on."

"A rebuttal to the bras on the Christmas tree?" Harper guessed.

"Something like that."

"What do you know, grandma?"

"Me?" Terri placed her hand on her chest. "I know nothing."

Harper studied her grandmother, and the way her eyes kept skittering away said what her words didn't.

"I don't believe you."

"I don't know what you think you see," Terri replied. "There's nothing I can tell you about who's doing this."

"Nothing you can tell me, huh?"

Terri set her phone aside and helped fill the last few bags.

"Not really. But while you're out, be sure and send me pictures of any flagpoles you might see."

"Are you sure you don't want to go with me?"

"Ava and Jack are coming today," Terri grinned, "or I would. You'll be okay, right?"

"I'll be fine," Harper replied. "I've finished grading and dropped off my exams for copying."

"I really appreciate this, dear." Terri patted her on her cheek. "You're a good girl. When are you going to find a nice boy and give me some more great-grandbabies?"

"Me?" Harper exclaimed. "You have Julianna."

"She's a little love," Terri remarked of her almost one-year-old great-granddaughter, who belonged to her cousin Tracey. "But you've always been the one who mothered your younger cousins."

"Yeah, well," Harper sighed. "I haven't found Mr. Right yet."

"It's because you've been away from Swan Harbor for so long," Terri stated matter-of-factly. "Now that you're home, start paying attention to what your heart is saying."

"You sound like Rachel and Eden."

"Do you doubt it?"

"That my heart is going to speak to me?"

"Yes."

Did she?

The memory of her exchanges with Clark brought a smile to her face. They were fun, a little flirty, and every time she listened to his piano recording, she wanted to swoon. Except, she kept trying to put a face on the person who was writing to her. And while it should have been impossible, when she thought of Clark, it wasn't Clark Kent she saw ... it was Aiden. When he'd looked up at her in the copy center with his slightly mussed hair and a lopsided smile, she'd felt something. Had that been her heart speaking?

"I'll try, grandma," she promised. "Is there anything else?"

"Don't forget those pictures," Terri reminded her.

Harper just shook her head and grabbed the baskets to take with her. She'd just set them on her back seat when her phone buzzed.

"Hey, Rach, what's up?"

"Is there any way you can give me a ride home?"

Her friend sounded weird, but with Riley crying in the background, Harper assumed that was why. "Where are you?"

Rachel gave an exasperated sigh and murmured to the baby for a minute before answering, "I'm at the pediatrician's office, and my mom was called into work early."

"Text me the address, and I'll be there as soon as I can," Harper answered.

"Thanks, Harper. Riley is wet and tired, and I can't find his pacifier."

"Nap time?"

Rachel groaned. "For both of us."

"Okay, I'm on my way. While you're waiting, keep an eye out for flying boxers."

"For what?"

"Flying boxers," Harper repeated. "It seems this time our underwear thief has run boxers up flagpoles."

"This I need to see." Then, Rachel started laughing.

"You found some?" Harper guessed.

"I did," Rachel giggled. "They're bright red and look like they have writing on them."

"Really?" Harper started her car. "If I bring a picture of those to my grandmother, she might make my favorite dessert."

"I'll keep an eye on them for you."

"And if someone comes to get them," Harper requested. "Take a picture."

Only in my hometown would Christmas bring bras hanging from the tree and boxers flying from flagpoles. What was next? Elves in nighties?

Elsa's Pediatric Practice
December 5
10:30 a.m.

"I'll be back by 2:00 p.m.," Elsa said to her new receptionist, Isaac, on her way out the door. "Send me a text if there's an emergency."

"Will do."

"You'll be okay here alone?"

"I'm fine." Isaac made a shooing motion with his hand. "Go, or Liam's going to be calling again."

"I'm going, I'm going."

"Have fun."

Elsa stepped outside and saw several women standing in a group staring up.

"What the heck?" She glanced up, and her lips twitched.

They were staring up at the flagpole that stood outside the building where her practice was located. But instead of the American flag flying proudly, there was what looked suspiciously like a pair of boxers. A pair of *red* boxers.

"What's going on?" Elsa asked Rachel.

"You haven't heard?" Rachel snickered.

"No."

"Instead of flags, Swan Harbor is flying boxers today," Rachel explained.

"Boxers?" Elsa paused. "As in men's underwear?

"Oh yes!" Lois laughed, never looking away from the bright red material flying above their heads. "Glynnis and I have already been to the town hall, the police station, the hospital, and now here.

"And the flagpoles at each of those places are flying boxers?" Elsa guessed.

"Yes." Glynnis shaded her eyes with her hand. "But these are the only ones that have said something. I just can't make out what they say.

Red ... say something ....

"Glynnis," Lois yelled. "Look at the waistband. It's gold."

Gold!?

"Looks like it to me too," Glynnis called back. "Did we bring the binoculars?"

Elsa's breath stuttered as she looked up at the boxers, and just as she suspected, they were familiar.

Crap!

"I've got them."

Lois returned with the binoculars, and Elsa slowly backed away from the group.

"Have, have fun, ladies," she told them. "I'll see you later. I'm running late for an appointment."

"We'll send you a picture if you want," Lois offered.

"No ... that's quite alright."

As she headed toward her car, she heard Lois yell, "I believe those are boxer briefs."

"Really?" Glynnis answered. "How can you tell?"

"The size," Lois yelled. "Bet they're meant to cup the owner's package nice and tight."

Elsa groaned and pulled open her car door.

"Can you tell what they say?" asked Glynnis.

"The word 'love' is printed all over them, then there's a picture, and underneath it says 'heart,'" Lois exclaimed. "But the wind is moving them too much."

You'll be in my heart....

At the last minute, Elsa couldn't stand it any longer and aimed her phone at the 'flag' to take a picture. And then, she stretched the screen to get a close-up look at the boxers.

Her heart flipped and sank into the pit of her stomach.

How?

Her phone buzzed before she could come up with an answer.

> Liam: Where are you?

Crap!

> Elsa: On my way.

She'd thought about sending him the picture, but at the last minute decided against it. After all, she could be wrong, right?

Except as she parked behind Liam's car and ran up the steps to their cottage, that sick feeling grew. She wasn't wrong, which meant someone had been in their home.

"It's about time," Liam began, but when he got a look at her face, tugged her into his arms. "What's wrong, love? You look upset."

"I am," Elsa groaned against his chest. "Why didn't you tell me?"

"Tell you what?" Liam tilted her chin, forcing her to meet his eyes.

Elsa studied him for a second and, seeing only confusion, continued, "You're still plugged into the gossip line, right?"

"I am," he replied hesitantly. "Are you feeling left out?"

"No." Elsa frowned, trying to figure out how he didn't know. "Have you checked your line today to see what the newest *'gossip'* is in Swan Harbor?"

Liam kissed her on her forehead and led her into the back room.

"I turn off the notifications when I'm teaching."

"And you had a class today?"

Since taking over as the chief paramedic, he'd made several changes at the

Swan Harbor Fire Department. One of them was more instruction for the new paramedics.

"Yeah. I'd just gotten home when I texted you. Why?"

Elsa took a deep breath and reached for her phone. "Because of this."

Liam sent her a confused look, but then glanced at the picture. She could tell the minute he recognized what was in the photo.

"Bloody hell!" He took off toward their bedroom.

"My thoughts exactly."

When she caught up with him, Liam was searching through his underwear drawer.

"Not there." He opened another drawer.

"Of course they're not there," Elsa pointed out. "That's because they're flying over my office."

He glanced over his shoulder with a raised brow. "Did you look to see if yours is still here?"

"No." Elsa glanced around with wild eyes, suddenly feeling as if she were being watched. "But women's panties aren't flying. It's boxers."

"Yet," Liam growled.

"Oh, alright," Elsa huffed, heading to the second bedroom.

"Where are you going?"

"To look in my suitcase," she told him. "I've been packing all my 'honeymoon' items."

The suitcase was lying on the bed. Except, instead of being open as she had left it, the top was closed.

"Have you touched it?"

"No, why would you? It was open, wasn't it?"

"Yes."

"I'm going to call Killian."

Elsa grabbed his shirt. "Wait."

"Alright." He brushed his hand down her spine. "I'm right here, love."

She gave him a grateful smile, took a deep breath, and flipped open the lid. "Someone has been in it."

"Is anything missing?"

The bikini panties that matched Liam's boxers were bunched up on top of everything. Elsa pushed aside a nightgown, several bikinis, and shorts, looking for one special gift.

"It's gone."

"What, love?"

"The black lace nightgown," Elsa murmured. "You know, the one—"

"—I ordered for you from the *Rebecca's Fantasy* catalog?"

"Yes."

"Bloody hell," Liam snapped. "That does it. I'm calling Killian."

"You can't," Elsa groaned. "We have to go."

He growled, and usually, that little sound caused her heart to speed up, but ....

"Alright." He took several pictures of the suitcase and grabbed her hand. "First, we'll choose our wedding cake flavor, and then I'll call Killian."

"That's fine. On the way, I can fill you in on the singers at our wedding and the latest on Aiden."

"And you said you weren't up on Swan Harbor gossip." He kissed her quickly. "You've been holding out on me."

Elsa smiled, but her thoughts were on her missing nightgown. She'd been looking forward to wearing it.

Aiden's Apartment
December 5
12:00 p.m.

Aiden was halfway out of his apartment when his phone buzzed, and only the manners his mum had instilled had him stepping back inside to check the text message.

> Liam: Hockey at Sonny's tonight at 6?

> Aiden: Do you really need me? I'd planned on spending the evening at the library.

> Liam: Come on, cuz. Ian has been waiting for over 300 years. He can wait a few more. Besides, we need you.

> Aiden: You realize I've never actually played
> hockey, right?

The return message was so long in coming, Aiden thought he was off the hook.

> Liam: Killian says everyone must start
> somewhere. Just bring your jock to protect your
> jewels. He also said to check your drawers for
> missing boxers.

> Aiden: Check my drawers? Bloody hell, what does
> that mean?

> Liam: Check the flagpoles. Sonny's at 6. There are
> skates, sticks, pads, and helmets at the rink.

Aiden was tempted to ignore the directives, both of them. But once again, his upbringing had him dropping his briefcase.

"Check for missing boxers," Aiden muttered, opening the drawer where he tossed his clean laundry. When the pile appeared to be about the right size, he dismissed the idea of missing boxers and went digging for his jock. It was old and pink from being washed with something red at one time, but it would have to do.

The gym bag was in a corner, and along with the pink jock, he tossed in a pair of old sweats and a soccer jersey. Anything else he'd need, Sonny's would have.

He slung the strap over his shoulder and grabbed his briefcase, already thinking about what he needed to accomplish at the library.

Aiden had started down the stairs when he got a look at the flagpole he'd been told to 'check.' "Bloody hell!" he exclaimed in response to the bright yellow boxers flying high above the Camelot Arms Apartments.

"Are they yours?"

"Wh—?" Aiden glanced over his shoulder into the laughing eyes of Harper Taylor. "Oh, uh, no."

She followed him the rest of the way down the stairs, still watching the boxers. "You know, it's like with the Christmas tree decorating."

Aiden tilted his head, trying to follow her thought process. "How so?"

"The colors," she murmured. "Bright, colorful bras, just like the bulbs hanging on the tree."

"And a royal gold pair of boxers hanging over Camelot Arms," Aiden guessed. "Just like a royal flag over Camelot."

"Yes!" Harper smiled, and when he looked at her, she took his breath. He'd never noticed how big her eyes were or how they sparkled with happiness. And her smile ....

Aiden flushed and glanced away, not wanting to be caught staring. "Do you live here?"

"In this apartment complex?" Harper thumbed over her shoulder. "No. I gave Rachel and Riley a ride home from the pediatrician's office."

"Ah, alright. Well, it was nice to see you again, Doctor Taylor. I'm off to the library."

"And I'm off to deliver cookies for my grandmother."

"Cookies?" Aiden's mouth watered, reminding him he'd forgotten to eat. "Captain Jack shared a few of your grandmother's peanut butter cookies with me. They were delicious."

"I'll tell grandma you said so," Harper smiled. "It will make her day."

He grinned. "Enjoy the rest of your day."

"You too, Doctor Jones."

Aiden had taken several steps away when it occurred to him that their formality was asinine. Not only were they colleagues, but they were going to attend a dance together.

"Doctor Taylor."

She looked back over her shoulder, and the way the sunlight bounced off her hair captured his attention. It appeared as if strands of gold were running through her dark tresses.

"Aiden?"

When she called his name, Aiden glanced up to see Harper watching him closely. She was nibbling her bottom lip. Almost as if she wasn't quite comfortable with what she'd said.

Unconsciously, a slow smile spread across his face. "I was going to ask you to call me Aiden. After all, Doctor Jones seems a bit formal, don't you think?"

"Okay, ... Aiden," she hesitated slightly. "And I'm Harper."

"Have a good day, Harper."

He'd just deposited his briefcase and gym bag in his car when he heard, "Oh, no," and saw Harper standing next to her car.

"What is it?"

She glanced up, and the distressed expression on her face had him heading back in her direction.

"Flat," Harper grumbled.

"Do you have a spare?"

"Oh, I couldn't," she began.

"Stop," Aiden silenced her. "I was brought up to help those in need. And you appear to be in need."

"But you have plans ..."

"So do you." He held out his hand. "Keys."

"I can change a tire, you know?"

"I didn't say you couldn't, did I?"

"No, but—"

"Bloody hell, Harper," Aiden retorted. "Give me your keys. It's too cold to have a pissing contest about changing a bloody tire."

Her lips twitched.

"What?"

"Nothing."

Aiden opened her trunk and moved a variety of junk around, looking for the release for the spare. As soon as he lifted the cover, he could tell his job had just gotten more complicated.

"Harper." He peered around the back of the car. "Were you aware your spare was flat?"

"I was afraid of that."

"You knew?"

"Well ..."

He shook his head, thinking he could definitely imagine his sister doing the same thing.

"The way I see it, is we take one of the two tires to the garage to be fixed ..."

"We?"

"Yes."

"No, Aiden," Harper argued. "I can't ask you to do that. I'll just call the mechanic."

"Don't you have cookies to deliver?"

"Yes."

"And were you supposed to be there at a certain time?"

She mumbled something, but when he didn't hear her, he slammed the trunk and rounded the car. "What was that?"

"Lunchtime," she repeated.

Aiden could see the huge baskets of cookies in the back seat, each holding multiple small bags.

"The only way that's possible, Doctor Taylor," Aiden said calmly, "is if I take you to deliver those baskets."

"I can't ask you to do that."

"You didn't ask," Aiden assured her. "I volunteered."

"You don't have to do this."

"I'm aware of that. However, if my mother or sister were stranded, I would want someone to help them.

The little secretive smile he'd seen earlier floated across her face again, and he had to bite his tongue to keep quiet.

"Are you sure?"

"Bloody hell, Harper," Aidan muttered. "Yes. Shall we?"

"Alright," Harper agreed. "As long as I'm not keeping you from anything."

"Nothing important," he murmured. "But since we're going in my car, call the garage and have them take care of yours. I can take you wherever you need to go when we're done."

When she didn't argue and took out her phone to make a call, Aiden carried the baskets to his car and stored them in the back seat.

"I'm going to leave my keys with Rachel. I'll be right back."

While she was gone, Aiden climbed into his car and tried to figure out why he wasn't disappointed about missing his library trip.

You like her

I barely know her.

But there's something about her that settles you.

Aiden watched as she walked toward him, and he had to agree with his subconscious. There *was* something about her that settled him.

"Are you ready?" he asked as soon as she climbed into the car.

"I'm ready." A teasing smile crossed her face. "But tell me, how are you at driving on the right side of the road?"

"The right side?" Aiden winked. "I'm sure you mean the wrong side."

Then, he did something entirely out of character and swerved a little into the opposite lane.

"Aiden!" Harper squealed.

For a minute there, he could have sworn he heard his heart speak, just as Captain Jack had promised.

SIX

Swan Harbor
December 5
1:00 p.m.

HARPER SENT A SURREPTITIOUS GLANCE IN AIDEN'S DIRECTION AS they drove through town. He looked like the same man she saw at the university every day, but he certainly wasn't acting like him. If she'd met this man first, she'd never have described him as quiet. When this man spoke, more words than she'd expected came out ... and he took her breath.

"What?" He met her look with a lifted brow.

"You're different from what I thought," fell from her mouth before she'd decided what—and how much to say.

"Different?"

"Yes."

"How so?"

They stopped at a light, and Aiden tilted his head in her direction. Then he smiled, and the way he was looking at her from the corner of his eye, caused her heart rate to jump up a notch or two.

He had dark wavy hair that he brushed back off his high forehead, dark brows and lashes, and blue eyes with flecks of amber ....

"You aren't wearing your glasses," she suddenly realized.

A gentle blush spread across his cheeks. "Contacts."

"I've never seen you in contacts," she responded. "New?"

"Not new." Aiden blew out a breath. "I ran out and only recently bought more."

"Ahh, that makes sense."

Was it taking the glasses off that caused the new behavior? Just like ....

"Bloody hell," Aiden muttered. "Will you look at that?"

"What?"

Before he said anything, she spotted what had captured his attention.

"Is that bloody hell because they're yours, or bloody hell because you can't believe anyone would wear those?" she teased, regarding the boxers that were flying above The Beach Shack.

The boxers were pale blue and so sheer she could see the restaurant's flag flying plainly on the other side of them.

"They're not bloody mine," he retorted, his face turning redder. "I've just never ..."

"I know." Harper aimed her phone at them and took a picture. "Swan Harbor takes some getting used to."

"Oh, don't get me wrong," Aiden hastened to assure her. "I like Swan Harbor. It's just a bit ..."

"Eccentric?" Harper offered.

He grinned, and that little zip she'd felt the other day standing outside his office reoccurred. But then he'd been talking to Sarah. Who was she?

Ask him.

Before she'd worked up the courage, he pointed to another flagpole, and the moment was gone.

"Have you always lived in Swan Harbor?" he asked, and the personal question surprised her.

"I went to grad school in Florida."

"Really?"

"University of," she explained. "But when I graduated, I heard Swan Harbor U was hiring, so ..."

He must have heard something in her voice because he gave her a look, and as clearly as if he'd spoken, she read, *Who hurt you?*

Joel.

Aiden's eyes flared as the name flitted through her mind, but that story wasn't one she was prepared to discuss.

"There's the turn to the Harbor Cross Nursing Home." Harper pointed to a hidden drive close to the hospital. "And there's—"

"Lois and—"

"—Glynnis," Harper supplied. "I ran into them earlier today."

"They're backtracking?"

"Not really," she explained. "More than likely coming full circle. They live in a retirement village nearby."

"I see."

Harper smirked as the tone of his voice said he didn't really see at all.

"There you are." Lois waved from across the parking lot. "Your aunt was getting concerned."

"Your aunt?" Aiden murmured.

"My Aunt Laura is the director," Harper whispered before turning to Lois. "I sent her a text."

"I know, dear," Lois tsked. "But you know how the residents can get."

"I'm here now." Harper grinned. "She can relax."

"And with your young man—"

"Oh, he's not ..." Harper tried to interject.

"—here to help?" Lois went on. "Aiden, isn't it?"

"Yes, ma'am." Aiden smiled at Lois. "How are you, Mrs. Duncan?"

"He remembered me, Glynnis," Lois whispered to her sister. "This is the young man who helped me locate my green bra the other night. He's such a gentleman."

"Thank you, ma'am." Aiden cleared his throat, and the twinkle in his eye caused Harper's heart to flutter. "Do I even want to ask what has captured your attention?"

Lois hooked her arm through Aiden's and directed him toward the flagpole.

"Those," she pointed up, "are Rupert's."

"Rupert?" Aiden sputtered. "As in your—"

"—Husband, yes," Lois exclaimed. "I bought those for Rupert for his last birthday. And yet, here they are, flying above Harbor Cross instead of covering Rupert's bony ass."

"Oh, I see," Aiden began, in his oh-so-very precise manner. "That is a problem."

"Isn't it?"

"Here, I can take the cookies," Harper offered.

Their gazes met, and she almost laughed.

I thought I could get away, his said.

With Lois? Good luck.

Don't leave me out here alone, he pleaded.

Sorry, Harper sighed. *But you don't know my aunt.*

His quick intake of air confirmed he'd received her message. But the wordless exchange they'd just had shaken her more than before.

You can read my mind?

I can.

Harper bit her lip, and when Aiden's gaze touched on them, they tingled.

Who are you?

He arched a brow, and yet again, she was struck with the thought that he resembled someone else.

"Harper!" Laura yelled. "We're waiting."

"I'm coming, Aunt Laura." She grinned at Aiden. "Lois can bring you in when she's done with you."

"But don't you need my help?"

"When you're done," Harper laughed. "I'll see you inside."

You're going to pay for this.

Promises, promises.

Aiden watched Harper until she disappeared into the building and wondered how he'd gotten himself into this situation.

You flirted.

Did I?

Yes! Where did this confidence come from?

You're asking me?

It's certainly not Clark who's been spending time with Harper.

But now what?

You can do it.

"I really should," he began.

"Oh, we'll have you in there in no time," Lois assured him. "Harper's a lovely girl, isn't she?"

She's beautiful.

He couldn't say that out loud, though. "I don't know her very well. But she seems quite nice."

"Oh, she's more than nice," Lois replied. "She's special."

"I see."

"Now." Lois pointed to Rupert's boxers. "Can you please rescue those for me?"

Aiden frowned. "Isn't there a law about messing with evidence?"

"Just a little one," Lois acknowledged. "I'm sure Killian won't mind."

Their eyes clashed for several minutes before she reached for the rope on the pole.

"If you won't do it, I will. Just keep a lookout."

When she started tugging on the rope and had to go up on her tiptoes, Aiden gave in. "Alright, I'll help, but if Killian asks, this was your fault."

She laughed. "Oh, don't worry. Nothing will happen to you."

"It better not," Aiden grumbled. But since she didn't respond, he assumed she hadn't heard him.

"Hurry," Glynnis whispered when he had the boxers halfway down.

"I'm bloody hurrying."

After only a few more tugs, he grabbed the prize. "Here you go, Lois."

"Oh, thank you," she gushed. "See, they say, '*Hey there, Hot Lips.*'"

"Very nice." Aiden tightly wrapped the rope around the pole. "Are we ready to go find Harper now?"

"I am. How about you, Glynnis?"

Each grabbed one of his arms and led him into the nursing home.

"Sandy, where's Harper?" Lois asked the woman standing just inside the door.

"She's making her way from room to room," Sandy replied.

"Was she being careful?" Lois followed up.

Aiden wondered what kind of trouble one could get into inside a nursing home. He just wasn't willing to ask ... yet.

"You know Harper's always careful," answered Sandy. "She's been coming here since she was a teen.

"That's good," Lois responded. "Because this is her young man."

"I'm not—," Aiden began, feeling the heat climb.

Sandy laughed. "Oh, don't worry. Harper told me you were a colleague. She started in the east hall if you want to help. Just be careful."

But as Lois and Glynnis led him toward the east hallway, he kept seeing the staff weave in and out of rooms.

"What—?" he barely got out before he ran into a woman heading in the opposite direction with her walker.

"Well, hello," she purred, throwing her arms around him and covering his lips with hers.

For a split second, Aiden's mind shut down, and all he registered was being surrounded by strong perfume. Then his brain clicked back on, and he grabbed the woman's arms and reared back. "Excuse me, Madam."

"Oh, there's no reason to excuse yourself, honey. You're quite the looker."

Aiden heard Lois snicker and side-eyed her. "A little help here."

"Oh, okay," Lois chuckled. "But you should see your face."

"That sounds ominous."

"It's nothing, really." She turned her attention to the woman who'd kissed him. "Come on, Yvonne. You've had your fun."

The infamous Yvonne winked. "I certainly did."

"Glynnis, help Aiden find Harper," Lois instructed before leading Yvonne back down the hall.

"Shall we?"

Glynnis grinned. "Sure, honey, but just be careful."

He followed her down the hall and waited while she stuck her head in and out of several rooms before locating Harper.

"There you are. I've got your young man."

"I'll be right out," Harper called from inside the room.

"I found her for you," Glynnis winked. "You're on your own now."

"Thank you for your help."

"Be careful," she whispered cryptically.

He waved her off, leaned back against the doorframe, and crossed his arms across his chest.

Then an unfamiliar pair of lips touched his, and when he opened his eyes, he found another woman had latched onto him.

"Minnie!" Harper pulled the woman away. "That's enough."

The older woman took several steps, then glanced back over her shoulder and blew him a kiss.

"What am I missing?"

Harper grinned. "You mean you don't know?"

"I have no idea," Aiden grumbled.

"Come with me." Harper pulled him down the hall and through a door that said, '*Staff only.*' "Look."

Since she'd taken his hand, Aiden's thoughts had short-circuited, and it took an extra moment for him to look in the mirror.

"Bloody hell," he muttered. The same dark hair and blue eyes, but several shades of lipstick were smeared on his face. "But why?"

Harper chuckled. "Mistletoe."

"Mistletoe?" he repeated stupidly.

"Yes," she explained. "You know the hemiparasitic plant that decorates doors and ceilings during the Christmas season?"

"I know bloody hell what mistletoe is," he barked, earning another snicker from her. "But I didn't see any."

"That's the plan." Harper handed him a wet towel to wipe his mouth. "It's attached closely to the ceiling—"

"Was that why no one walked a straight line?"

"Very good, Doctor Jones." She led him from the bathroom and pointed at the ceiling tiles. As soon as he glanced up, he could see he'd been snookered. "Bloody brilliant. How did you not—?"

"—Get caught under one?"

"Yes."

"I've been coming here since I was a teenager," she replied. "I know where they're hung."

Do you now?

You wouldn't dare.

Aiden followed Harper up and down the hallway, and while she delivered the cookies, he checked to see if the resident had diabetes or was on a special diet. But after having his cheeks pinched and getting more kisses than he'd had in a while, he finally realized she'd set him up.

"Is Mr. Montague good to go?" Harper stopped outside the last room.

Aiden gave her a suspicious look.

"What?"

Except he didn't buy her innocent expression, and before he glanced at the color coding on the door, he checked the frame for mistletoe.

"You don't trust me?"

He advanced on her slowly, looking one way and then the other.

Harper's eyes grew wide, and her pulse fluttered rapidly in her neck.

"Aiden," she muttered breathlessly. "What are you doing?"

For every one step she took, he took two until they stood toe to toe, her back against the wall. She's so petite, he thought, gazing down into her upturned face. He placed one hand on the wall next to her head and pinned her in.

"You weren't very nice."

"Oh, come on," she forced out. "You didn't mind sharing a few kisses with these women. Now, did you?"

"What do you think?" Aiden leaned forward just enough so he could feel the gentle puff of her breath against his mouth.

"What do I think?" she practically purred.

"Yes, look." Aiden pointed up, assuming her eyes would follow his finger.

"I don't see anything," she uttered a second before sliding under his arm and into the last room.

"Bloody hell," Aiden muttered, turning around to lean against the wall. "What are you doing?"

"Waiting for you," he heard before someone pinched his cheeks, and then kissed him again.

Why was it he volunteered to help her?

Because you like her.

"I'm ready." Harper breezed out of the room. "Time to head to the rehabilitation center."

"I'm not sure my cheeks can stand it."

It was only the way his heart flipped when she giggled that had him following her out the door.

After all, he was trying to listen to it.

Swan Harbor Pier

December 5

3:00 p.m.

Finn was slowly meandering along the pier, his thoughts on where he was going to hang the plant he was carrying when his phone buzzed. "Miss me, love?" he teased in a husky voice.

"Of course, I miss you," Ava assured him. "But that's not why I'm calling."

"Is there a problem?"

"I hope not."

"What is it?"

"It's Becca."

As soon as Ava said her name, Finn knew where she was going.

"This is about her husband, isn't it?"

"How did you know?"

"Because I know you," he said out loud. But he was thinking because I investigated your friend's husband.

"You do, don't you?"

"Ava, love, what do you need me to do?"

"Well," she eased into the story. "Becca is meeting Sam at Papa's Pizzeria and giving him the divorce papers. I just thought maybe ..."

"You want me to check on your friend?"

Ava sighed. "I just don't want him knocking her confidence. She's been doing so well."

"I'll check on her." His voice lowered. "But it's going to cost you."

Her breath caught. "What do you want?"

Everything and anything. "You know that thing you do with your talented mouth?" Her hum was low, sexy, making him wish she were standing right in front of him. "That's what I want."

"I think I can arrange that," she promised.

"I'll be looking forward to my reward."

With images in his head of Ava looking up at him as he was rewarded, Finn sauntered up the walk toward the pizzeria. He arrived to find a rather large group of women congregated outside the shop. Several of whom had their faces pressed against the window.

Finn pulled one woman aside. "Anita, is everything okay?"

"So far," she confirmed. "But that's why we're here."

"To keep an eye on Becca?"

"Oh, no," Giennie, the local realtor, exclaimed. "We're here to watch that slimeball husband of hers. If he says something we don't like, he's dead meat."

Finn winced. "You don't mean that literally, do you?"

Giennie's eyes met his, and in them, he saw determination.

"We take care of our own."

"Ignore her." Anita pushed Giennie out of the way. "She's just messing with you because she heard you were thinking of encroaching."

"Encroaching?" Finn turned troubled eyes back to Giennie. "I would never."

"That's good," Giennie deadpanned. "Or I might have to sic Paddy on you."

The image of Giennie's large, ex-football player husband flashed through Finn's mind.

"I ..." Then he noticed the twinkle in Giennie's eyes, telling him they'd played him. "Nice try, ladies. But it seems Becca has help if she needs it. Carry on."

"Thanks for stopping by Finn." Anita smiled. "Ava's lucky to have you on her side."

Finn acknowledged her comment, but couldn't keep the goofy grin off his face. "It is I who am the lucky one."

Giennie snickered. "Can I send Paddy to you for some 'sweet talk' lessons? That man has breathed in too much sweat or something."

Finn chuckled. And with one more look inside Papa's windows, assuring him all was as it should be, he waved goodbye to the women. He liked that Swan Harbor was a place where people looked out for others. That small-town charm, as his wife called it. And with his job of *checking on Becca* over, he could set his sights on collecting his reward.

Finn: Becca has her army. I'm ready for my prize.

Instead of a verbal response, Ava sent a picture that was worth a few thousand words that had him rushing home.

"Ava, love," Finn called, slamming the door behind him. "Where are you?"

"I'm up here," her voice wafted down the stairs.

He took them two at a time and found her going through her lingerie drawer.

"What are you looking for?"

"My babydoll," Ava replied. "The one that matches your sheer blue boxers that are flying above The Beach Shack."

Finn grunted, annoyed, and a bit embarrassed because someone had been in his home and had taken something of his. But it wasn't just the fact that someone had taken his boxers. It was that he hadn't noticed.

You're getting soft.

He had to agree his heart certainly felt mushy, but other parts of his anatomy ....

"How did you get a picture of my boxers?" Finn asked, curious why he hadn't seen them when he'd passed the restaurant.

"I found the blue one." Ava held up the nightgown. "But I can't find the red one."

"The red one that matches my sleep pants?"

"Yes. And Harper took the picture."

"Harper?"

"Yes. What are you going to do?"

"Check for my sleep pants." Finn tugged on the drawer, and as expected, found them missing. "Then I'm going to hang this all over the house." He held up the sprig of mistletoe he'd brought home.

Her dark brows rose. "And then?"

"Collect my reward."

"But, but," Ava stuttered as he sauntered toward her. "What about our things? Shouldn't you call Killian?"

"Bloody hell, no," Finn retorted. "I don't plan on discussing my underwear situation with my son."

"But Finn." Ava slid her hands up his chest and around his neck. "I liked those boxers and my red nightie."

He cupped her arse and pushed her hips into the cradle of his. "I'll buy you more. Now ... my reward ..."

SEVEN

Swan Harbor University
December 12
11:30 a.m.

Harper stood in front of her classroom, waiting for the last few students to finish their final exams, and had to fight to stay focused. It had been a week since Aiden had come to her rescue, and moments during the time they'd spent together still caused her heart to speed up.

The way he'd looked with lipstick smeared on his face. His exasperated expression when yet another resident pinched his cheeks or kissed him. But it was what she saw in his eyes as he'd advanced on her under the mistletoe that continued to take her breath. Was that her heart talking, or was it just that she'd not had a man treat her like he did ... in, well ... ever?

"Merry Christmas, Doctor Taylor." Mia set her exam on the pile. "Nice sweater."

Harper glanced down at the sweater her grandmother had sent her while she'd been going to grad school in Florida. Santa was sitting in the sand under a decorated palm tree, sipping an umbrella drink.

"Thank you, Mia." Harper looked out the window at the gray sky. "One of Florida's sunny days would be nice right now."

"Definitely. No snow in Florida."

"That's true." Harper grinned. "Have a Merry Christmas and enjoy your break."

Harper watched Mia leave, surprised to see Aiden hovering just outside the door.

The first thing she noticed was he was wearing his glasses. But even through them, his gaze was so intense she had to hold on to the table to keep from falling.

The longer he stared, the more he mesmerized her ... then ... he smiled. There was something so endearing, yet sexy, that if she hadn't been holding onto the table, her legs would have given out.

Cute sweater, she read from across the room.

Hey, you're just jealous you don't have one, she sent back.

He blushed and ducked his head, and the thought, *he's awkward,* floated by ....

Then the last few students brought their tests forward, and when she looked back up, Aiden was gone. There was a part of her that wanted to ponder what had just happened, but that would have to wait since she had a lunch date.

She left the exams in her office, and when she walked outside, saw that it had snowed. There was a hush in the air that wasn't usually present since many students were already gone for the holidays. Except, it felt like it was more than that. Not only did the world around her feel different—*she* did too.

On her way across campus, she thought about what might be different. It took several seconds, but she finally decided the biggest difference was the feelings within herself. Almost as if optimism had replaced the negativity she'd brought from Florida, and hope had pushed aside cynicism. Was that because she was listening to her heart? Was it the town, her friends, family—or was it Aiden?

Her mother, Doctor Beverly Taylor, an economics professor, was waiting just inside the doors of the student union.

"Hi, Mom." Harper stamped the snow off her boots. "All done with exams?"

"Finished today," Beverly shared. "Now, I need to grade."

Harper groaned. "Me too."

"Perils of the profession, I'm afraid," laughed Beverly.

"I thought that was worrying about tenure," Harper replied, knowing that was her next professional goal.

"Well, that too," Beverly sighed. "Plus, the many committees."

"No one's pushed me into any yet," Harper answered. "But I know my time will come."

"Just wait. Meet you at the usual table?"

Harper nodded and slowly let out the breath she'd been holding while she decided what to eat. However, the look on her mother's face, as she slid into a chair across from her, said she'd relaxed too soon.

"So, tell me about Aiden," Beverly began by saying.

"Wow," Harper laughed. "You didn't even wait until I started eating."

Beverly's dark eyes sparkled, making Harper wonder what she'd heard from her aunt or grandmother.

"What can I say?" Beverly's eyes flared when Harper took off her coat. "Oh, my word, Harper Deanne! I can't believe you wore that sweater!"

Harper had to fight not to giggle. "Come on, Mom. It's cute. Who can resist Santa on the beach?"

"It's not Santa that I mind." Beverly waved her fork toward the sweater for emphasis. "It's that palm tree, and the way it's outlined."

"What?" Harper asked innocently, pushing the button on the battery pack, lighting up the tree.

"That's why." Beverly jabbed her fork at the sweater. "The tree looks like a man's thingy."

"Thingy?" Harper snickered. "Come on, Mom. You can say the word. It looks like a man's pe—"

"Beverly, Harper." Dean Montague approached their table, forcing her to swallow the rest of the word. "This year's festivities are off to a bang-up start, aren't they?"

"Hello, Reginald," Beverly murmured, making Harper feel guilty for embarrassing her mother. "There's never a dull moment in Swan Harbor, is there?"

"No, there isn't." He turned to Harper just as she shut off her sweater lights. "My grandfather enjoyed the cookies you dropped by last week. That was kind of you."

Harper had always had a soft spot for the elder Montague, who'd substituted at Swan Harbor High well into his nineties. As a reporter who'd traveled all over the world, his stories always sounded exciting.

"I'm glad he enjoyed them," she replied. "I knew the peanut butter ones were his favorite."

"They are. Thank you again." He said goodbye, leaving her alone with her mother.

"You don't think he heard you, do you?" Beverly whispered.

"I doubt it," Harper tried to assure her mom. "But it was what you were thinking."

"I'll never understand your grandmother."

"You just got the nice genes." Harper snickered. "And Aunt Rhonda got the bawdy ones."

"Don't get me started on your aunt." Beverly rolled her eyes. "Let's talk about you. Aren't you still doing that research study?"

That her mother moved away from Aiden on to her secret match wasn't a total surprise. They'd had the same conversation after each four-week period when her matches had changed.

"You know I am. But only for a few more weeks."

"It ends on New Year's Eve, right?"

"Yes."

"What's the matter, honey?" Beverly's stare said she was trying to read Harper's mind. "It's not going well?"

"No, it's going fine," Harper sighed. "And my match 'Clark' seems nice. It's just getting very complicated."

"How so?"

"You know me," Harper went on. "Things fall out of my mouth. And since we can't 'say' anything that could hint at our identity, I'm always checking and double checking my responses."

"I would think that would be difficult," Beverly agreed. "So, no discussion about families or jobs?"

"None." Then she chuckled at the memory of the conversation she'd been having with Clark for the past several days. "Right now, we're arguing over the best band of all time."

"Queen," Beverly immediately responded.

"That's what I tried to tell him." Harper shook her head. "But he swears it's the Beatles."

"The Beatles?" Beverly echoed. "Any specific reason?"

"He thinks the harpsichord in the song '*In My Life*' is amazing."

"He has a point."

"I know," Harper grumbled. "I'm trying to come up with a new question to ask him."

Beverly hummed. "How about ...?"

Swan Harbor Library
December 12
12:30 p.m.

Aiden pulled into a parking spot at the library and looked out the window. The snowflakes were larger and more plentiful than they'd been just an hour before. Was it a mistake to spend a few hours on research? After all, he'd not grown up driving in the snow, especially on the wrong side of the road.

If you get stuck, you could call Harper.

The thought brought her back to the forefront of his mind, a place where she'd spent quite a large amount of time over the last week. He couldn't forget the way her brown eyes had grown even larger when he'd boxed her in. Or at least when he thought he'd gotten the best of her. Except she'd skirted away before he'd ....

Do you really think you'd have kissed her?

He wanted to believe the answer was yes. But part of him suspected he was fooling himself. That was the only reason he answered truthfully—no, but damn if he hadn't wanted to.

"Listen to your heart when it speaks," Jack said. "It always knows."

"I'm trying, Jack." Aiden grabbed his briefcase and headed into the library.

The smell was the first thing he noticed—one that was universal in libraries—no matter where you were. Old books, a little must, and whatever cleaning products they used.

"You must be Aiden Jones," a brunette who appeared to be in her early thirties greeted him. "Captain Jack said you would stop by sometime."

"I am. Are you Amanda?"

"Amanda Kane." She shook his hand. "I've laid out a pile of newspapers for you. There's also a list of where you could find others on microfilm. I've also included several books written about Swan Harbor. Can I get you anything else?"

When she stopped talking, it took Aiden an extra second to process everything she'd said. Especially since she'd said it all with a single breath.

"This is very nice of you," he began. "I wasn't expecting this much help."

"I like to be helpful." Amanda smiled. "That's our motto here at the library. Be helpful. So, if there's anything you need, just let me know. I just want to be ... you know—"

"—Helpful," they finished simultaneously.

Amanda led him to a table in the back corner where she'd left stacks of material for him.

"Thank you, Mrs. Kane." Aiden set his briefcase on the table, ready to begin.

"Are you sure there's nothing else you need?" she asked again.

"I'll let you know." Aiden pulled out a chair, located a notebook, and reached for a book.

In the Beginning; The Origins of Swan Harbor, written by M. Prince in 1965.

He almost flipped through the pages looking for mention of the pirate or pirate ship. Instead, he opened to the first chapter.

Chapter One - The Beginning

In March 1692, Prince Geoffrey and his band of like-minded travelers arrived at the port in what is now Boston, Massachusetts. They had been forced to leave their home in England for refusing to sign an oath of allegiance, pledging their support to the Jacobites. America offered them an opportunity to start over. Determined to provide a place for the new settlers to call home, their caravan began traveling north. Geoffrey was looking for a place where the land was fertile, the water was plentiful, and the opportunities were endless. But after four weeks of traveling by foot and wagon, he'd begun to think he was searching for the impossible.

And then, almost as if they were being given a sign, they spotted a wedge of beautiful swans in the distance.

"We must follow them," he told the others.

There was much grumbling among the men of the group until Anne Michaels stepped forward.

"We follow the swans," she proclaimed in a soft, albeit forceful, voice. "Look, they are being guided by a black swan."

Everyone gasped and glared at her with identical frightened expressions.

"One black swan in a bevy of white? Isn't that an omen?" one asked.

"Black swans are a reminder to reclaim your personal freedom," Anne explained. "Isn't that what we're doing?"

The arguing continued, but Geoffrey stepped forward and gently touched Anne on the shoulder. She'd been the one to help his mother, Caroline, when he'd been born. And when she had become ill, it had been Anne they'd called.

"She's right," he cried. "We left England for a fresh start. Those swans will lead us to the water.

Within hours, they'd decided, and while several family units peeled off in other directions, the majority remained.

The swans led them farther north, past what is now Portland, and then they flew east and disappeared.

"What do we do now?" they asked Geoffrey.

"Why, we follow, of course."

Using whatever tools they had brought and could find, the settlers cut through the heavy foliage that lined the path. It was lush, and once they broke through, they discovered ...

Sheriff's Department
December 12
1:30 p.m.

"Killian, line 1," Amy said over the intercom. "It's Madge Tanner."

"Bloody hell," Killian murmured. "You wanted to talk to her, right?"

"Enjoy," Rusty laughed, closing the file he'd been looking through. "I'm meeting Rene for lunch."

"Wanker," Killian muttered. "Tell your wife hello." He answered the phone. "What can I do for you, Madge?"

"Killian," she snapped, her voice coming across loud and shrill. "I need to know if you have my Jimmie's boxers."

"Why would you ask me if I have your husband's boxers?"

"Because." She cleared her throat. "Boxers were flying all over the town last week."

"Well, yes, there—"

"So, shouldn't you have collected them all by now?"

"We've collected them," he cut in.

"Then can you tell me if you have Jimmie's boxers?"

"Let's try this," Killian suggested. "Give me the specifics, and once I've gone through all the information, I'll let you know."

"That's the best you can come up with, young man?" she huffed. "The last time this happened, Ernie was on top of things."

"I'm working as quickly as I can," Killian assured her. "Now, what are you looking for?"

"Boxers," she stated. "They're size large and have dancing hot dogs on them."

"Dancing hot dogs?" Killian repeated.

"Yes!" she went on. "You know a wiener in a bun with legs, and they're dancing?"

Killian held in the groan, but barely, when she continued.

"Do you know how long the boxers have been missing?" he interjected when she'd taken a breath.

"Well, I can't pin it down exactly," Madge explained. "I believe Jimmie wore them during the week of Thanksgiving. But I washed them on the Friday after."

"You're sure you washed them on the Friday after Thanksgiving?"

"I always do my laundry on Fridays, Killian."

"That wasn't what I was asking, ma'am."

"Well, what was it then?"

Killian pinched the bridge of his nose and prayed for patience.

"I was asking if, on the Friday after Thanksgiving, Jimmie's boxers were in the wash."

"Well, of course, I washed Jimmie's boxers!" she exclaimed.

"Were Jimmie's dancing hotdog boxers in the wash?" he reworded the question.

"Sure."

"Alright then, Mrs. Tanner," Killian replied. "I have all the information I need."

"You'll call me back?"

"Aye. As soon as I know something."

When she said goodbye and hung up without going on, he thanked his lucky stars and added her information to the *'boxer theft'* file.

But as he was making notes about the flying boxers, a piece of his conversation with Rusty from a few weeks back rolled back around.

"And on December 12," Rusty read on, "skivvies were flying ..."

"Skivvies were flying?" Killian murmured.

Which had been something they'd read from the notes in December 2000.

He grabbed the file and flipped it open.

Bras on the tree on December 1.

Check, he thought, already happened.

December 4—dozens were seen hanging ....

Could that have been the boxers 'hanging' from the flagpoles? Or was something else coming down the line?

December 12—skivvies were flying ...

"Killian." Dylan strolled into their office. "Have you come to any conclusions?"

"Madge is looking for Jimmie's dancing hotdog boxers," he quipped.

"That wasn't quite the information I was expecting," Dylan grumbled.

Killian pointed to the report from 2000. "Do flying boxers count as 'were seen hanging' or 'skivvies flying'?"

"What do you think?" Dylan turned the question back.

"Flying skivvies," Killian retorted. "But why aren't the 'gifts' in the same order?"

Dylan shrugged. "Call Ernie. Did you ask Amy for his number?"

"I left a message," Killian admitted. "He hasn't called back."

"Call Rupert."

"Rupert?" Killian raised a brow in question. "Why, Rupert?"

"I think they're neighbors."

"Alright." He grabbed the phone.

"'Lo," Rupert barked.

"It's Killian, Rupert. Do you have a moment?"

"I'm retired," Rupert grumbled. "It's snowing outside. I have several moments. Why? Need me to help solve this case?"

"No," Killian sputtered, not willing to admit how little he knew about the situation. "I was hoping you'd seen Ernie Luka lately."

Rupert hummed. "Depends on what you mean by lately."

"Recently, then," Killian settled on. "Have you seen Ernie recently?"

"Recently?" Rupert hummed. "No, I can't say I've seen him recently. He …"

The word hung in the air for so long, Killian lost his patience. "Bloody hell, Rupert. Do you know where Ernie is or not?"

"Of course I do."

"And?"

"He's fishing in Florida."

Killian clenched his teeth so hard, he felt the pulse in his jaw begin to tic.

"Do you have the phone number?"

"Sure. Let me ask Lois."

Killian fully expected Rupert to return and yank his chain some more. To Killian's pleasant surprise, Rupert returned, rattled off the number, and hung up.

"Goodbye to you too," Killian retorted, dialing the number for Ernie Luka.

"Yo." Someone answered the phone on the third ring.

"Is this Ernie Luka?"

"Who wants to know?"

"This is Killian Reade. I'm a detective in the Swan Harbor Sheriff's Department. Do you have a moment?"

"So, you're the new guy, huh?" Ernie laughed. "Heard you brought some excitement to the town and took care of Santora for good."

"I was lucky, sir."

"Oh, don't be modest," Ernie went on. "Now, what can I do for you?"

"Tell me about the case in December 2000," Killian requested.

"December 2000?" Ernie repeated. "Which case would that be?"

"The one where stolen bras ended up on the town Christmas tree," Killian reminded him.

"The bras?" Ernie hesitated a second before adding, "Oh! The bras!" His chuckle grew into a full-belly laugh. "I already solved that case, son. This one's for you. Good luck." Then the phone went dead.

"Bloody hell!" Killian muttered just as his brother arrived.

"What happened?" Liam asked.

Killian quickly shared what he could, but his thoughts were still spinning.

"Maybe lunch will help you figure things out. Come on, I'm starving."

"You're always starving."

On the way out of the department, Killian stopped at Amy's desk when he heard his name.

"Yes, Mrs. Patterson," Amy replied. "Killian is the detective handling those."

He shook his head and mimed that he was going to lunch.

"He's at lunch now, Mrs. Patterson. But as soon as he returns, I'll give him the message." She was quiet for several seconds before continuing, "Yes, ma'am. Panty wreaths. I've got it."

As soon as she'd hung up, Killian shook his head. "Don't tell me more underwear has disappeared."

"Actually reappeared," Amy laughed. "Panties folded into Christmas wreaths."

"I'll deal with it after lunch," Killian sighed. "What's next with these thieves?"

"Look at it this way," Liam quipped on their way out the door. "At least they're not lacy."

"That was bad."

"Hey," Liam laughed. "Aren't you the one who always says, 'you work with what you have?'"

EIGHT

Sally's Diner
December 12
2:30 p.m.

Liam wiped his mouth, tossed his napkin on his plate, and pushed it aside. Killian, sitting across the table from him, had been a horrible lunch companion, lost in his own thoughts.

"You'll never believe what was zipping along the gossip line today," he tossed out.

"What?"

An answer not unlike he'd gotten before from his brother, he decided.

"Seems Joe Gordon's wife, Rita, came home early from the office and found him playing Santa with the neighbor."

Killian grunted, pushing Liam to add, "Apparently, the neighbor gave a whole new meaning to sitting on Santa's lap."

"Bloody hell, Liam," Killian grunted. "Did you have to put that image in my head?"

Liam shrugged and angled so he could stretch one long leg along the bench. "Just thought I'd share."

"I wish you hadn't."

"Thought it might make you a better lunch companion."

"Sorry." Killian ran his hand through his hair and leaned back. "I keep thinking of my call with Ernie. What was so funny?"

"The answer, of course."

"The answer to what?"

Liam rolled his eyes. "And you call yourself an investigator. The answer to the question. What did you ask him?"

"To tell me about the case in December 2000," Killian grumbled.

"And that's when he started laughing?"

"Aye," Killian muttered. "Repeated the words 'the bras' twice and then said he'd already solved that case, and this one was for me."

"Is this case like any other you've worked?"

"Bloody hell, no!"

"Then maybe that's the problem," Liam pointed out. "Perhaps you're trying to solve in one way when what you really need is to go another."

"What the bloody hell does that mean?" Killian groused.

Liam shrugged. "No idea, but it sounded good, didn't it?"

Killian muttered under his breath for a few minutes but then suddenly frowned. "Isn't Joe Gordon the high school hockey coach?"

Liam grinned. "It's about time you tuned in. But yes, he's the hockey coach. Rita tossed his arse out in the cold."

"Does this mean Rita is your next matchmaking case?"

"Let's not rush things," Liam cautioned. "I'm still working on Aiden."

"I thought Aiden was involved in that matchmaking project at the university."

"He is," Liam hummed. "But, I think he has a thing for Harper, and ... they're going to the dance together."

"Isn't that a good thing?"

"For Aiden?" Liam grunted. "No. Too many things to keep track of. In fact, here comes the man I want to talk to."

"Hayden?" Killian asked, just as the younger man arrived to clear their plates.

"Need anything else?"

"I do," Liam spoke up. "Aren't you part of that project at the university?"

Hayden frowned. "What do you know about that? I know you aren't involved."

"Not me directly," Liam hedged. "But ..."

"He's matching our cousin with yours," Killian interjected.

"Which one?" Hayden laughed. "I have several."

"Harper."

"I heard my Aunt Laura talking to Aunt Sally a few days ago about them."

"Really?" Liam leaned closer. "What were they saying?"

Hayden shrugged. "I don't know."

"How could you not know?" Liam sighed. "You didn't listen?"

"No."

Liam blew out a breath in annoyance. "So, back to the project. Can you 'share' with me who Aiden's 'match' is?"

"Why?"

What could he say that would get Hayden on his side? Finally, he opted for the truth.

"I believe Aiden likes Harper. And I know they're going to the Gala together. But with the match hanging out there ... I just worry he won't take a chance."

Hayden shifted his weight from one leg to the other and then glanced across the room.

"How's it going with Katrina?" Liam tossed out.

"It's not," Hayden admitted.

"Have you asked her out?"

Hayden winced. "I tried, but she was busy and ..."

"How about a deal?" Liam proposed. "You help me, and I'll help you."

"You think you can help me?"

Liam scoffed. "I know I can help you."

The younger man's gaze drifted around the room to land on the girl again.

"Okay. Let me get my computer."

"I certainly hope you know what you're doing," Killian retorted. "You don't want to piss off their aunt. Or Terri Patterson, their—"

"Speaking of ..." Liam tipped his chin toward the door.

"What?" Killian barely got out before four women arrived, led by Hayden's grandmother. "Ladies."

"Killian," Terri exclaimed. "You need to come with us."

"What is it?"

"Panty thieves," a gray-headed woman Liam hadn't met piped up.

"And it can't wait until after lunch?"

"No," Dorothy, one of Swan Harbor's biggest gossips, insisted. "How would you like to have your panties taken?"

"Madam, I assure you, I don't wear panties."

Liam snickered at his brother's discomfort. "No, just skivvies with kittens on them."

"Those were yours?!" Terri chuckled, confirming she'd seen Killian's kitten boxers flying above the sheriff's department.

"Never mind that," Killian grumbled. "Don't get your panties in a wad. I'm coming."

"It's why we're upset," Terri insisted. "Someone wadded up our panties and wove them into wreaths."

"Let's go."

"Thank you," Terri beamed. "And here comes Hayden to entertain Liam."

"Have fun."

Killian gave Liam a dirty look, but as soon as Hayden slid across from him, he forgot all about his brother's problems.

Hayden powered up his laptop. "Okay. Each individual taking part had to fill out a questionnaire. They chose an alias and were given their first match at the end of September. That was based on their relationship with their families, what type of families they wanted, etc. The next match was based on career and life goals. With me so far?"

"I'm not bloody daft," Liam retorted. "But if this only involves Swan Harbor University, there are only so many unattached individuals."

Hayden gave him the look many his age had perfected. The one that said, '*Are you sure you aren't daft?*' and continued.

"It's not just SHU," Hayden explained. "There are ten colleges and universities, all in the northeast."

"Alright, that makes more sense. And the last matches?"

"During Thanksgiving week, the matches were based on interests outside of work," Hayden went on. "Let's see who Aiden's match is."

Liam watched Hayden's fingers fly across the keyboard until finally, he looked up with a smile. "Rosalind is Aiden's match."

"I bloody know that," Liam grumbled. "Who's Rosalind?"

Again, Hayden's fingers flew across the keys, and the look on his face gave Liam his answer.

"It's Harper, isn't it?"

"Yes," Hayden admitted.

"How about the first two matches?"

Once more, Hayden went back to his computer. "I don't believe it," he murmured after several seconds.

"Harper?"

"Yes," Hayden nodded, closing his computer. "All three parameters matched them."

Liam grinned, trying to decide whether he said something to his cousin or if he should let the experiment play out.

"What happens at the end?"

"The matches decide if they want to meet," Hayden explained. "The ones who do will be rolled over into a longitudinal study the sociology department is planning. Now, I helped you …"

"You did," Liam agreed, "and I promised to help you. Here's what you need to do …"

Swan Harbor Library

December 12

3:30 p.m.

Aiden had written several pages of notes, but when he found no mention of Ian Jones in the book, he'd pushed it aside. Then, he began sorting through the articles Amanda had laid out. Except instead of focusing on what he should do, his thoughts kept straying to his latest message from Rosalind.

Clark,

Okay, I'll agree that the In My Life harpsichord solo is pretty good. But since you play the piano, which present-day performer do you admire?

Rosalind

Something made him lay down his pen to answer.

Rosalind,

While there are many wonderful pianists, such as
Jim Brickman and John Tesh, I really enjoy Yanni.
There's just something about his combination of
piano, synthesizers, and a full orchestra that
speaks to me.

Here's a question for you to go with the season.
What's your favorite Christmas song?

Clark

He'd barely set his phone down when a message from his sister arrived.

Sarah: Have you found anything more about when
Ian first arrived in Swan Harbor? I've been trying
to find out more about the silver coins. I found out
that in the fall of 1715, a tattered ship hobbled
into port in what is now The Carolinas. I can't find
the name of that ship, but … it was a Spanish
galleon. And there was mention of the ship
carrying silver and gold, which could have been
used to restore the ship. Then, a ship called El
corazón del Rubí sailed off the waters along the
Delaware coast that fall. And the Ruby Heart was
a Spanish galleon, just like ….

"Hope's Haven," Aiden murmured.

Could Captain Jack's Fine Dining, the restaurant that was in the Spanish galleon, and anchored one end of the Swan Harbor pier, be El corazón del Rubí? Was that ship part of the Spanish Treasury Fleet? They believed it to be Hope's Haven, the ship the pirate Ian Jones had left for his heir. Were they the same?

Something had him separating the newspapers, and a headline stretched across the top of the Swan Harbor Daily News caught his eye: **Who are you?** With a small picture of Captain Jack's Spanish galleon below.

"Bloody hell," he whispered when he saw whose name was on the byline.

"What?" Liam had arrived and was looking over his shoulder.

"Nothing," Aiden remarked, deciding he didn't want to get into something he'd not investigated yet. "What are you doing here?"

Liam pulled out a chair and sat down, making Aiden think his visit was intentional instead of accidental.

"I heard you're going to the Christmas Gala after all."

Aiden grinned, as he'd wondered how long it would be before his cousin found out.

"I am. But who told you? Was it the infamous Swan Harbor gossip line?"

"Not this news," Liam laughed. "I found this out from my fiancée."

Aiden remembered when he'd rescued Harper the week before, she'd said she'd picked up Rachel and Riley from the pediatrician's office.

"And Elsa learned about it from Harper's friend, Rachel?"

"Something like that," Liam admitted.

Aiden shrugged as if it were no big deal that he was going to the dance. When in reality, he was looking forward to it. He just hoped he wasn't too awkward.

"We're helping each other out."

Liam hummed, but somehow the hum said, '*I don't quite believe you.*' "You have a tux, right?"

"My tux?" Aiden frowned. "I wasn't aware I'd need a tux."

"But didn't you say you had a tux for my wedding?"

Aiden gave Liam a sheepish smile. "I was going to rent."

Liam rolled his eyes. "Come on, cuz. You can't impress the ladies in a rented tux."

"But..." Aiden glanced at the table, thinking of all the work he still wanted to do.

"It will be here waiting for you," Liam assured him. "If we're lucky, it won't take long."

Aiden capitulated, only because he knew his cousin was right on a couple of counts. After spending a few hours with Harper the previous week, the work would wait, and he did want to impress her.

Aiden told Amanda he would return momentarily and followed Liam out of the library to find that the snow hadn't let up.

"Maybe we should do this another day," he replied, nervously noting his car already had a thin layer of snow covering it.

"We're only supposed to get 6" to 8", Liam reported, hustling him along. "We'll be fine."

"I guess."

Aiden followed his cousin down a side road, and into a small store that specialized in formal wear.

"Liam," a saleswoman greeted them. "I hope you aren't here to pick up your suit."

"No, Heidi," Liam assured her. "But I need you to work some magic on my cousin, Aiden. Think that's possible?"

She grinned. "I'll try."

"You're a peach."

When Heidi turned her dark eyes on him, Aiden felt like a fly being watched by a spider.

"Come with me," she stated.

"Trust her," Liam winked. "She knows what she's doing."

Aiden was several steps behind her, and by the time he caught up, she was holding a tux shirt, pants, and jacket.

"You're a 16½ shirt, right?" asked Heidi.

"I believe so. But it's been a while since I bought shirts," Aiden admitted.

She hung the clothes in one of the dressing rooms and pointed him toward it.

"Do you have black dress shoes?"

"Yes—" he began.

"I've seen those," Liam interrupted. "How old are they anyway?"

"A few years."

"A few?" Liam snickered. "Five, six …"

"Ten."

"Yes, he needs shoes," Liam added.

"Size 12." Heidi took off without asking if she was correct.

"How does she know what size shoe I wear?" Aiden whispered.

"She studies men closely," Liam murmured out of the corner of his mouth.

"Come, come." She hurried Aiden into the dressing room. "I'll be waiting right out here for you."

"You're in excellent hands." Liam winked. "I'll see you at the bachelor party."

Aiden ducked inside the dressing room and hurriedly changed into the pants and shirt, noticing his socks felt damp. It had come time for him to pick up some warmer shoes and clothes.

"Are you ready in there?" Heidi called.

He quickly slipped into the shoes she'd brought him and stepped out of the dressing room. "Where do you want me?"

She pointed to a set of mirrors. "Right there."

When he moved into position, she smoothed her hands across his shoulders and down his back, her hand landing on his arse just a little too long.

Heidi knelt in front of him, tugged the pant leg straight, and lined up the hem on the top of his shoe. "Which way do you dress?"

Aiden gulped and could feel the heat rising. *Bloody hell, Liam. You did this on purpose.*

"I ..."

Giennie's Gym
December 12
8:30 p.m.

Harper wearily climbed off the bike she'd ridden during her spin class at Giennie's Gym and draped a towel around her neck.

"I'd forgotten how much fun that was.

Rachel sent her a dirty look. "You don't have extra baby weight. I thought he was going to kill me."

"You look terrific," Harper assured her friend. "But I have to admit, Paddy was a bit sadistic tonight."

"It's because Giennie told him he could learn a thing or two from Finn Reade," her Aunt Laura confided.

"That's what happens after you've been married for years," Becca muttered when she passed by their group.

Harper gave her aunt a confused look, feeling as if she'd stepped into the middle of a story.

"Becca finally got her scumbag husband to sign the divorce papers," Laura confessed. "But their teenage son didn't take it well."

"I see."

"No, you don't, honey," Laura laughed. "And I hope you never have the issues Becca had with a man."

Aiden would never do to you what Joel did.

Harper agreed she didn't really understand what they were referring to. However, she understood a broken heart.

"Is Becca going to be okay?" she asked, knowing her aunt and the other woman had been friends for years.

Laura looked off in the direction Becca had gone and nodded. "I think she's going to be better than okay. She got the loan to start her business, and that's really helped her confidence."

And having confidence in oneself was important. That was something Harper understood.

"I'll see you girls later." Laura left to talk to another group.

"Let's grab our coats, and while you get Riley, I'll warm up the car."

"Sounds like a plan," Rachel agreed.

Once in the locker room, Harper slipped her sweats over her shorts and allowed her thoughts to float to the men in her life.

Aiden had made a point of stopping by her classroom earlier in the day. When he'd smiled, her beating heart had practically sung the Hallelujah chorus. Plus, exchanging flirty messages with Clark made her feel giddy.

"What are you thinking?" Rachel asked, her expression all-knowing.

"Why do you ask?"

Rachel rolled her eyes. "Because you have that Harper look."

"That Harper look?"

"Yes," Rachel groaned. "The one that says you're trying to solve a problem. Were you thinking about Aiden? Or was it, Clark?"

"A little of both," Harper admitted. "I'll tell you in the car."

"I'll hold you to that," Rachel said, on her way to pick up Riley.

Harper exited the gym, and the wind whipped around her, sending a chill through her. The biting cold had her rushing to the car, jumping inside, and starting it before searching for her gloves.

She'd just found the second one when Rachel opened the back door, letting in more cold air.

"Brrr," Harper groaned. "Hurry."

Rachel laughed. "You've gone soft."

"Guilty. I'd kill for a little of Florida's warmth right now."

Rachel fastened Riley's car seat in the back and jumped into the front. "If you think this is cold, you're going to be crying in January and February.

"Why did I move back here again?"

Rachel side-eyed her. "You know why. Your heart was talking."

Harper wasn't so sure it had been speaking to her before she'd moved back, but since—maybe.

"So," Rachel circled back to the earlier conversation, "Aiden or Clark?"

"I was just thinking about Clark's last message," Harper explained. "He wants to know my favorite Christmas song."

"And you can't decide," Rachel guessed.

"No." Harper waved toward the stereo where they were listening to *Trans-Siberian Orchestra*. "Is it *Christmas Canon* or *Wizards in Winter?*"

"That's a tough decision," Rachel muttered tongue in cheek.

"It is ..." Harper's voice faded when her headlights bounced off a car that had slid off the road. "Oh, no."

"What is it?"

Harper pulled to the side of the road and stopped. "I think that's Aiden's." She jumped out of the car to check.

The wind blew straight through her sweats, and once again she cursed the fact she hadn't worn her warmer clothes.

"Is he inside?" Rachel called, opening her door a little.

Harper brushed the snow off the window and peered in, her heart rate slowing when the car was empty.

Aiden!

Where was he, though? They were miles from his apartment, and if he'd tried to walk in this weather ....

She took several steps back, finally taking her phone out of her pocket to use the flashlight. When the beam landed on footprints heading toward Camelot Arms, her blood froze.

"He's walking." She climbed back into the car. "Why didn't he call for help? Do you think he's wearing enough warm clothes? How far are we from your apartment?"

Where are you, Aiden?

"He'll be okay," Rachel's calm voice pierced the fear shooting through her.

"How can you know that?" Harper snapped. "He's never been through a Maine winter before?"

I'm coming.

"I know because he's the one your heart's talking to you about."

Harper wanted to scoff at Rachel's assertion, but could there be something to those words? Throughout her entire life, she'd heard the statements, '*Your heart wants what it wants*' and '*When your heart speaks, it's best to listen,*' but had never really believed …

NINE

Swan Harbor
December 12
9:00 p.m.

AIDEN!

The sound of her voice reverberated inside long before her car stopped behind him. He knew it was her without even turning around. She'd heard his call.

Harper!

Aiden!

A door slammed, and he slowly turned to see anguish on her beautiful face.

"Are you okay?"

I'm fine, he conveyed, just before she wrapped her arms around him, sharing some of her warmth.

"You're not fine," she scolded. "Come on."

I am too fine!

Right! she tossed back. But Aiden could hear the disbelief in her voice, even though the word was silent.

"Let's go." Harper wrapped her arm around his waist and, in the few minutes they'd stood there, his limbs had stiffened.

Lean on me.

It took tapping into a reserved energy source for him to move. Left foot, then right foot was on replay inside his head as they walked toward where she'd parked. When they were close enough, another woman jumped out, and he realized it was Harper's friend, Rachel.

"Put him in front." Rachel reached out to help. "You have seat warmers."

"Good idea. I'd forgotten about those."

"See," Rachel teased. "You are getting soft."

Aiden climbed into the car, and when his wet pants hit the warm seat, his muscles relaxed even more.

"You're sure you're okay?" Harper asked again before requesting a blanket from her trunk.

I hope she can find it.

What?

There's junk in your trunk, Aiden teased silently.

Her dark eyes twinkled in the low light inside the car. "Be nice."

He intended to allow her to help him for just a few minutes while he thawed, and then he'd take over. But as the warmth seeped in, lethargy had him fighting to keep his eyes open.

"Here." She shoved something into his hands, and more blessed heat spread up his arms.

Angel, he thought.

"You've forgotten my name?" she teased.

"No." The one-word response was all he could push out, sending the rest silently. *But you're my Angel.*

Harper leaned over him to fasten his seatbelt, and as her silky hair brushed across his face, tiny prickles of awareness followed.

"I probably stink," she told him nervously. "We were on the way home from the gym."

You smell like an Angel.

"If you believe that, the cold has affected your sense of smell." She shut the door and ran around the car.

Logically, he knew he'd not been out in the elements long enough to cause any lasting damage. Except he was having a hard time trying not to shake. And while his hands and backside were warm, he could barely feel his feet. As they were still in his wet shoes.

Bloody hell, he was cold.

You shouldn't have been walking in this weather.

Aiden glanced sideways, unsure he'd heard what he thought he'd heard.

I wasn't going to just sit in the bloody car.

Why didn't you call for help?

Bloody phone died.

Men!

It could have happened to anyone.

Harper parked, and when Aiden's eyes met hers, his heart expanded, and his breath lodged in his chest.

"Let me." She was so close her warm breath whispered across his face.

When the seatbelt loosened, he was cognizant enough to know she'd gotten out of the car. Except before he could process the next step, Harper opened his door.

"I can do it." Aiden forcibly lifted his legs up and out of the car.

Harper put her arm around his waist and guided him toward the stairs. Once again the thought, *she's so petite*, wafted through his mind.

"Do you need any help?" he heard Rachel ask when they reached their floor.

"No," Harper denied. "You take care of Riley. I'll talk to you later." Then she reminded him she didn't know where he lived.

His apartment was located around the corner from Rachel's. But when he stopped outside the door, his thought processes were still so slow, he couldn't figure out what to do next.

"Which pocket?" she asked as if she'd read his mind.

"Right." He responded, and then it clicked. *They needed his keys.*

Except, did he really want her digging in his pockets? Especially when he was so cold. Bloody hell, no! By the time his thoughts were making themselves known, though, she'd already retrieved the keys.

Home sweet home flew through his head when they walked into the apartment, and she flipped on a light.

It's not so bad.

It's bare.

You should try living with a ninety-year-old. This is practical.

"You need to take off those wet clothes," she said. "Do you need some help?"

"No."

"How about something warm to drink?"

"Tea, please."

"Go change." Harper pushed him toward the hallway.

Aiden nodded and shrugged off the blanket she'd wrapped around him, dropping it on the sofa. Before leaving the room, habit had him plugging in his phone. That he'd gotten stuck with a dead battery still made him feel like a bloody ponce.

I'll be right back.

I know.

He disappeared down the hallway, where he quickly exchanged wet clothes for dry. Then waited on the sofa for Harper.

"I wasn't sure how you took your tea," she began, only to have her words die mid-sentence.

Their eyes met, and he wanted nothing more than to reach out and tug her into his arms.

Thank you, Angel.

I'm no Angel.

Aiden's breath caught when the sound sent a zip straight to his groin. The stirring in his nether regions confirmed for him he wasn't dead.

You're my Angel.

She rolled her eyes, but the little smile flirting with her lips told him more than what she'd said. His words meant something.

"Here." Harper shoved the warmers he'd been holding into each sock. "Your feet need to warm up."

"Thank you."

She brushed his hair off his forehead, and he couldn't help but wish she would settle on the sofa next to him. Just as he was preparing to scoot over, she sank into an oversized chair he'd discovered at a used furniture store.

"Are you any warmer?"

"Getting there."

"Where's your heavier coat?" she asked what he'd hoped she'd stay away from.

"I haven't bought one," he admitted sheepishly.

"No winter shoes? Warmers in your car, a blanket, an extra charger for your phone," she rattled off. "What were you thinking?"

Her show of temper surprised him, and he wasn't sure how to respond.

I'm sorry, I'm such a plonker.

Aiden's Apartment

December 12

10:00 p.m.

Harper wanted to bite her tongue for being so rude, but the Britishism threw her. "A plonker?"

"An idiot." Aiden took several sips of his tea before continuing, "I had it on my *'to do'* list for this weekend."

"London has cold weather."

His gaze lowered and touched on her University of Florida hoodie and old sweatpants, and she could hear him thinking the same thing about her. Neither was completely prepared, and it could have been worse.

Aiden ducked his head and glanced up under his brows, and her heart flipped a few times.

I'm sorry.

No, I'm sorry. You *scared me, and when I'm scared ...*

You snap?

"Something like that," she murmured, noticing he was fighting the need to close his eyes.

"Aiden, do you want me to call about your car?"

"I can ..."

Let me take care of you. Rest.

Angel ....

She didn't know where the endearment had come from, but she had to admit, she kind of liked it. Even though she hadn't heard him say it out loud yet. But something told her hearing the word in his husky voice could be the beginning of her undoing. Was she ready?

Your heart is speaking. Listen to it.

Aiden was relaxed against the back of the sofa, his lashes dark against his high cheekbones. And that errant lock of hair falling on his forehead made her fingers itch to push it back.

Slow down, Harper, she scolded. Take things one step at a time. But even after the sharp talk she had with herself, it took several seconds before she could look away.

His phone was charging on a small table beside the door, and she was thankful he didn't have a passcode. Since she'd forgotten to ask where he wanted it towed, she had his car taken to the garage. Then, because it was late, she called her grandmother.

"Hello?" Terri answered hesitantly.

"Grandma, it's me," Harper whispered. "On the way to bring Rachel home, I found Aiden walking in the cold. His car had slid off the road."

"Aiden's okay, though?"

She looked back at the man still asleep on the sofa. *He's more than fine.* Out loud, she replied, "Just cold. I'm not sure when I'll be home."

"Okay, dear. Thanks for calling."

As soon as she set the phone down, it rang. This time, it was Liam.

"Hello," she answered quickly, knowing the questions were going to come fast.

"Who is this?" Liam snapped. "Where's Aiden?"

"It's Harper Taylor, Liam," she began. "Aiden's fine, but he was in a little accident, and I found him walking home."

"Bugger that. What happened?"

In as concise a manner as possible, she explained what had happened and that she'd had Aiden's car towed to the mechanic.

"What time did you find him?"

Harper shrugged, even knowing Liam couldn't see her. "Around 9:00 p.m."

"He's not hurt?"

"Just cold," she assured him.

"I left him around 4:30 p.m. Where had he been?"

"Where had he been?" she repeated. "I don't ..."

Then, as plain as if he'd uttered the word, she heard Aiden say, *Library. The Library?*

Her gaze met Aiden's across the room. "He was at the library, Liam."

Aiden sat up a little straighter and held out his hand for the phone.

"Hold on a minute. Aiden wants to talk to you."

She unplugged the phone and handed it to him. Then, to give him some privacy, she went into the kitchen to make more tea. The gentle murmur of his voice was comforting, and by the time she returned to the front room and refilled his cup, he'd hung up.

"Everything okay?"

Aiden gave her a crooked smile. "It's fine."

"Were you really at the library?"

"Yes." He sighed and rolled his eyes, disgust written on his face. "Liam showed up around 3:30 and took me to be measured for my tux. Afterward, I went back to gather my stuff, intending to leave, but …"

"Something captured your attention, didn't it?"

"How did you know?"

"You have no idea how many times I've gone to the library to study and stayed until closing. But—"

"—Your parents always knew where you were."

"This is Swan Harbor," she reminded him. "And my dad is the captain of the police department. There aren't many places I could hide."

"Is that why you went to graduate school in Florida?"

"Maybe partly," she acknowledged. "But their offer was the best."

"Do you miss it?"

"Florida?"

"Florida and being on your own."

She wasn't ready to tell him that Joel had trashed many of her memories, and she wanted to build new ones. Nor could she admit that something had led her back to Swan Harbor—and that was even before Aiden had moved to town.

"Rachel was right," she settled on. "I've gone soft after living away. My only regret is I never made it to Key West to see the sunset, but overall, I'm happy to be home."

"I'm glad you're here too," he murmured, and the intensity in his gaze had her metaphorically squirming in her seat.

"So, tell me," she searched for a way to diffuse the heat crawling up her neck. "What caught your attention at the library?"

A corner of his mouth ticked up as if he knew what she was doing.

"Searching for information about Ian Jones."

"He's the one the Spanish galleon supposedly belonged to, right?"

The gossip line had been buzzing for weeks with the news that Aiden was a long-lost relative of Killian and Liam Reade. And that at one time, Aiden's ancestor, had owned Captain Jack's ship.

"He is," Aiden agreed. "What do you know about that ship?"

Harper smiled, the memories of sailing on the ship when she was a child flowing through her head.

"I know it's been a fixture in Swan Harbor for years," she began. "When I was a child, Captain Jack and my uncles used to take us out to sea. Until he docked the ship at the pier and turned her into a fancy restaurant, that is."

"When was that?"

"Late '90s or early 2000s, I think. I'm glad you've discovered who she belonged to. I always felt that she seemed so lonely." Harper hesitated for a second, letting the memories wash over her. "For the longest time, it was just the ship and her companion, Jonesy."

The melancholy tone of her voice surprised him for some reason.

"I've heard plenty from Captain Jack about Jonesy." He hesitated for a second before pushing forward. "What were your thoughts about Captain Jack and his belief that Swan Harbor's hope is tied to a swan?"

She chuckled. "When you're from Swan Harbor, you don't question statements like that."

"Never?"

"Well, not out loud," she admitted with a laugh. "But you know, when Jonesy was in Swan Harbor, things always seemed—well—different."

"How so?"

"I don't know," she shrugged. "Makes no sense because when it's all broken down, he's only a mute swan. Migrates just like other birds. Leaves in the fall, returns in the spring, until ..."

"This year," Aiden supplied.

"Yeah. Have you met him?"

"Jonesy?" Aiden shook his head. "No, but I've been privy to plenty of conversations about him with Jack."

"I remember once when I was about ten and on the beach with my family." Her eyes sparkled as if the memory was a good one. "Jack and Jonesy appeared to be having a staring contest. I asked the Captain if he could understand what the swan was saying."

Aiden laughed. "And let me guess, Jack said something cryptic."

"How did you know?"

"Because everything Jack says is cryptic."

"That's the Captain," Harper acknowledged. "That day, Jack told me it wasn't time for him to understand what Jonesy was saying. That when it was time, he'd know."

"Which left you more confused than before you'd asked," he guessed.

"It did," she laughed. "Did you find anything new?"

Aiden's heart raced a little faster, thinking about what he'd found. He looked around for his briefcase, wanting to share, but then remembered where he'd left it.

"Bloody hell, my briefcase is in the car."

"Come now, Doctor Jones," she teased. "If it were that interesting, I bet you'd remember more than you think."

He wanted to say something clever, but when he couldn't think of anything, cleared his throat.

"It was a newspaper article."

"Really?"

"Written in 1965 by C. Montague. Could that be ...?"

"Mr. Montague, yes!" Harper exclaimed. "Cecil Montague was a reporter and traveled the world. He's 105 and still sharp."

"You think he'd talk to me?"

She laughed. "I'm sure he'd love that. Did he write an article about Ian Jones?"

"Not about the pirate per se, but the ship."

"I thought you knew the ship belonged to your pirate relative."

"We do," Aiden nodded. "We also know the collection of silver pieces of eight that belonged to him came from a ship in 1715. Where did the ship come from, though? When did he first come to Swan Harbor and meet Hope? And why?"

"So many questions."

"Yes," he agreed. "My sister sent a text yesterday that could answer the question about the ship."

"Really?"

"Are you really interested in hearing about this?"

"Why would you ask that?"

"I just," he shrugged, unsure how to explain what he was thinking.

"Aiden," the husky tenor of Harper's voice sent a shiver up his spine. "I *want* to hear what you found out. My family has been in Swan Harbor for generations, and who knows, maybe finding something out about your Ian will lead to information about my ancestors. Besides, I ..."

Her voice trailed off, and their gazes locked.

You what?

Want to get to know you.

Really, Angel?

Yes, really.

Why?

She rolled her eyes, and a corner of her mouth kicked up.

Because of this. How can we do this?

He shrugged. *I've no clue.*

Has it ever happened to you?

Never. You?

No, tell me what you found.

"I sent a picture of the article to my sister. Do you want to read it?"

"Read it to me," she instructed. "I don't have my contacts in, and my glasses are in the car. And besides ...."

"Besides?"

"You have a sexy voice," she quipped.

She'd said it teasingly, but that didn't stop the heat from creeping up.

"Alright."

Aiden pulled up the message he'd sent to his sister earlier in the day.

The article was titled, *Who Are You?* and featured a small picture of Captain Jack's ship in the corner. The article continued.

This Spanish galleon has been a 'resident' of Swan Harbor for longer than anyone can explain. While it belongs to Captain Jack Swan, little is known about her origins. But could our very own pirate ship have once been a part of the Spanish Treasury Fleet of 1715?

Aiden glanced up before he continued. Harper had taken off her shoes, tucked her legs under her, and was leaning her head against the cushions. "You're tired."

"A little," she admitted. "Do you want me to go?"

No! But that was being selfish.

"Do you want to go?"

"I want you to read the rest."

He grinned, unwilling just yet to let on how happy that made him. "Alright."

On July 24, 1715, twelve ships, collectively known as the Spanish Treasury Fleet, left Havana, Cuba, bound for Spain. They carried gold coins, bars, silver coins, chests of jewels, emeralds, rubies, pearls, and Chinese porcelain. However, as they sailed along the coast of Florida, the fleet encountered a hurricane. Eleven of the twelve ships were thought to have perished. As of the writing of this piece, while many of the vessels have been discovered, I've been focused on one—the Nuestra Señora de Concepcíon.

According to my research, the Concepcíon, as I'll call her, was blown off course on July 30, 1715, and presumed to have sunk. But what if somehow the Captain steered the ship around the winds from the storm? If so, could that ship have sailed farther up the Eastern Seaboard, eventually landing in Swan Harbor? Is that why our ship has no name? Is she the Nuestra Señora de Concepcíon?

Aiden finished the article and was going to show Harper the picture he'd found, but when he looked up, she'd fallen asleep.

Angel?

There was a part of him that wondered if he should wake her. The other side, though, didn't want her to go.

That invisible connection between them propelled him across the room, where he dimmed the lights and lifted her gently into his arms. Then he carried her to the sofa, and settled her beside him, tucking her close. With her head resting on his shoulder, he leaned his own against hers and finally allowed himself to relax.

Sleep, Angel, he thought just before he drifted off.

TEN

Aiden's Apartment
December 13
7:00 a.m.

Harper slowly swam toward wakefulness, the warmth surrounding her giving the impression of being wrapped in a down sleeping bag. But ... that didn't fit with the hardness pressed against her breasts or her hips. Nor did it work with the smells tickling her nose.

Oh!

Her nerve endings stood, taking notice when she realized *what* she was feeling. One eye opened, then the other, and slowly she tilted her head back enough to see the underside of a chin.

Aiden!

She had slept with Aiden!

The memory of the night rushed back, and she had to fight to lie still. Confronting him wasn't something she could handle ... yet, anyway.

They were lying on the sofa, face to face, his hard body pressed against her much softer one. Too fast, too fast, she thought, her pulse racing.

"Your thoughts are awfully loud," Aiden murmured in his morning rough voice.

"Sorry," Harper squeaked.

"'S'alright." He rubbed his chin back and forth against the top of her head and groaned, the sound reverberating through her body.

The pull between them whenever he was close was there. She wanted to bury her nose in his sweater and enjoy being in his arms.

"Hmm, Harper."

He kneaded her back muscles for several seconds before ... suddenly stopping. Then, almost as if he were using only his tactile senses, his hands moved around her back.

"Bloody hell, Harper," Aiden cried, jumping off the sofa. "I'm s-s-sorry."

She pushed up into a sitting position and brushed her hair back, immediately feeling the need to reassure him.

"Aiden, it's okay. We fell asleep."

He gave her a look, embarrassed yet endearing.

"I didn't mean ..." he hesitated before coming back with, "Are you alright?"

Harper studied his expression, and suddenly the uncomfortable feelings disappeared. He hadn't tried to take advantage of her or of the situation. And as soon as he'd realized where they were, he'd moved—and apologized.

"Aiden."

She took a step closer and unconsciously laid her hands on his chest. His eyes flared, but when she went to remove them, he covered them with his.

You're fine.

"I didn't mean to fall asleep."

"Neither did I." Aiden glanced over her shoulder, and she held her breath, wondering what was next. "I *am* sorry."

Something had her giving him an impish smile. "Just be glad I'm legal. Otherwise, my dad might come looking for you."

He blanched, pushing her to tease a little more. "I told you he's the police captain, right?"

"Yes." Aiden swallowed hard, but then the look on his face transformed as he realized she'd been teasing. "That was mean."

"What?"

"You know what?" he exclaimed. "It's not nice to tease because there's always a payback ..."

"I don't think I'm scared." She stepped back enough to put a little space between them. "I should go, though. Grandma's probably worried."

"Thank you for rescuing me."

"Do you need me to take you to the garage to get your car?"

He glanced at his watch, then shook his head. "No, that's alright. Liam said he'd take me."

"If you're sure." She grabbed her keys and started toward the door. "I'll see you later."

"Thanks again ..." The word hung in the air, making her wonder, would he use ...? "Harper," he finished with a grin as if he'd known what she was thinking.

She headed toward her car, but the memory of how she'd felt in his arms lingered. Should she have stayed ... just to see?

What did your heart say? Did you even listen?

There'd been moments when she'd listened, but fear held her back.

"Harper!" Aiden called just as she opened her car door. "Wait!"

"You're out here without a coat again," she scolded. "Didn't you learn anything last night?"

"Sorry," he muttered sheepishly. "I didn't want to miss you."

A little thrill ran through her at his admission, making her tongue-tied for a second.

"At least you put shoes on," she quipped.

Their gazes clashed, and he hesitated, giving her the impression he was working his way around to something.

Harper had to grab hold of her car door to stay upright. Hoping—wanting to feel his arms around her once more.

"Aiden?" she hesitated, hoping it would prevent her from doing something foolish.

"Can I have your number?

"My phone number?"

"Yes. After all, we are still going to the Gala together, right?"

"We are," she replied breathlessly.

"And last night," he continued. "We decided we wanted to get to know each other, right?"

"We even slept together," slipped out of her mouth.

His face turned red, and she wanted to bite her tongue. "I'm sorry. I was teasing, and sometimes my tongue gets ahead of my brain."

"Mine too." Aiden gave her one of those lopsided, adorable grins that caused her knees to weaken.

"Give me your phone." Harper held out her hand and added herself as a contact. "You can call or text me now, and I'll have yours."

"Alright. Drive safe."

"I wasn't the one on the side of the road last night," she quipped.

"Am I ever going to live that down?"

"Someday."

Harper started her car and let it warm up for a few minutes, and their eyes met. *See you soon, Angel.* As she backed out of the parking spot, she glanced at him once again, and the look on his face stayed with her all the way home.

Swan Harbor Zoo
December 13
4:00 p.m.

Aiden pulled into a parking space at the Swan Harbor Zoo and gathered the papers he'd brought to share. He'd used his time wisely since Harper had left his apartment. A trip to the store had netted him a warmer coat and boots. And his time at the library had given him new information. Which was why he'd gone searching for Captain Jack.

He found him sitting on a bench in the aviary, eye to eye with a white swan.

"Jonesy, I presume?" Aiden murmured so as not to startle either the man or the animal.

Captain Jack looked up, and his expression was atypical for the older man.

"Young Aiden. Come and sit." Jack waved toward where the swan was swimming slowly in circles. "Meet Jonesy."

Aiden settled on the bench and studied the swan for several seconds. He tilted his head in one direction and then in the other.

"Jonesy's a beautiful bird. There's something about his expression that makes me—"

"—Feel as if he's listening to every word you say," Jack murmured.

"Yes." Aiden turned his attention back to the older man, whose expression was still somber. "Is that what has you vexed? Is there anything I can do?"

Jack took a deep breath and leaned forward, balancing his elbows on his knees. "Jonesy needs to be free. He's a wild bird and not meant to be cooped up in this," he waved an arm around, "artificial environment."

"But Emma said—"

"I know my great-niece is a veterinarian," Jack interrupted. "And I trust her to care for my dog, Bandit. But she admitted that avian medicine wasn't her specialty, and I just ..."

"Want the best for Jonesy?" Aiden guessed.

"Of course!" Jack exclaimed. "I've spent the last fifty years watching over him. I can't stop now."

"Fifty years?" Aiden repeated. "Jonesy has been coming to Swan Harbor that long?"

"Yes." A tender smile crossed Jack's face. "Ava's birth brought us hope and Jonesy."

Aiden knew the story behind that was an emotional one. And the deeper he dove into the history of the town, the more curious he grew.

"I know you thought Finn being in Swan Harbor helped the town's hope," Aiden began. "But how do you think hope and Jonesy are connected?"

Jack glanced up. "What have you found out about Swan Harbor's discovery?"

"That a wedge of swans led the earliest settlers to this location," Aiden replied. "I found a book written by M. Prince in 1965."

"Margaret Prince," Jack murmured. "A friend to my sister, Rose, as well as to Terri Patterson. She was Dylan's grandmother and passed way too young."

"Another woman who didn't live beyond forty-five?"

"Another Swan or Prince woman," Jack reiterated. "Ava is the only woman in either family to live beyond forty-five." He lifted his head suddenly as if something concerning him flew through his brain. "Is your mother living?"

"Yes," Aiden answered. "Why?"

"Geoffrey and Christine are the connection between the Swan and Prince families. Their daughter, Hope, fell for a Jones, bringing in your family."

"And you're wondering if whatever is causing the women of those two families to die carries over into mine?" Aiden surmised.

"Something like that."

"What do you think it is? A curse or something?" Aiden tossed out with a laugh.

The look Jack sent him had Aiden taking another look. "Wait, I was just joking."

That Jack and the Swan family had known loss wasn't something Aiden could deny. And he had to admit it was curious—as well as a little frightening —to think about. Especially if whatever it was, touched his family. The thought of anything happening to his mother or sister was terrifying. Also, if he were to marry, and there was something there, would his wife be susceptible as well?

"Do I believe in curses?" Jack sighed, and to Aiden, it sounded like the older man bore the weight of the world on his shoulders. "I believe the destinies of the Swan and Prince women are interconnected. Because of that, their futures are cut short way too soon. Was it because of a curse, the power of suggestion, or was it just fate? Those are answers I can't give you. However, I *do* know that with Jonesy's appearance, the town's hope burned brighter."

"Why, though?" Aiden repeated. "Why do you feel Jonesy and the town's hope are connected?"

"As you read in Margaret's book," Jack explained. "Swans led the first residents to our little pocket of the world. A swan is a symbol of purity, beauty, grace, and love. Many believe that when swans are present, they improve communication and are also a sign of marital fidelity. Additionally, since they combine the elements of air and water, they embody eternal life, or forever. And isn't hope the first step to forever?"

Aiden hummed as in many ways that made sense, but he still couldn't completely buy into it. Mostly because he felt as if Jack was leaving several essential facts out of his story.

"I understand what you're saying about wild animals wanting to be free," Aiden acknowledged. "How do you know Jonesy really wants to be free, though? In here, he's warm and has plenty of food and attention. Wouldn't it be better to wait until spring?"

Jack humphed. "You've been talking to Emma, haven't you?"

"Not exactly," Aiden hedged, unwilling to admit he'd overheard her complaining to Elsa one day at Sally's.

"What did you say earlier?" Jack went on, not pushing the issue. "That his expression makes—"

"Me feel as if he's listening," Aiden replied.

"Have you ever known someone with whom you feel as if you can hear their thoughts?" Jack wanted to know.

Harper!

"Hear their thoughts?" Aiden echoed. "Why do you ask?"

Jack's twinkling dark eyes met his as if he were privy to a secret.

"Harper?"

Aiden could feel the heat climbing. "Why would you ask if it was Harper?"

"You'll never meet a more caring individual than Harper," Jack smiled, not even bothering to answer the question. "I've known her since she was born. She's a special girl."

"We get along well," Aiden conceded, fighting the smile that threatened.

"Of course, you do," Jack laughed. "Everyone gets on with Harper. But I digress. What I was trying to explain is that, just like you, I feel Jonesy is listening to us. I'm trying to do the same."

"And by listening to Jonesy, you think he's telling you he needs to be free."

"I do, but I don't think you found me just to talk about Jonesy. What have you got there?" He pointed to the folder on Aiden's lap.

Aiden opened the folder and pointed to the picture of the ship he'd copied. "Have you read Cecil Montague's article speculating your ship was once a member of the Spanish Treasury Fleet?"

"We talked about it a few times," Jack admitted. "Nothing ever came of it, though. Why?"

Aiden quickly explained Sarah's speculations that Hope's Haven had once been called El corazón del Rubí. "But once I mentioned the Nuestra Señora de Concepcíon—"

"She took off after that bone," Jack guessed.

Aiden laughed. "You could say that. Sarah found out the Concepcíon had a distinct mark somewhere. It was meant as a talisman to help *'steer the ship true.'*"

"If my ship was once the Concepción," Jack murmured, "and she survived the hurricane, it worked. What is the mark?"

"A lily."

"Another symbol of purity," Jack noted with a grin.

"More importantly," Aiden added. "It's a symbol harkening back to the Madonna."

Jack stood and glanced down at Aiden. "What are you waiting for, my boy? Let's go search for that lily.

Swan's Spirits
December 13
10:00 p.m.

Finn stretched his arm along the bench seat, watching the gentle ribbing going on around him. Life had never been better for the Reade men. He was married. They were celebrating Liam's last night as a bachelor, and in February, it would be Killian's turn. There'd been knocks along the way, but together, they had all survived … and thrived.

"Good looking bunch, aren't they?" Jack saluted with his glass of bourbon. "Much has changed this year."

"I was thinking the same thing," Finn agreed. "They've been wonderful changes."

"The best."

Jack blinked several times, and Finn was once again reminded of everything he'd lost, pushing him to add, "Something tells me next year will be even better."

"You think so?" Jack's dark eyes glittered in the low light of the room. "I spent some time with Aiden today. He has his eye on Harper Taylor."

"I heard that's not all you and Aiden talked about today," Finn retorted. "Climbing up onto the ship's bridge in this weather could have been dangerous."

"Aiden said it was cold enough to freeze the balls off a brass monkey," Jack laughed. "I told him he'd seen nothing yet."

"But did you find what you were looking for?"

"We did." Jack pulled up a picture on his phone and slid it across the table. "That had been burned into the wood in the center of the wheel."

Finn glanced at the photo. "A flower? On a ship?"

"A lily," Jack corrected. "Or more precisely, a Madonna lily." He then explained why they'd been looking for it.

"So, Captain Jack's Fine Dining was once part of the Spanish Treasury Fleet, thought to have sunk in 1715," Finn hummed. "Makes you wonder how it ended up in Swan Harbor."

"And how Pirate Ian Jones ended up with it," Jack added. "But Aiden said Sarah is working on it. That she's like a dog with a bone when she wants something."

"I heard Sarah and Miriam are coming for Christmas," Finn commented, working to manipulate the conversation to fill in a hole or two.

"That will," Jack began, but when Killian pulled up a chair, he switched topics. "What brings you to the old person's side of the room?"

"Hey, speak for yourself," Finn grumbled, for several reasons.

"I'm not coming to listen to you complain about Jonesy," Killian retorted.

Jack held his hands up in surrender. "No Jonesy talk tonight."

"Good."

"Hey, Killian," Rupert snickered. "What kind of underwear do sexy monkeys wear?

"Chim-pant-zies," chuckled Jimmie. Then the entire table started laughing.

"You wanted to know why I moved." Killian thumbed over his shoulder. "I never knew there were so many underwear jokes."

"They *do* know how to get going," Jack agreed. "By the way, have you solved the case yet? I heard something about your panties being in a wad."

Killian groaned. "Yes. That's the latest."

"And no clues?" Finn asked.

"None," Killian sighed. "Did you check the evidence room for your boxers?"

Finn's heart skipped a beat because he hadn't let on that it was his boxers flying high above The Beach Shack. And he had no intention of discussing his underwear with his son.

"I picked up mine," Jack piped in. "My boxers with the skull and crossbones were flying at the pier."

"Dad?"

"I," Finn searched for an answer that wasn't a lie, "haven't had time to look," he finally settled on.

"Better make time," Killian smirked. "You wouldn't want them to slip through your fingers."

"That was just as bad as Rupert's joke." Finn changed the subject, which was better for his peace of mind. "How are Paris and the puppies?"

He and Ava had discovered the mother dog and her new puppies right after they'd been born. Thankfully, they had gotten them to Emma, who had performed her veterinary magic on them before any harm was done.

"According to Emma, they're perfect for five-week-old puppies," Killian shared. "Our cats are having a good time with them."

"Paris doesn't mind?"

"No," Killian laughed. "She gives you that look that says, '*Children*' and goes back to sleep."

"The next time you come over," Finn suggested. "Why don't you bring Paris? I know Ava is eager to see how she likes her new home."

"My dad with a dog." Killian shook his head in mock disbelief. "Never thought I'd see the day."

"My son with three kittens and building a new house," Finn tossed right back. "Never thought I'd see the day."

"What can I say?" Killian held his glass up. "There's just something about those King women that draws you in—"

"—And won't let go." Finn clunked his glass against his son's.

"Amen to that." Killian took a sip of his rum, and right on cue, turned his attention to Jack. "How about you, Captain? Any chance of a wedding in your future?"

Jack gave Finn a pointed look. "Did you tell him?"

"About Edythe?" Finn shook his head. "That's your story to tell."

Jack downed the rest of his bourbon and pushed out of the booth. "Not tonight, boys. This old man is going home to Bandit. I'll see you at the church."

"Couldn't you have been more subtle?" Finn grumbled. "You're a detective for bloody sake."

"Sorry," Killian sighed. "That wasn't one of my finest moments."

"No, it wasn't," Finn agreed. "Just remember, without a last name, I've gone as far as I can. For tonight, though, I'm going to follow Jack and make sure he gets home. I'll see you tomorrow."

He made the rounds saying goodnight, paid the bill, and stepped out into the frosty weather. When the north wind whipped around him, he had to agree with Aiden. It was cold enough to freeze off a monkey's balls. Maybe he'd look into some place warm to take Ava for a few weeks in the winter. After all, he'd been wanting an excuse to buy his wife one of the bikinis he'd seen in the *Rebecca's Fantasy* catalog.

ELEVEN

Elsa & Liam's Cottage
December 14
4:00 p.m.

Her wedding day dawned cold and clear, and Elsa spent most of it feeling like a princess. An early appointment at the Foxy Lady for a manicure/pedicure and hair. A healthy lunch, a peaceful afternoon, and all she had to do was slip into her dress. Then a carriage ride to the church where her happy beginning would be waiting … the first day to the rest of their lives.

"Quit daydreaming, El," Emma scolded. "I left you in here thirty minutes ago, and you're still not dressed."

Elsa gave her a sheepish smile. "Sorry."

"Thinking about Liam?"

"And how I feel like a princess," Elsa admitted.

"Well, at least your carriage won't turn into a pumpkin," Emma laughed. "Now, get your dress on. Our moms will be here in five minutes."

Since learning of her mother's Alzheimer's diagnosis, Elsa's emotions had been on a roller coaster. Some days, Patty was more cognizant than others. On those days, her mother knew who she was. But many times, she didn't. It made her feel as if she were walking on a tightrope every time she went to visit.

A quick glance at the clock had her pushing away her worries to step into her wedding dress. The bodice was fitted with a sweetheart neckline, long slim sleeves, and a flowing train.

Elsa glanced in the mirror to see her mother standing in the doorway, wearing an expression she hadn't seen in months. Her hands were clasped together, and when their gazes met, she had her answer.

"You look just like a princess," Patty exclaimed.

Elsa smiled. "I feel like one."

"Do you need some help?"

"Please." Elsa turned her back toward her mother, wondering what Patty was thinking. Wondering if she understood the significance of the dress.

"There." Patty gently smoothed her hands down the back of Elsa's gown. "All done."

Elsa hesitated for a breath. "Thanks, mom."

"You're very welcome." Patty dumped the contents of her purse onto the bed and began pushing things aside. "I know I put them in here."

"What are you looking for?"

"Oh, you remember," Patty replied, not really answering the question. "I saw them this morning and thought, '*Oh, those would look good.*'"

No, thought Elsa, *I don't know.*

"Here they are," Patty exclaimed, holding a necklace aloft. "I knew I'd put them in there."

"Your pearls?" Elsa's breath caught. "Do you want me to put them on you?"

"No, silly." Patty crammed everything back into her purse, including a bag of chips, a frame with no picture, and what looked like the set of keys her caregiver had complained about losing. "These are for you."

"For me?" As a teenager, she'd begged to wear the necklace, knowing it had belonged to her grandmother. And Patty's response had always been, '*On your wedding day.*' Had she remembered her promise?

"Of course, for you. Turn around." Patty waited expectantly for Elsa to turn around, then she carefully fastened the necklace. "Perfect."

Elsa studied her image in the mirror. The way the pearls fit in the hollow of her throat made them look like they were made just for her.

"You look beautiful, honey," Patty murmured. "I wish your father were here to share this day with you."

At the mention of her father and that it was by her mother, tears rushed to Elsa's eyes.

"I know, mom. I wish he was too."

Patty hugged her, then stepped aside. "Who did you say was giving you away again?"

"Uncle Jerry," Elsa sighed, knowing she'd told her mother many times.

"Uncle Jerry?" Patty frowned. "Do I know him?"

"Yes, mom," Elsa explained patiently. "Jerry and Charlotte have been friends of our family forever."

"Oh, okay."

Elsa grabbed a tissue and dabbed at the wetness on her face. She refused to allow anything to ruin her day.

"Patty, are you about ready to leave?" Ava asked, when she entered the room with Emma.

"Leave?" Patty frowned. "But ..."

"You and I are riding in the limo," Ava reminded her. "While Elsa and Emma follow in the carriage."

Patty nodded and looked at Elsa for confirmation. "Okay, well. If you say so." She picked up her large bag and left the room without saying goodbye.

"We'll see you girls there." Ava waved, and Elsa could hear her directing Patty from the house, and then it was quiet.

"Thank you for loaning me your mom to help plan the wedding," Elsa sniffed. "I'm not sure I could have done it alone."

Emma laughed. "Trust me, El. It was my pleasure. She got to plan a wedding and wasn't constantly asking when Killian and I were getting married."

"That was your fault for waiting so long to set a date," Elsa scolded.

"It wasn't setting the date," Emma clarified. "But sharing the date."

"True." Elsa smoothed her skirt down and touched the red velvet of Emma's dress. "You're not mad about wearing this, are you?"

"It's your wedding, El. I'm here for you."

Elsa blinked rapidly, fighting the tears that threatened. "Remember when I moved to Swan Harbor in August?"

"Yes," Emma grinned. "And you were a mess."

"I was," Elsa agreed. "I had no job, no place to live, and no boyfriend. You and your new friends fed me ice cream and gave me hope."

"I remember that," Emma replied. "Sadie fed you the same line she'd fed to me."

Elsa nodded. "She said, 'things will work out, Elsa. You're in Swan Harbor, and the heart always wins.'"

"And she was right."

"Think we're going to get through this evening without crying?"

"Probably not," Emma sniffed. "But I would be remiss in my maid-of-honor duties if I wasn't prepared."

She plucked a few tissues from the box and shoved them into Elsa's bouquet.

"Emma!"

"It's better than having snot running from your nose," Emma pointed out. "Right?"

There was something about that statement that made Elsa giggle.

"You win," she agreed, tucking an extra tissue inside. "Let's do this."

Main Street Church
December 14
5:00 p.m.

Liam glanced at his watch to see that only five minutes had passed since the last time he'd looked. "You're sure you have the rings?"

"You already asked me that," Killian sighed. "And the answer is the same. Yes, I have them."

"And the suitcases are in the car?"

Ava and Finn had gifted them their honeymoon. Tickets to Aruba and a home on the beach for a week. And since they were driving to Portland and spending the night there, he'd been worried they'd forget something.

Killian pulled a piece of paper from his suit jacket. "The rings are in my pocket, the suitcases are in the car, and the tickets, instructions, and your passports are in that bag Elsa is going to carry onto the plane. She's bringing it with her. You need to relax."

Logically, he knew that, but after everything he'd put Elsa through before admitting he loved her, he wanted their wedding day to be perfect.

"I know, I know."

Liam searched for something to keep him busy and opened the door to the sanctuary just a crack.

"Bloody hell, Liam," Killian grumbled. "What are you doing?"

"Distracting myself," Liam admitted. "I'm checking on Aiden."

"Aiden? Why?"

"You know why. If he has questions while I'm gone, I'm sending him to you."

"What kind of questions?" Killian asked suspiciously.

Liam peered through the small crack to see Aiden escorting Harper down the aisle to her seat.

"Look at that." Liam jammed his finger through the crack. "Do you see that?"

They exchanged places, allowing Killian to look through the door.

"Do I see what?" he asked, confusion written all over his face.

"Where he seated Harper."

Killian looked out again. "Alright, I see where she's sitting, but I fail to see the problem."

"Bugger that." Liam pushed his brother out of the way and checked again. "Aiden likes Harper. Plus, I have it on good authority she likes him. Except he sat her next to another man."

"He did?" Killian looked again.

"Yes," Liam snapped. "A good-looking bloke too."

Killian glanced back out and jammed his thumb over his shoulder toward the guests. "Either your nerves have affected your vision, or you need glasses. Look again."

Liam took a breath and peered out once more. "It's Devin Hall."

"And?"

"He's a physical therapist at the hospital, which is how he knows Elsa."

"And?"

"Harper's cousin," Liam finished sheepishly.

"Aye." Killian punched him in the arm. "There."

"Ouch!" Liam rubbed his arm where Killian sucker-punched him. "What was that for?"

"To give you something else to think about," Killian explained. "Relax. Everything will be fine. Worst case scenario, another underwear escapade. And since just about the entire town's here—I think we're safe.

Liam nodded and shut the door quietly. And for the next few minutes, he relaxed. Until the music changed, ratcheting up his nerves. "Is it time?"

"It's time." Killian gave him a little nudge toward the door.

"But what if—?"

"Open the bloody door." Killian forcibly pushed him. "Or do you not want to get married?"

"I want to marry Elsa almost more than I want to breathe," Liam admitted. "But what if I disappoint her?"

"Liam, she loves you, and you love her," Killian said quietly. "I'm sure you'll disappoint her, just as she will you. But you talk it through and move forward ... together. That's what marriage is."

"Listen to my little brother," Liam quipped. "He's sounding so grown up."

"Just open the bloody door."

Liam took a deep breath and stepped into the sanctuary. Their family and friends filled the small church, and suddenly, he was calm.

You start with hope, add a whole lot of love, and build the future brick by brick. And today, they were laying another brick.

His gaze bounced around the church, making eye contact with a few. When he noticed Aiden was sitting next to Harper, he smiled. *Good going, cuz,* he thought.

Then the music changed, and the rear doors opened, giving him his first look at his bride. His heart stopped, and he wanted nothing more than to run up the aisle and claim her as his.

Elsa floated toward him, and he thought she'd never looked more beautiful. It was only sheer will that kept his feet locked in place until it was time to step forward. He shook Jerry's hand, kissed Patty's cheek, closed his fingers around Elsa's hand, and felt whole.

"You look beautiful," he whispered.

"Thank you."

A single tear escaped from the corner of her eye and trickled down her face. Liam cupped her jaw and gently swept it away.

Once again, the music changed, and as Tyler and Rachel sang, Liam stared into Elsa's eyes, mesmerized by the look of love.

We start with a little hope ...

I love you ...

Harper side-eyed Aiden. *Did I just see ...?*

Yes.

That there were couples who could have silent conversations wasn't something she'd thought was unique to her and Aiden. She'd seen it in action her entire life. Her parents, aunts and uncles, and now, friends. Was that part of listening to your heart? Somehow, that fit.

I, Liam, take you, Elsa ....

From the corner of her eye, she saw her Uncle Danny link his hand with her Aunt Sally's. Across the aisle, Liam's father gave his new wife, Ava, a sizzling look. What must it be like to have that special someone who would always be your person?

To have and to hold from this day forward.

Rupert and Lois, and Madge and Jimmie, sitting in front of her, who'd been married over fifty years, exchanged private looks.

Would the feeling be freeing, or would you worry it would disappear?

It wasn't until Aiden held out his white handkerchief, she realized her emotions had bubbled up and spilled over.

Thank you.

My pleasure.

He smiled, and she got lost in the blue of his eyes. Suddenly it felt as if time had stopped, and they were the only two people left.

I now pronounce you husband and wife.

Harper tore her gaze away from Aiden's and focused on the couple. Only through rote, was she able to clap, stand, and follow everyone out of the sanctuary.

"Need a ride, Harp?" her cousin, Devin, asked.

"No." She regathered her thoughts. "I drove."

"See you there."

"Are you alright?" Aiden's husky voice rippled across her skin, waking her nerve endings and creating a new awareness of him.

"I'm fine."

"Really?" He raised a brow in disbelief. "You looked ..."

"Weddings just make me emotional," she used the handy excuse.

"Well, if you're sure."

"I am." She grinned. "Aren't you supposed to go have your picture taken?"

A ruddy hue dotted his cheekbones, and he sighed dramatically. "I guess. You'll be alright?"

"I'm fine," Harper assured him again. "I'm just waiting for Rachel."

He nodded, told her he would see her at the reception, and disappeared into the sanctuary.

What was going on with her? It was as if ...

"Harper, there you are." Rachel came from around the corner. "Are you ready?"

It was quiet for several minutes while they drove out of the parking lot and started toward the Lighthouse Inn, where the reception was being held.

"You sounded wonderful, Rach."

"Thanks." Rachel's eyes sparkled. "Singing with Tyler is ..."

When Rachel didn't immediately complete her sentence, Harper tossed out some options.

"Good? Bad? Fun? Boring?"

"Wonderful," Rachel replied softly. "Tyler's voice is husky and just so sexy. He could sing me out of my panties if he tried."

"Rachel!" Harper exclaimed. "Isn't that how you ended up with Riley?"

Rachel giggled. "Well, there is that. But he has his little girl, Bethany, and it would be so perfect if we ..."

"Rachel," Harper cautioned. "Be careful. Tyler isn't ready for a relationship yet."

"Okay," Rachel sighed dramatically. "I'll be nice. He did ask me if I'd be interested in singing at his club."

Tyler James owned the club, Siren's Song, which anchored one end of the pier, opposite the pirate ship.

"What did you tell him?"

"Maybe."

"You told him maybe, when I know you were jumping up and down inside."

"I had a reason, though," Rachel hummed. "Remember when we were in school, and I had to sing in front of people?"

"Are you referring to how your stomach hurt because you were so nervous?"

"Yes!" Rachel sighed. "Singing at the church is different, but I'm not sure I have what it takes to sing in front of a crowd."

"Don't sell yourself short," Harper encouraged.

"I'll try not to."

Harper parked and let the car power down for a few seconds before getting out.

"Are you okay?" Rachel asked quietly.

"I'm ..." instead of giving her pat answer about being fine, she let it hang, unsure what to say before finally settling on, "confused."

"Okay." Rachel angled sideways. "I'm listening. Does this have anything to do with Aiden?"

"Why would you say that?"

"Please!" Rachel rolled her eyes. "There were enough sparks flying between you two, it could have powered the church."

"Really?"

"Yes!" she huffed. "Look. I know Joel's behavior has made it difficult to trust in what you're feeling. And I know you feel obligated to see this experiment through . Especially since you do have a connection with your matches. But your heart is speaking. Don't you owe it to yourself and Aiden to see what it's trying to tell you?"

Did she?

Don't you want a happily-ever-after like your parents?

"I'll try."

"Promises, promises," Rachel grumbled. "I know how stubborn you can be."

"Who, me?"

Rachel just shook her head, but as Harper followed her into the inn and handed over her coat, she promised herself she'd be open.

Lighthouse Inn
December 14
10:30 p.m.

Aiden took a drink of the champagne and set it on the bar. Dinner was over, the speeches completed, and the cake cut. And now that he'd finished his obligatory dances with family, he'd wanted to ask Harper to dance. Except every time he started toward her, she was dancing with someone else.

"Is there a reason you're here?" Liam asked. "Instead of on the dance floor with Harper?"

"Is there a reason you're here?" Aiden quipped. "And not with your new bride?"

"She's dancing with my dad."

"And why aren't you dancing with Ava?" Aiden asked before someone mentioned Harper again.

"Because she's dancing with Jack," Liam explained. "But answer the question."

Aiden huffed. "I tried."

"And?"

"She's always dancing with someone," he murmured. "I didn't want to butt in."

"Why the bloody hell not?" Liam grumbled. "If you like someone, you have to be willing to fight for them."

"I don't know." Aiden shrugged. "She looked like she was having fun."

"Who's she dancing with?"

"I don't bloody know." Aiden nodded to the side of the room where he'd last seen Harper. "Do you know him?"

Liam laughed. "That's Rod—her brother. He works with me."

"Oh."

"I get the feeling something else is holding you back," Liam suddenly tossed out. "What is it?"

"When I'm with you and Elsa, Ava and Finn, or Killian and Emma,"

Aiden began. "It always feels like there's a conversation going on around me. One that's silent and only shared between each couple."

Liam studied him for several seconds, then turned to look off into the crowd.

"To be honest, cuz, I'm not sure what it is. But after I came to Swan Harbor to warn Killian about the danger, something changed. It was as if Elsa's beautiful blue eyes were saying things to me. Had they always done so? Or was I only just paying attention? I don't know. But it's there. Why? Do you have that with someone?"

"Harper," he admitted. "But during your wedding, it was different."

"Different, how?"

Aiden searched for a way to explain what he was thinking.

"It was as if I could *feel* her emotions. I know that makes no sense, but ..."

"It makes about as much sense as anything else that happens in Swan Harbor," Liam pointed out. "Now, there are only a few more dances before Elsa tosses the bouquet, and I get to whisk my bride away. Go get the girl."

Aiden took another sip from his glass, set it on the bar, and started toward the dance floor.

"Aiden," Liam waylaid him. "While I'm away, you can ask Killian or my dad for help. Surprisingly, Finley Reade has some moves for an old guy."

"Who're you calling an old guy?" Finn retorted, passing Aiden as he came off the dance floor. "Watch it, or I'll take your woman again."

Liam chuckled. "Get your own woman."

Aiden wanted what his cousins and uncle had found. A woman who loved him and wanted to be with him no matter what.

The music switched to a much slower song, and the closer he got to Harper, the more nervous he felt. A racing heart and sweaty palms were not what he needed.

His eyes met those of the man she was dancing with. Just as he opened his mouth, he heard her say, "What are you looking at, Ben?" Then she turned and met his gaze. "Aiden!"

Harper smiled, and Aiden's heart settled. "May I?"

He wasn't even sure if she said yes or just drifted into his arms, but once she slipped her hand into his, he knew she wasn't going anywhere for the rest of the evening.

Their eyes met, and hers so warm, something inside shifted.

"What took you so long?"

"Excuse me?"

She laughed. "That sounded very British."

"That's because I am British," Aiden reminded her.

"Oh, I know," she shrugged. "But sometimes you sound more so than others."

Aiden frowned. "Is that good or bad?"

"Neither. It just is."

He wasn't sure who had the upper hand, but saying nothing more, swung her around in a couple of intricate steps.

"Now, what did you mean about it being about time?"

I've been waiting for you.

His breath caught. *You didn't look lonely.*

She giggled. *So, you did notice.*

Bloody hell, of course.

The music slowed even more, and needing her close, he tucked her against his chest. She fit perfectly under his chin, and their hearts seemed to beat in sync.

Aiden couldn't help but think that this was where she belonged. Something told him she was feeling the same thing. He could *feel* her emotions.

One song bled into another, and much too soon, he heard the announcement for all the single women to line up.

"I think that means Liam and Elsa are leaving."

"And throwing the bouquet."

Rachel walked by and tugged on Harper's sleeve. "Come on."

He hesitated, loath to let her slip from his arms.

"I'll be back," she promised before following Rachel into a group of women.

"Everyone ready?" Elsa called.

There were several screams, and then Elsa turned around and tossed the bouquet over her shoulder. It flew through the air and landed directly in Harper's arms.

He should feel a little freaked, Aiden thought, pulling open the door for the newlyweds.

"It's on you now, cuz," Liam said, as he and Elsa ran out the door.
And that couldn't be truer.

TWELVE

Ava & Finn's Cottage
December 16
1:00 p.m.

AFTER SHE COMPLETED EACH TASK, AVA MADE A CHECKMARK ON her '*to-do*' list. With every mark she made, she was that much closer to number nine. That one sent a variety of feelings shooting through her system—fear, anticipation, and excitement. Somehow, she felt ... powerful.

Are you brave enough?

For most of her life, she'd felt like Rapunzel. She'd been the girl trapped in the tower, waiting for her very own Flynn Ryder. A man who loved her for who she was and not for what she was worth. And finally, after fifty-one years, she was free.

Finn had shown her what it was like to be loved and had given her many firsts. A trip to the zoo, a carousel ride, a hickey, and that all-powerful first time of hearing 'I love you' said to her by someone who was not her father.

Ava jotted an email, attached some forms, and hit send. Then, she made a checkmark next to the number eight, and with that done, it was time. Her heart raced, her hands got sweaty, and a giddy feeling arose within.

Are you sure?

Once she was sure she had time to make her purchase before Finn returned from the gym, Ava took out the *Rebecca's Fantasy* catalog.

Her nerves had her rushing through the pages featuring barely-there nighties and right to the toys. She bypassed the lotions, took a second look at the oils, and turned the page to find ....

"Oh, my," she murmured, noting the variety of sizes, colors, and materials.

How was she to choose which one would be best? And then about halfway down the page, she read, "The O WOW is guaranteed to make you scream with pleasure."

The description sold her, and after quickly filling out the order form, Ava buried the magazine and checked off number nine.

"Ava," Finn called, his husky voice wafting up the stairs.

"Up here," she replied, making sure she left nothing out in the open.

He bent over her from behind and nuzzled just under her ear, sending her pulse racing.

"You smell good."

"Thank you." Ava casually laid her arm across her list.

"Finn's gift, huh?" he chuckled. "What did you get me, love? You're acting awfully nervous."

"Nervous?" Ava shut her computer and pushed away from her desk. "You're imagining things."

"Nice try, Mrs. Reade." He quirked his mouth, causing his dimples to pop, and offered his lower lip. "Something the matter, love?"

Finn tugged her into his arms, and just like always, his heat reached out and grabbed her heart.

"Nothing's the matter," she barely got out before his lips were on hers, giving her one of those soul-sucking kisses that caused her knees to go weak and muddled her thoughts.

"I was just going to shower. Care to scrub my ... back."

For a second, Ava allowed herself to get lost in his dark eyes. "Sounds tempting. But I need to go."

"Go? Where are you going?" Finn followed her into their bedroom.

"Terri's," she reminded him. "I'm almost finished with my quilt."

The first time she'd met Terri, she'd brought out a quilt that Ava's grandmother Rose had started over fifty years earlier. Time and sorrow had prevented it from being completed.

"Will it fit on our bed?"

"No," Ava sighed, "it's not big enough. I'm not sure where I'll put it."

"I'm proud of you."

She cupped his jaw and kissed him tenderly. "I'm proud of me too. I'll see you in a few hours."

"Ava," Finn called when she reached the bottom of the stairs. "Ask Terri about Edythe. Without a last name ..."

She nodded, and on the short drive to Terri's, thought about his comments. There had been many changes in the past year—a health scare, finding her family, and a man who loved her. They just needed to find Edythe. The best was yet to come, for all of them—she hoped, anyway.

"Hi, Ava." Harper waved her inside. And just like the first time she'd arrived, Terri was sitting in front of an enormous television screen watching her soap opera. "As you can see ..."

"I'll wait," Ava laughed. "I forgot to check the time."

"I just can't stand that Kristin," Terri tossed over her shoulder when the commercial came on. "What's she doing sleeping with the son? Especially when years ago, she slept with the father. Just awful."

"It's a soap opera, grandma," Harper reminded her.

"I know it's a soap opera," Terri grumbled. "Doesn't mean I have to like it."

"She's been complaining about the storylines for years," Harper confided, as soon as the commercial was over.

"But she continues to watch," Ava guessed.

"Every day," Harper confirmed. "She laid your quilt on the sofa if you want to get started."

"You don't have plans to quilt today?"

Harper sighed. "I have a meeting at the university, and then I'm going to Sally's. She wants my help with the gingerbread house-making party."

"The parents don't stay?"

"Oh, they stay," Terri added when another commercial came on. "But they stand in the corner and gossip."

When Harper was gone, Ava took her quilt and spread it out across her lap. She reached for the thread and had to fight with an orange kitten for it. "And who are you?"

Terri clicked off the T.V. "That's Ginger, one of Harper's kittens."

"One of?"

"Yes," Terri nodded. "Fred is the other."

"Fred and Ginger," Ava laughed. "What do they think of the Christmas tree?"

Terri sighed. "They broke a few ornaments before we removed all the bottom ones."

"Emma complained about the same thing," Ava laughed. "Said her cats knock them off and play soccer with them across the floor."

"That sounds about right."

Terri showed her how to get started, and as soon as she was comfortable, Ava asked, "Did you know the woman who broke Jack's heart?"

The older woman said nothing right away but then stood up to take a photo album off a shelf. "I was hesitant to show this to you because I wasn't sure what you knew. But since you asked …"

Ava took the album, surprised to see her hand shaking when she opened the book. "Rose and Ray Dawson are excited to announce the engagement of Jack Swan and Edythe Burnett …."

Sally's Diner
December 16
5:00 p.m.

When Harper drove into Sally's parking lot, a quick glance at the clock told her she was only a little late. Time had gotten away from her when she'd stopped by her office after her meeting.

"Did you get sidetracked?" Rachel asked when Harper walked inside the diner.

"Yes," Harper admitted sheepishly. "I stopped by my office for five minutes and—"

"Got caught in a rabbit hole," Eden guessed.

"Sorry," Harper said again, storing her coat in the back. "What do I need to do?"

Sally was busy scurrying from table to table, leaving bowls of gumdrops and licorice.

"Nothing until the kids arrive," she murmured on her way by.

The bell over the door jingled, and Harper looked up, expecting to see a child's smiling face. Instead, her mother and aunt walked in.

"Mom," Harper exclaimed. "I didn't expect you tonight."

"Laura called, and I ..." Beverly began.

"What she's trying to say is we came to see Sally's decorations." Laura snickered.

"Decorations?" Harper glanced around the diner but saw nothing new.

"Look up, Harper," Eden murmured.

"Am I standing under mistletoe?"

"Not exactly," Beverly muttered, her face an interesting shade of red.

Harper glanced up, first with just her eyes, almost scared to look. But then ... she tilted up her chin.

"Oh, my goodness. Why haven't you taken them down?"

"Why?" Sally sent her an exasperated look. "Do you know the business I'll have with people wanting to check out my décor?"

"Are they clean?" Harper sputtered.

Sally giggled. "I hadn't thought about that, but ..." she shrugged as if it wasn't her problem.

"You know," Beverly mused, staring up at the ceiling. "There is something creative about it."

"You complained about the decorated palm tree on my sweater," Harper exclaimed. "But you think *this* is creative."

"Well, at least these are covered," Beverly muttered, which had Sally and Laura doubling over with laughter.

Harper shook her head and studied the ceiling objectively. Jocks! Men's jocks were hanging from every ceiling tile in Sally's. And in every conceivable color.

"I didn't know they came in so many colors."

"It is pretty amazing, isn't it?" Sally agreed. "Heads down, our first customers are here."

"Heads down, she says," Laura muttered. "What do you want to bet none of the mothers will keep their heads down?"

"Look who just showed," Rachel whispered. "It's Tyler and his daughter."

"Deep breath, Rach," Eden whispered.

"I'm cool," Rachel assured them. "Really."

For the next two hours, Harper moved from table to table, helping with gingerbread house construction. The icing on graham crackers at one table, licorice for trim on another.

"Skip has one that color," she heard when she passed by a group of women.

"Tyler, did you say the red one belongs to you?" someone teased.

"No, mine's the green one," he quipped.

And the easy camaraderie he shared with the women had her thinking of Aiden. Would he claim the blue one or the pink one? Or would he be so embarrassed he'd just smile?

Since the wedding, he'd been on her mind—a lot. Except she wasn't sure how she felt about that.

"Are you thinking about Aiden?" Eden asked as they wiped down a table.

"Why do you say that?"

Eden rolled her eyes. "I think Rach would claim you have that 'Harper' look and are trying to solve a problem. What did he do?"

"Do?"

"To put that look on your face?"

Harper shrugged, struggling to figure out what had been going on in her head.

"You know when you go to a wedding, and they say, 'you may kiss your bride'?"

"Yes."

"What do you think?"

"When they kiss?" Eden frowned. "I guess I've not given it much thought. Why?"

"Because," Harper's tone softened. "I see a man who's kissing a woman as if she's his end-all and be-all. After watching Liam kiss Elsa, I've realized I've never truly been kissed."

"You've never been kissed?" Rachel hummed. "Then who was it kissing Bobby in the back of the movie theater when you were sixteen?"

Harper groaned at the memory. "But don't you think there are 'differences' in kisses?"

"How so?"

"I don't know for sure," Harper murmured. "When his lips touch mine, though, I'll know. The world will stop, and all that will matter will be what's happening between us. Something tells me that at that moment, everything will feel *so* perfect, I won't want it to stop. When that happens, I'll know he's the person I'm meant to kiss for the rest of my days."

"Wow," Eden and Rachel muttered simultaneously.

"Am I expecting too much?" Harper sighed.

"That's how I felt when your Uncle Danny kissed me the first time," Sally remembered fondly. "And after almost forty years, he still makes my heart go pitter-pat. Just keep listening to your heart. It will happen."

"I'm trying." Harper's thoughts jumped between Clark and Aiden. But after everything with Joel, was she ready?

Aiden's Apartment
December 16
8:30 p.m.

Aiden flipped the water a little hotter and leaned against the wall, letting it pound on his shoulders. He'd spent hours in the library, hunched over a table and a microfiche machine, and crawling around a dusty basement. But even after jogging a few miles around the track at Giennie's Gym, his back was still stiff. However, the information had been worth it.

While he dried and slipped on a pair of sweatpants, what he'd learned kept playing over in his head. Except no matter which way he examined it, the information had not been something he'd anticipated. And when he shared the news with the others, he wasn't sure what to expect.

He'd located a poster buried in the archives that at one time had belonged to the sheriff's department. Ian Jones's picture showed a man with dark hair touching his shoulders, dark eyes, and a square jaw. Except it wasn't the depiction of the man that shocked him. That had been the words claiming he was wanted for murdering Isabelle Williams. Who was she, and why had he killed her?

He'd spread his notes across the table, and was preparing to organize them when someone knocked. Assuming it was the pizza he'd ordered, Aiden grabbed the money and answered the door.

"Surp—" Harper's voice died mid-word, her gaze glued to the middle of his chest.

Aiden glanced down and realized he'd forgotten a shirt.

"Sorry. I just got out of the shower and ..."

She visibly shook her head, as if she thought that would help organize her thoughts. "I'm sorry. I should have—"

"Hey," Aiden touched her arm. "You're fine. Do you want to come in?"

"Are you busy?" she asked hesitantly.

"I thought you were the pizza I ordered," he explained. "Did you need something?"

Once again, he caught her staring at his chest, and he had to fight the need to cover. Her eyes seared his skin, making him want to pull her into his arms to see where things would go.

"I brought you a present." Harper reached around behind her and handed him a box.

Aiden glanced inside. "Christmas bulbs?"

"And a tree." She dragged the six-foot live tree into his apartment.

"You brought me a tree?"

He quickly set the box aside and took the tree from her.

Harper tossed a grin over his shoulder before running back outside, only to return with a stand.

"When I was here the other day, you didn't have one, and so ..."

"You brought me a tree."

"Yeah."

Their gazes locked, and he wasn't sure what to say or what to do.

Is this okay?

It's more than okay.

Really?

Really.

"Good. Where should we put it?" Harper turned in a circle before rushing to the corner next to his keyboard. "How about here?"

"Alright. But the needles are bloody sharp," Aiden grumbled. "I'll be right back."

"Okay."

He leaned the tree against the wall and hurried down the hall, grabbed the first clean shirt he could find, and pulled it over his head.

When he returned, Harper was running her fingers over the keys of his keyboard. "Do you play?"

"Some," he admitted. "Do you?"

Harper laughed, a lighthearted sound. "Sure." She played a one-finger version of *Twinkle Twinkle Little Star.*

"Very nice."

"Why, thank you." She mock-bowed. "Now, it's your turn."

"I don't think so." Aiden picked up the tree and waited for her to position the stand, so he could slide the trunk into it. "I'm rusty."

He knew he'd recorded the song for Rosalind, except that had been different. They hadn't been in the same room. Meaning if she hadn't enjoyed the music, he wouldn't have to see her disappointment.

"But you saw the extent of my skills. I bet ..."

A knock on the door cut her off.

"Saved by the pizza." Aiden winked. "Let me get that."

"Chicken," he thought he heard her mutter when he turned away.

Aiden laughed and after paying for the pizza, grabbed some plates, a bottle of flavored water, and glasses. When he'd set everything on the table, and she still hadn't sat down, he sent her a silent message.

Harper?

"Yes?"

Aiden was still a bit wigged out by her uncanny ability to hear him when others couldn't.

"Come eat." He took her hand and directed her toward the table.

"Oh, but I didn't come here expecting to be fed."

"I know." Aiden guided her into a chair and pushed it in, lightly resting his cheek against hers. "But did you eat?"

"I, I ate some gumdrops and graham crackers."

"I thought I smelled sugar." He lightly nuzzled her cheek.

She gave him a look that said, '*What did you just do*'? Aiden had to admit it was as if someone had taken over his body. He imagined it to be his Clark to Superman transformation.

"Pizza?"

"One piece."

"One piece." He set it on her plate. "Got it."

Harper took a bite, and her moan of delight had his pants immediately tightening.

"I'd forgotten how delicious Papa's is," she murmured around a mouthful, the grease causing her lips to glisten.

Aiden swallowed and forced his attention away from her mouth and onto the food on his plate. "Tell me about the gingerbread decorating. Did the kids have fun?"

Her eyes grew larger, whatever she was thinking, causing them to crinkle at the corners.

"Sure. What kid doesn't enjoy making a gingerbread house? But I think the mothers had the most fun."

"Really?" Aiden frowned. "How so? I would have thought the mums spent most of their time telling little Timmy and Susie not to eat the decorations."

"Speaking from experience?"

"Perhaps," he replied, wearing a coy expression.

"You can't stop there," Harper encouraged. "Did you eat all the gumdrops?"

"Guilty," he admitted. "Well, except for the green. I don't care for those."

"Agreed. Which ones are your favorite?"

"Why the red, of course."

"Mine too."

I'd share it with you.

She laughed. "But what if I wouldn't share with you?"

"Hey," he retorted. "That's not fair."

"Sorry," she quipped. "No one gets between me and red gumdrops."

"I'll remember that."

For the next few minutes, he was content to finish eating and just listen to her talk. She was interesting and made the empty spaces easier to handle. With her, he was experiencing a camaraderie he'd never found with any other woman.

"So," he circled back after they'd eaten and put away the remaining pizza. "You didn't say. Why did the mums enjoy the decorating?"

Harper giggled, and the sound went straight to his heart.

"Because of the decorations."

"Don't tell me," Aiden remembered a comment from his cousin Killian. "The underwear thief struck again."

"Very good, Doctor Jones." Harper handed him a strand of lights and started wrapping them around the tree. "Sally's ceiling is decorated with jockstraps."

Aiden gulped. "Did you just say—?"

"Jockstraps," Harper repeated. "I did."

"And they were hanging ...?"

"From Sally's ceiling. Yes! And you know what?" she went on conversationally. "I learned something new."

He was torn between running into the other room to check for his jock and just letting her talk.

"I learned," she went on before he'd responded, "that they come in all colors."

"Really?"

"Yes. In fact," Harper laughed. "There was one that was pink."

Aiden could feel the heat climbing up his face. "Uhh, pink, you say?"

"Yes!" She peered around the tree, her eyes alight with laughter. "And not just any pink either."

Aiden frowned. "Pink is not pink?"

"Oh, no!" Harper shook her head. "See this?" She handed him a bright pink bulb. "This is hot pink, or you could even call it magenta. But this," she pointed to a lighter bulb on the tree, "is light pink or baby pink."

"I see."

Her laughter was tinkling. "No, you don't. But that's okay. Anyway, the pink jock was lighter, almost as if ....

Something red was washed with it.

"Exactly," she hummed.

Aiden clamped down on his thoughts, asking instead, "Why is she leaving them hanging?"

"Sally thinks it will be good for business."

He looked at her, assuming she was teasing. "You're serious."

"Very." Harper frowned. "In a weird way, it was just as creative as the bras."

"What's next?"

"Who knows?" She disappeared behind the tree, and suddenly, the lights popped on. "There."

Aiden stepped back and studied the tree. It was a little lopsided, and the lights were only half-lit. He slipped his arm around Harper and pulled her snugly against his side.

"What do you think?"

She glanced up. "It's kind of ugly."

"Ugly?"

"Yes."

Their eyes met, and almost unconsciously, he cupped her cheek with his left hand. "Harper."

Aiden could feel her pulse racing and the sting of her nails where she dug her fingers into his side.

"I hope," Harper took a deep breath, and her pulse raced even faster, "you like your tree."

"I do. Thank you."

He was going to kiss her and slowly leaned toward her until his mouth was hovering just above her lips. Her breath drifted across his. Harper's eyes drifted shut.

Angel ....

Just before their lips touched, his phone buzzed.

"Bloody hell!"

"You'd better get that," she murmured, stepping backward. "I'll see you later."

"Harper?"

With a wave, she was gone before he could find out what had happened. Where was Liam when he needed him?

THIRTEEN

Calliope's Dress Shoppe
December 17
11:00 a.m.

Harper meandered around the racks, party dresses in every color slipping through her fingers. But concentrating on the Gala was impossible. Her thoughts kept seesawing between Clark and Aiden—two men, two responses. With one, she needed a new question. With the other, an answer.

"What about this one?" Eden held a long green dress up in front of her.

"It's okay," Harper murmured, without really looking at it.

Eden hung up the dress and pulled out a red one. "How about this one?"

Harper gave a one-shoulder shrug and moved on to another rack.

"Intervention time?" Rachel murmured.

"Definitely," Eden replied seconds before each looped an arm through hers. "You're coming with us."

"Wait," Harper sputtered. "I need—"

"To talk about what's going on inside your head," interrupted Rachel. "We're here for you, and yet, you are elsewhere."

"Rachel's right," Eden agreed. "Maybe if you talk through what's going on, then we can shop."

Harper sighed, equal parts annoyance and thankfulness.

"Do I have to?"

Eden sent her a look that probably had the second graders she taught sitting up and paying attention.

"I'm not one of your students."

"Then stop acting like a brat," Eden uncharacteristically snapped back. "You wanted us to come shopping. Yet you've spent the entire time staring at your phone or pouting."

"Talk to us," Rachel pleaded again. "When we were carrying everything to Aiden's apartment last night, you were in a good mood."

"And today," Eden went on. "Your mood sucks. What did Aiden do?"

"Why do you ask that?"

"Harper," Eden gave an exasperated grunt and pulled her into Paula's Pastries. "Find a table. I'll get your favorite."

Harper grabbed a table in the corner and hung her coat over the back of her chair. How was she supposed to explain to her friends how she felt when she couldn't explain it to herself?

Her phone buzzed, and without even looking, she knew it was from Clark.

> Rosalind,
>
> You're cheating. I didn't ask what your favorite Christmas songs were, but song. Can you choose just one?
>
> Clark

"Clark or Aiden?" Eden set a cup of hot chocolate and a plate of crullers on the table.

"Clark. He's still trying to get me to commit to one song," Harper answered.

Rachel laughed. "Do you think he really cares?"

"I think the limitations are hindering the questions we might want to ask each other." But until she said that out loud, she hadn't realized how true it was.

"Because you can't ask personal questions?"

"Yeah," Harper nodded. "We text back and forth. It's just all superficial."

"Isn't that what you do when you date someone new?" Eden pointed out.

"True," Harper acknowledged. "Except when the person is in front of you, there's body language, the tone of their voice—it's just different. Plus, in my head, Aiden and Clark are merging."

Eden frowned. "How so?"

"When I picture the man on the other end of these texts or listen to the music recording Clark sent, it's Aiden's face I see." She blew out a breath. "It's more confusing than I thought it would be."

"And Aiden," Rachel prodded. "What happened?"

Harper grinned. "He opened the door last night without a shirt on, and wow!"

"Wow?" Eden repeated.

"Under those tweed jackets, he's built." Harper waggled her brows and fanned herself.

"Aiden?" Rachel exclaimed.

"Yes," Harper smiled. "He seemed surprised but pleased I brought him the tree."

"Okay," Eden nodded. "I'm with you so far. Then what caused Zombie Harper?"

"Or did you use the mistletoe?" Rachel laughed. "Is that why you're Zombie Harper? Did he kiss you?"

"I didn't use it," Harper admitted. "It was in the box, except I chickened out."

"So, no kiss?" Eden pushed a little more.

"But only because I chickened out," Harper blurted.

"Why?" Rachel exclaimed. "After your big speech about kisses, I thought that's what you were going to find out. What happened? Were you thinking about Joel?"

"No," Harper hummed. "Or at least, I don't think so. Then Aiden cupped my face, and he was so close, I could see the flecks of amber in his blue eyes. I could feel his warm breath blowing across my mouth ..."

"And?" Rachel shrieked. "You didn't jump him?"

"His phone buzzed, and all I could hear was his husky chuckle when he was on the phone with Sarah."

"So, you ran instead of asking him who Sarah was?" Eden surmised.

"I did."

"It's been days," Eden pointed out, "and you have some kind of mental connection with him. Why haven't you asked him?"

"She's chicken," offered Rachel.

"You could text him," suggested Eden.

"No," Harper sighed. "I want to see his face. But I did get a text from him that I need to answer."

"That said?" Eden asked.

Harper pulled up the texts on her phone and flipped it around.

Aiden: What happened? Did I overstep?

"Meaning, he knew something was wrong," Eden pointed out.

"And cared enough to ask what it was," added Rachel. "Most guys would let that fly over their heads."

"What should I say?" She glanced at the text once again, and several thoughts flew through her head.

Eden rolled her eyes. "Meet him for lunch and talk to him."

"Tell him about Joel," Rachel encouraged. "It would help him understand where you're coming from."

"Do you think we're there, yet?" Harper frowned. "I'm not sure."

"You almost kissed," Rachel muttered. "It's time."

"Hey, isn't that Aiden?" Eden pointed out the window.

Harper glanced outside to see Aiden lift his chin as if someone had called his name. He then opened his arms, and a beautiful woman ran into them.

"Who is that?" Eden whispered.

A sick feeling in the pit of Harper's stomach swirled. "I bet that's Sarah."

"Oh, Harper," Rachel sympathized as Aiden and the mysterious woman disappeared. "I'm sorry."

Harper dropped the rest of the cruller on the table, as what she'd just eaten threatened to come back up. "I'm so stupid."

Sally's Diner

December 17
1:00 p.m.

In the time it had taken them to finish their lunch, Aiden had reworked how to present his information more than once. But as soon as Sally carried away their plates, he forgot everything.

"Just spit it out," Captain Jack suggested. "Treat it like ripping off a Band-Aid."

Aiden winced. "Thanks for putting that image in my head."

"Whatever works." Jack shrugged.

"I'll do it," Sarah offered.

"I can bloody do it." Aiden pushed the envelope with the picture of the poster across the table. "I found that in the archives."

Jack studied him for several seconds before opening the envelope and taking out the photo. His brows arched, and then a smirk crossed his face.

"Ian Jones was wanted for murder?" He shook his head. "This can't be right."

"You don't think Ian could have killed someone?" Aiden exclaimed. "He was a bloody pirate."

"Oh, I think he could have killed. If he needed to," Jack clarified. "I just don't believe he killed a woman, especially this close to Hope's death."

Aiden pulled the picture back to check the date. "January 10, 1720. That was about a month before he left the ship and silver in Swan Harbor, right?"

Jack nodded. "Remember when you gave me the date of Ian's death?"

"You said he went back to England and died of a broken heart," Aiden replied.

"Because whatever he did after leaving Hope's side tore at his soul," Jack spoke with conviction, almost as if he was privy to information not yet obtained.

"What do you think he was doing?"

"What were Ian's last words to Hope?" Jack murmured. "I promise you, Hope, I'll find the key. And, on that day, we'll both be free."

"Which means the journals aren't the key," Aiden guessed. "Ian was in Boston searching for it."

"Maybe." Jack shrugged. "Maybe not."

Sarah had been sitting next to him quietly, but as Jack wound down, Aiden could feel her energy spark.

"Apparently, my sister has some information to share."

Jack laughed. "Like a dog with a bone, I believe, was how you described her."

"Bloody hell," Aiden snapped when Sarah elbowed him. "What was that for?"

"Comparing me to a dog," she retorted.

"Sorry." He waved his hands over her notes. "Carry on."

"We know the ship in Swan Harbor is indeed the Nuestra Señora de Concepción," she began. "But further research always leads back to the same conclusion ...."

"That the ship sank in the hurricane and was never recovered," Aiden added.

"Right." Sarah moved aside several pages of notes to focus on one with a timeline. "I still believe that at some point, the Concepción's name was changed to the El corazón del Rubí."

Jack frowned. "Why do you believe that? Is it just because the ship is a Spanish galleon?"

"Yes."

"And I can put Ian Jones on the El corazón del Rubí in November 1718," Sarah imparted with a *so there* grin.

"Bloody hell, Sarah," Aiden grumbled. "Why didn't you tell me?"

She shrugged. "I wanted to see your face when I told you."

"And you should see your face, Aiden," Jack chuckled. "I think she's one-upped you."

Aiden gave his sister a disgruntled look. "Okay, Baby Sister, continue."

His lips twitched when her mouth tightened at his use of a nickname she hated.

"While I couldn't find anything definite to back this up," Sarah went on. "There were rumors that Ian Jones was carrying around a large ruby that was shaped like a heart. His claim was that Queen Victoria had given it to him after the war, but who knows."

"Why was he flashing around a ruby?" Aiden asked, trying to piece together a few more things.

"I don't know," Sarah hummed. "But some rumors can be traced back to a blacksmith."

"A blacksmith?" Jack's face lit up. "And this was in November 1718? Could he have been having their rings made?"

"Possibly."

"So, Ian Jones was seen in the Boston Harbor before coming to Swan Harbor and finding Hope," Aiden said. "But did you find out anything around the time of the poster?"

Sarah gave him one of her Cheshire cat grins, setting Aiden's teeth on edge.

"Bloody hell, spit it out."

"I found mention of Ian visiting the same blacksmith in December 1719." She pointed to the timeline that had dates and pictures lining it. "This time, the rumors aren't of the ruby heart, but of pieces of eight."

"Grandfather's pieces of eight," Aiden murmured.

"Perhaps," she agreed. "He had the silver melted into jewelry. But this is the only picture that I can find."

Sarah laid a piece of paper on the table, and Aiden's gaze met Jack's. "Isn't that ...?"

"Yes, it is," Jack answered quietly.

"But what does it mean?"

Jack shook his head. "I don't know, Son. But I'm more convinced than ever that Jonesy needs to be free."

Sarah frowned. "Why is it I laid out a possible timeline for Ian Jones between 1718 and 1720, but I'm the one lost?"

Jack's face softened. "We're sorry. But we've seen that picture before."

"Where?"

Aiden pulled up the photos on his phone and scrolled through, locating the picture from Ian's journal.

Sarah smiled. "Bloody hell, this means I was right. But what happened to it?"

"I don't know," Aiden shrugged.

"If we find it," Jack murmured. "Something tells me it leads us to the key Ian was searching for."

Aiden's pulse raced as he stared at the picture of a heart with a lighthouse in the center. *Where are you? And what part of the story do you hold?*

The Pier
December 17
3:00 p.m.

Emma climbed out of her car and had to force herself to open the door of Captain Jack's. She found the older man pacing back and forth in the dining room, wearing a look of fierce concentration.

"Okay, Jack, I'm here," she announced, noting Aiden was sitting next to a woman with striking blue eyes.

Jack glanced up. "Have you met Sarah, Aiden's sister?"

"Hi, Sarah." Emma crossed her arms, took a deep breath, and prayed for patience. "Would someone tell me what's going on?"

"This is about Jonesy," Jack began.

"Well, of course, it's about Jonesy," Emma grumbled. "Except you know where I stand on that."

Jack pointed at Sarah. "She's uncovered some information that I feel pushes the need for Jonesy to be free."

"Do you want Jonesy to die?"

A pained expression crossed Jack's face. "You know I don't want that!"

"Jack," Emma tried again, deciding guilt was the only thing that would get through to him. "I agree Jonesy should be free. But remember how sick he looked in October?" He nodded, and she continued to push, "You said yourself, he usually migrated in early October, and it wasn't until he was in the aviary, he pepped up."

"But that was when your mother and Finn were falling for each other," Jack argued. "That added to the town's hope."

As a scientist, she still had a hard time buying into that, but it was a point she ignored for the time being.

"Finn and mom got married," Emma shrugged, "and Jonesy is fine."

"He is," Jack admitted. "Except, remember the pictures in Ian's journal; the chest, the heart with the lighthouse, a key, and then a picture of two connected hearts."

"Meaning?"

"Sarah found out where Ian Jones was after Hope died," Aiden replied. "The words we read in his journal led us to believe the journals were the key."

"They're not?"

"We don't think so." Jack gave her a concerned look, and she knew he was thinking about the fact that women in her family rarely lived beyond their forty-fifth birthday. "We think when put together, those pictures lead to the key."

"Why do you think that?"

"Because the picture drawn below the connected hearts is Jonesy ... and another swan."

Emma raised her brows. "So, we have the chest and the key. What about the other two pictures?"

"Well," Jack winced. "We're working on that."

"I'll make you a deal," Emma offered, thinking it would keep Jack off her back for a while at least. "You find the heart with the lighthouse and figure out the connected hearts. Also, find a place for Jonesy where the water is warm, and he has shelter from the elements. If you can take care of those things, we'll talk."

When Jack smiled, some of the weight she was carrying on her shoulders dissipated.

"We can do that." He turned to Sarah and Aiden. "But now, I'm going to show off the lily burned into the wheel. Would you care to accompany us?"

"Not this time." Emma glanced at her watch. "I'm meeting mom for coffee in a few minutes."

She left the restaurant and strolled up the pier toward Les Pâtisserie, where she was meeting Ava. Unfortunately, the walk didn't help clear her head, as when she arrived, her thoughts were still a jumbled mess.

When she arrived, Ava was waiting in front of the shop. "Mom, why aren't you inside where it's warm?"

"I just arrived," Ava murmured, still staring off toward the ship. "What's that old fool doing climbing up on the bridge in this weather?"

Emma laughed and pushed her mother inside. "He's showing Sarah the lily."

It was quiet while they placed their orders and found a table. Ava poured hazelnut creamer into her cup and stirred it for several minutes before taking a sip.

"Sarah, as in Aiden's sister?" she finally asked.

"Yes. Apparently, Sarah showed up today, and the information she brought convinced Jack and Aiden the journals aren't the key."

"Oh, dear." A pucker formed between Ava's brows. "So now what?"

"According to Jack, we have the chest and the key," Emma explained. "We need the heart with the lighthouse and to figure out how two hearts are connected. And then ..."

"Jack's still going on about freeing Jonesy, isn't he?"

"Yes," Emma sighed. "I told him to figure out those last clues and find warm water."

"Do you think that's possible?"

Emma glanced out the window, and the gray sea stretched out before her. "Not without help. The water's just too cold."

"Poor Jack," Ava murmured.

"I know Jack complains and frets about the swan and the key," Emma frowned. "But I think taking care of Jonesy gives him purpose. Without it, he'd be lost."

"Maybe." Ava glanced around to make sure no one was paying any attention to them. "I found out Edythe's last name. It's Burnett."

"And?"

"Finn is trying to find her, and the child she was carrying all those years ago."

"Do you think that's a good idea?"

The fact Edythe had called off their wedding and disappeared, pregnant with his child, had to be something that chipped away at Jack's heart. But how would he feel if she walked back into his life?

"I had to try," Ava whispered. "The thought of Jack not knowing whether he has a son or daughter out there hurts right here." She placed her hand over her chest.

Emma said nothing but hoped they knew what they were doing.

"Do you have any more stops?" Ava asked as they finished their coffee.

"I need to go to Joanne's Gems," Emma answered. "My charm bracelet is done, and I'm dropping off Killian's signet ring to be cleaned."

"I'll walk with you." Ava pulled on her coat. "You can tell me about Paris and the puppies."

"You know, you can come and visit Paris any time you want, right?"

"Oh, I know," Ava grinned. "But I'll be happy when her puppies are weaned and can go to their homes. And she can come to her new home. Do you think she'll like it?"

"Mom," Emma exclaimed. "We've gone over this. Paris will love it."

"You're still bringing her with you tomorrow, right?"

"Tomorrow?" Emma asked as they arrived at the jewelry store.

"We're practicing baking, remember?"

"Oh, that's right. But yes, I'll bring Paris. Do I need to bring anything else?"

"No." Ava's blue eyes twinkled. "I think we have it covered."

"Emma, Ava," Al greeted them. "How are things?"

"Good." Emma smiled, handing him Killian's ring. "I'm bringing you that to clean and need to pick up my bracelet."

Al put the ring in a small pouch, handed her the ticket stub and disappeared into the back. When he returned, he put on the bracelet.

"It's good as new."

"Thanks, Al." She stuck the ticket into her phone case so as not to lose it.

"Have you heard from the newlyweds?"

Ava nodded. "They're enjoying Aruba and sent us a few pictures of the beach. It's gorgeous."

"Tell Elsa her necklace is ready to be picked up when she gets home," Al reported.

"Will do. Thanks again."

As soon as they walked outside, Ava grabbed Emma's sleeve.

"Do you need to go right home?"

Emma noticed that Patti's Pampered Pet Store was just across the street. "Let me guess."

"Maybe they're having a sale." Ava hooked her arm through Emma's and pulled her along.

"Hold on, mom." Emma took bigger steps to keep up with Ava. "You're acting like a new mother."

"That's what I feel like," Ava exclaimed. "Are you coming?"

Emma followed her inside, thinking one of them needed to have a cool head.

FOURTEEN

Terri Patterson's Home
December 18
10:00 a.m.

Logically, Harper knew she needed to pull herself out of bed. She also knew that she and Aiden had made no promises. But she'd thought they were working toward something.

And that's why you ran?

She ran because she was a chicken. Except now, with that admission, what did she do about it?

Talk to him! Answer his text.

Except, she couldn't. Not until she decided what to say. Instead, she was watching a Superman marathon, as he was her dream man.

One side was awkward and unsure, while the other was confident and caring.

Like Aiden.

She forced that thought away and went back to the movie. There had been many actors who'd portrayed Superman, but none of them pulled off both sides as well as Christopher Reeve. When he transformed from Clark into Kal-

El, his voice and intonation were different, his facial expressions changed, and he even seemed to stand taller.

Except, watching Clark's shy puppy behavior around Lois Lane caused feelings she wasn't ready to face, rise to the surface.

"Harper!" her grandmother yelled. "Come, take care of your kittens."

"Okay, grandma." She forced herself to climb out of bed and pulled on her robe.

When she did, she caught sight of an orange flash as it raced by her door.

"Ginger?" Harper ran into the hallway.

The kitten was gone, but trailing across the floor was a strand of cream-colored yarn.

"No, no, no!" Harper followed the yarn to the front room, where she found part of the afghan hanging from her grandmother's crocheting basket.

Terri poked her head around the corner, carrying another one of her afghans. "Did you find them?"

"I found this." Harper gathered the afghan and rolled up the extra yarn and then followed the trail that led down the hall. It ended in her grandmother's bedroom as if the kitten had gotten bored and moved on to something else.

Once she'd collected all the yarn, Harper left the afghan in the bedroom and went searching for her mischievous kitten. She found hair ribbons spread across the bathroom floor, and claw marks on the toilet paper. But no Ginger.

"I've got them," Terri called. "They're eating."

Instead of going to check on the kittens, Harper crawled back into bed and resumed watching the movie. She just didn't have the energy to converse.

The movie reached the scene where Lois was interviewing Superman and wondering if he could read her mind. It was only fitting for Harper to compare her ability to converse silently with Aiden.

"Your grandfather and I had that ability," Terri murmured.

Harper glanced up, surprised to see her grandmother standing just inside the room.

"You did?"

Terri settled on the bed next to her before continuing. "I know you don't remember your grandfather, but he was such a handsome man. Such a hard worker, too. Then he had a stroke, and everything changed."

The story continued of how Terri's oldest child, and Sally's husband, Danny, had quit medical school to help.

"The stroke changed Dean," Terri went on. "He was angry and said words that weren't always kind. I knew people wondered why I stayed with him when he wasn't the same man I'd married. Do you know why, though?"

Harper brushed her hand across her cheek, surprised when it came away wet. "Because you loved him."

"I did," Terri confirmed. "But sometimes even love isn't enough."

"Then why?"

"Because Dean and I could still converse silently." Terri's smile was sentimental. "Even after his stroke, when the words he spoke out loud weren't always the nicest, the words from here," she touched her chest, just over her heart, "were still the same words of love. Over and over, he told me he was sorry. That he loved me. It kept me going."

"You listened to your heart."

"I did," Terri acknowledged. "And you know what it's telling me now?"

"That your granddaughter is being an idiot?"

Terri laughed. "I wouldn't quite put it like that. More like my granddaughter is hurting. Do you want to talk about it?"

"I don't know."

"How about this?" Terri suggested. "I'll tell you what I know, and you can fill in the blanks."

Harper shrugged, assuming her grandmother knew little.

"Joel, that boy you liked in Florida, broke your heart," Terri began. "Except after you got involved in that research project at the University, your heart began to heal. Then something happened, and when you looked at Aiden again, your heart spoke. How am I doing so far?"

"How?" Harper's mouth dropped open.

"I raised six children," Terri reminded her. "Plus, did you really think your mother could keep a secret?"

"And I discussed the research project with her," Harper realized. "How did you know about Aiden, though?"

Terri chuckled. "When sparks ignite, the gossip line takes flight."

"Oh, brother."

"It's always been that way," Terri reminded her. "Just with cell phones—

it's much faster. So, tell me what happened with Aiden. I heard he had you cornered under the mistletoe at the nursing home, and you skittered away."

Harper's face flamed as that had been the first time she'd felt overwhelmed by his nearness. "I freaked," she finally admitted.

"Why? You like him, don't you?"

In as succinct a way as possible, she told her grandmother about hearing him on the phone with another woman. She then told her about coming back to her apartment after submitting her dissertation and finding Joel and her roommate in bed together.

"It was awful," she shuddered. "I thought he was ..."

"There has to be more," Terri pushed.

Harper sighed, the memory putting a nasty taste in her mouth. "A few weeks after catching them, I'd fallen asleep on the sofa. When I woke up, he had pinned me in and was kissing me."

"That I hadn't expected," Terri admitted.

Harper barked out a dry laugh. "Oh, I didn't either. But I had the last word. I kneed him in the gonads and pushed him onto the floor."

"Your father would be proud."

"Yeah," Harper sighed. "Every time Aiden gets too close, something happens. First, it was the memory of Joel. Then it was the phone call to another woman."

"Have you talked to him?"

"No, Aiden sent me a text, but I don't know what to say."

Terri tilted her head, and the look in her dark eyes made Harper feel as if she could read her mind. "Every story has two sides. Aren't you supposed to go to the faculty holiday party tonight?"

"Yes."

"Talk to him."

"But what if ...?"

"Talk to him, Harper," Terri reiterated. "Your heart and his heart are connected. You need to listen."

"I'll try." Harper's attention went back to the television. Except if she talked to him, would she like what he had to say?

Sheriff's Department
December 18
1:00 p.m.

Killian stepped into Sally's Diner, the place crowded and alight with the buzz of conversation. Then, just as he'd expected, there was silence as everyone looked up to see who'd arrived. Once they'd looked their fill, the talking would resume.

"Are you here for lunch, Killian?" Sally asked expectantly.

Killian gave her a stern look and pointed up. "I'm here about the crime you forgot to report."

"Oh, well," Sally shrugged and waved for him to follow.

They wound their way around the tables to her office in the back next to the kitchen.

"I assume you're looking for this." She handed him a piece of paper. "Those are the names of the people who've collected their ... garments."

Killian glanced at the list of names and recognized one or two.

"You didn't get phone numbers?"

"No. But you work for the sheriff's department," Sally pointed out. "I'm sure Amy can get them for you."

He could tell his patience was wearing thin and moved in another direction.

"When did you first notice your new ... decorations?"

"You mean, when did the jocks first appear?" Sally laughed. "Hmm, two days ago. The afternoon of the gingerbread house decorating."

"You didn't open that morning?"

"Oh, no. We never open on the day of the decorating," she clarified. "I sleep in that day, and then I go shopping."

"And why was it you didn't report the break-in?"

"No one took anything," Sally pointed out. "Plus, did you see the lunch crowd? The new decorations are good for business."

Killian fought not to roll his eyes. "I need to collect—"

"No, you don't," Sally interrupted. "They're not hurting anyone, and let's face it. There's a greater chance someone will claim them here than if they're in some box in your evidence room."

She had a point, but he hated to admit it. "Fine," he retorted through gritted teeth. "But if someone claims one—"

"—I'll write their name and number."

"See that you do." Killian closed his notebook and stood to leave.

"Don't forget your lunch on the way out."

"I didn't order anything."

Sally laughed. "You're one of our regulars, Killian. Your usual is waiting."

He grabbed his lunch, returned to the office, and tossed the piece of paper on Amy's desk.

"Can you get those phone numbers for me?"

"Sure thing, Killian."

"Bloody hell." He dropped into his desk chair. "Have you been to Sally's and seen her new decorations?"

Rusty laughed. "No, I haven't had the pleasure. But Rene took Roland to the gingerbread house decorating and told me. She said, 'Well, I'm just glad your old, gray one isn't hanging on display.'"

"Thanks for that image," Killian muttered.

"You're welcome." Rusty gave him a cheeky smile. "It's what partners are for."

"Killian, Line 1," Amy called over the intercom.

"You want to answer it?"

"My name's not Killian." Rusty laughed. "Go right ahead."

"This is Killian," he answered hesitantly.

"This is Dorothy Mann. I need to report a theft."

"What are you missing, Mrs. Mann?"

"My snowman."

Killian exchanged looks with Rusty. "Your snowman?"

"Yes," she hummed. "Last night, I went to bed, and it was on the lawn. Then this morning, I went out to get the paper, and it was gone."

"Missing snowman," Killian repeated. "I'll send someone out to take your statement."

"Bloody hell," he grumbled after he'd hung up. "Now people are stealing snowmen. Did you know about this?"

Rusty tossed a piece of paper onto his desk. "I was just getting ready to tell you."

The list contained at least ten names, each with 'missing snowman' written after each.

"Why would someone take snowmen?" he murmured.

Rusty shrugged. "Based on last year's underwear escapades, perhaps the thieves are looking for someone to wear what they've taken."

Killian groaned. "Not what I needed to hear."

"It is what it is," Rusty offered.

Liam's comment about the way he was trying to solve the crime kept bouncing against Ernie's laughter. What was he missing?

He pulled out his notes and looked over what he'd written:

Bras hanging from the town Christmas tree.

Skivvies flying from flagpoles.

Panty wreaths hanging on multiple doors.

Jockstraps hanging from the ceiling at Sally's Diner.

He compared them to the notes he could piece together from December 2000. Each incident had been checked, meaning something was going to occur before December 26. The question was, what could it be?

Ava & Finn's Cottage
December 18
3:00 p.m.

As soon as Ava heard Finn on the phone, she snuck outside to check the mail. Logically, she knew it had only been forty-eight hours since she'd placed the order, but it was never a bad thing to be too careful. Especially if the package wasn't discreet, as the website had promised. Of course, if there was writing on the box, it would be more than Finn she'd have to worry about. And that was something she definitely hoped wasn't the case.

When she peered inside the mailbox, she saw a nondescript package wrapped in brown paper. *Already?*

"What are you doing?" Finn's husky voice startled her, causing her to drop the gift in the snow.

"Now look what you've done," she scolded. "I was just getting the mail."

He hummed and twisted his mouth, so his dimples popped. "You looked as if you were on a secret mission."

Ava noted that the gift was addressed to Finn. "No secret mission. But what's this?" She shook it and listened for a rattle.

"What does it look like?"

She studied it for several seconds. "I'm not sure. But I could open it and let you know."

"Oh, you could?" He grinned and advanced on her. "That's really unnecessary."

"Are you sure?" Ava teased. Then something inside had her tossing the mail in his direction and taking off.

The snow was deeper and softer than she'd expected, and she hadn't gotten far before she tripped, landing face-first.

"Ava."

Finn touched her arm, and her hours of self-defense classes kicked in. She rolled sideways, catching him unaware, and tugged him off his feet.

"Bloody hell," he muttered.

She was halfway up when he pulled her back down and rolled on top of her. "Now what are you going to do?"

The heat from his body on top countered the cold of the snow below. "No, the question is, what are you going to do?"

His lips toyed with hers, and all she wanted to do was sink in and enjoy the feel of his mouth. Slowly, her arms went around his neck. He groaned, taking the kiss deeper, and the imp inside had her shoving a handful of snow down the back of his shirt.

"Bloody hell." Finn rolled, just enough so she could scamper up and take off toward the door. "That wasn't very nice."

"Oh, I quite liked it." Ava laughed. "You should see your face. And guess what?"

He stopped in the middle of the yard and propped his hands on his hips. "Let me guess. Another teen moment?"

"Yes!" She beamed. "My first kiss in the snow."

"Come here." Finn crooked his finger. "I'll give you another kiss in the snow."

"That is tempting," Ava teased, noticing the sway of curtains across the street. "But we don't want to give the neighbors a heart attack."

"No?"

"No." Ava sent him a teasing smile. "Besides, look who's here."

When Emma drove into the driveway, she tossed the package to Finn and ran toward the car.

"Paris is here," she giggled, barely waiting until Emma parked before opening the passenger side door.

Paris jumped out and bounced around for several minutes before settling next to Ava to be pet.

"I didn't expect you this early."

"Killian said he would meet us," Emma laughed. "I called to ask him why he took our snowman, and he said, 'bloody hell, not ours too,' and hung up."

"Someone took your snowman?" Ava frowned and glanced back toward the front of the house where they'd arranged a family of snowmen. "Finn? Did you move one of our decorations?"

"Our snowman?"

"Yes." Ava pointed toward the front where there was once a snow family—mother, father, and child. Except the female snow person was missing.

"Bloody hell."

Emma giggled. "Call Killian. You can say 'bloody hell' together."

"Did Killian say why people are stealing snowmen?" Ava asked as they followed Finn and Paris into the house.

"He doesn't know. But he told me about Sally's newest decorations. Have you seen those?"

"No," Ava grinned. "How about dinner at Sally's tonight?"

"Oh, that will go over well," Emma laughed.

"Hey," Ava muttered tongue-in-cheek. "All we're doing is looking at the decorations."

"True," Emma hummed. "Cookies first?"

"Of course." Ava nodded toward the kitchen. "I'll be right back. I'm going to grab some dry clothes."

Aiden's Apartment
December 18
5:00 p.m.

While waiting for Sarah to get ready for the faculty holiday party, Aiden's phone buzzed. When he saw the message was from Rosalind and not Harper, he couldn't stop the feeling of disappointment that zipped through his system.

> Clark,

> If you're going to make me choose, fine. I would pick Christmas Canon because I love it when the children's choir joins the orchestra.

> Here's another seasonal question for you. What's your favorite Christmas story? Are you a Frosty, Grinch, or A Christmas Carol kind of guy?

> Rosalind

He decided he'd respond to the message later and pulled up the text he'd sent to Harper.

> Aiden: What happened? Did I overstep?

Except just like all the other times he'd checked, there was still no response. What had gone wrong? How had he completely misread her signals?

"Did you hear from her?" Sarah asked, coming into the room and dropping onto the sofa.

"What?"

She gave him her patented '*Please, I'm not a nutter*,' expression. "The woman you've been hoping to hear from all day."

"No," Aiden grumbled.

"Is she the one who bought you the tree?"

"How do you know I didn't buy the tree?"

"Please," Sarah laughed. "How many years have I known you? Have you ever picked out a tree on your own?"

"No. But that's because I knew you or mum would take care of it."

"Maybe," she agreed. "But it's what, December 18? Way too early for you to have a tree."

"Perhaps living in Swan Harbor put me in a Christmas mood a little earlier this year."

Sarah studied him for several minutes. "Possibly, as it feels like Christmas is in the air. But I don't think so. Spill."

"Why didn't I know you were coming to town this early?" Aiden asked instead.

"I told you why. I wanted to see your face when I shared what I'd learned."

"No, that's not it."

"I wanted to come sooner than mum," Sarah tried a different tactic. "Thought I could do research here just as easily as at home."

"And when is mum coming?"

"The twenty-third. Quinn is going to London and flying here with her."

"Tell me why you wanted to get away from Cornwall," Aiden repeated the same question. "You had dad's entire home to yourself."

Her eyes flared when he'd mentioned his father, pushing him to ask, "Did Dad try to contact you?"

"Not Dad," Sarah shuddered. "One of his business partners."

Aiden sighed. "Tomorrow, we'll talk to Killian. I'm sure he'll have a few suggestions."

She nodded and waved toward the tree. "What's her name?"

"Harper."

"Cute."

"Harper is beautiful," he responded cheekily.

Sarah rolled her eyes. "And what did you do?"

"Bloody hell, why do you think I did something?"

"Because you probably did."

"This time," Aiden admitted. "I don't know."

"What happened?"

"I just said, I don't know," he snapped.

"You really like her, don't you?"

"I do."

Except once the words were out there, he had to acknowledge the like was quickly heading toward something else.

"What happened?"

Aiden thought back on their time together. Pizza, flirting, decorating the tree, and then ....

"Everything was going well," he murmured. "Harper turned on the tree lights, I slipped my arm around her, and she looked up at me and licked her lips."

"Did you kiss her?" Sarah butted in to ask.

Aiden frowned. "No. We were close, but before anything happened, the phone rang. Then she made an excuse and disappeared."

"Did you tell her it was your sister?"

"It didn't come up."

"Will she be there tonight?"

"Harper teaches in the College of Education. So, she should be. Why?"

"Well, Big Brother." Sarah stood and grabbed her wrap. "Let's go so you can talk to Harper."

"But I don't want to leave you alone."

Sarah chuckled. "Did you know that there's someone at Swan Harbor University who has published several articles about pirates and the Spanish Treasury Fleet?"

"Really?" Aiden asked, surprised he hadn't learned that from Jack or the librarian. "Who is it?"

"Doctor Hall," she murmured. "Joshua Hall. Know him?"

FIFTEEN

SHU Holiday Party
December 18
6:30 p.m.

Harper poked at the ice floating in her glass while listening to the conversation going on around her. She was sitting at a table with her mother, father, Aunt Laura, and Uncle Josh. Her mother was filling her aunt in on the latest university gossip. Josh and her father were talking about the hockey team. And she was waiting for ....

Angel ....

The word reached her ear, sank, and swirled around her heart.

"Harper, isn't that the man who was with you when you brought the cookies to the nursing home?" Laura leaned over to ask. "Who's that with him?"

She didn't want to look, but steeling herself for the impact, Harper glanced over her shoulder. Aiden was standing just inside the room, the heat from his gaze searing her with its intensity.

The woman she'd seen him hugging was standing next to him, but they weren't touching. She was pretty, Harper grudgingly admitted. Black hair, blue eyes, tall.

"That's Aiden," she confirmed. "I don't know the woman."

Her mother gave her a funny look but didn't put her on the spot.

"She's not a new faculty member. In fact, she looks like him."

His sister flew through Harper's mind.

Yes.

Harper gasped and whipped back around. *Your sister?*

Yes.

She closed her eyes and dropped her head. *I'm a fool.*

You aren't.

But with Aiden and his sister crossing the room towards her, Harper knew the time would come when she'd need to own her actions.

"Good evening," Laura took the initiative. "Aiden, isn't it?"

"Yes, ma'am." Aiden's gaze touched on everyone before meeting Harper's. "This is my sister, Sarah. She surprised me by showing up several days early."

"That was a pleasant surprise, I bet." Laura nodded to the man next to her. "This is my husband, Josh, Harper's mother, and my sister, Beverly, and her husband, Greg."

Harper noticed Sarah and Aiden exchange looks when Laura introduced her uncle.

"You wouldn't be Doctor Joshua Hall by any chance, would you?" Sarah exclaimed.

"It depends," Josh's eyes twinkled. "Why do you ask?"

Sarah rattled off the title of some article, but Harper let the words fly over her head. She only had eyes for Aiden.

"I did write that," she heard Josh say.

"You'll have to forgive my sister, sir," Aiden mock-confided. "Since we discovered that the pirate Ian Jones was our ancestor, she's gone a bit nutter."

"Hey, watch it," Sarah laughed.

She turned back to Josh and rattled off a question about a Spanish galleon and the efficacy of ...

Harper tried to listen, but she kept getting lost in the heat of Aiden's eyes. They needed to talk.

"Would you care to dance?"

I thought you'd never ask.

His breath hitched when she slipped from her chair. "Excuse us."

As he led her toward the dance floor, where a small band from the music department was performing, Harper felt like she was floating. Then he pulled her into his arms, and just like at Elsa and Liam's wedding, it felt like home.

His chin brushed against the top of her head, and that current between them sparked. The feel of her hand in his, the smell of his cologne, and the heat they generated wrapped around her, forcing her to acknowledge it was time.

"I'm sorry." She pulled up her big-girl panties.

Aiden studied her closely. "What are you sorry for? I thought …"

Harper leaned back just enough to meet his gaze and admitted to overhearing him on the phone with Sarah.

"And you thought she was someone I was involved with from England?"

"Yes."

"But you knew I had a sister," Aiden frowned. "Didn't you?"

"I did," Harper sighed. "But either you never said her name, or I didn't hear it."

"I'm sorry." He looked across the room. "I thought I'd done something …"

"Aiden." Harper waited until his gaze was once more on her. "When I was in Florida, there was a man, and he cheated on me, so …"

"Once bitten, twice shy?"

"Something like that," she acknowledged.

Aiden tightened his arm around her waist, pulling her hips a little closer to his. "We'll take it as slowly as you need to go."

"We will?"

"Of course." Aiden spun her around a few times. "Is that alright?"

Harper made the mistake of looking up. Their eyes met, and her breath lodged at how right it felt.

You feel it too, don't you?

Except she couldn't get her tongue to work. She could only nod and bask in the feeling swirling around them.

"So," Aiden teased. "That's your father, huh?"

"Yes."

"You aren't going to sic him on me, are you?"

"Just mind your p's and q's, and I won't have to," Harper teased right back.

As the music wound down and they walked back to the table, her hopes for the evening increased substantially. Even if it meant her father asked him a tough question or two.

Ava & Finn's Cottage
December 18
7:30 p.m.

"Was it worth it?" Finn asked Ava after he'd parked and powered down the car.

"Dinner at Sally's so I could see her decorations?" Ava laughed. "Sure. I want to see you in one of those red ones."

Finn shook his head. "Is that what you got me for Christmas?"

"Maybe." She winked and, without waiting for him to open her door, jumped out to meet Emma, Killian, and Jack.

He'd enjoyed their meal, but when Jack had mentioned that he and Aiden didn't believe the journals were the key, he'd seen Killian's face. His son was concerned but trying hard not to show it.

"Let me get that." Finn unlocked the door and let the ladies proceed them inside. "Are you alright?" he asked Killian softly.

"Aye," Killian replied without hesitation.

Finn glanced at Jack and picked up the conversation they'd been having at Sally's.

"If the journals aren't the key, then do you have any ideas?"

"It's on the last page of the journal," Jack replied. "The chest, the key, the heart with the lighthouse, and the connected hearts."

"When the heart speaks ... listen?" Finn suggested.

"No," Ava scoffed. "Connected hearts equal true love."

Jack frowned. "Why do you say that?"

She caught Finn's eye and sent him a secretive smile.

"Didn't you ever watch fairy tales? The handsome prince always rescues the beautiful princess, and there's a true love kiss."

"But this isn't a bloody fairy tale," Killian snapped.

"We know that Killian," Jack jumped in. "Except in a way it makes sense.

When couples fall in love, the hope seems to burn brighter. After all, look at what happened to Jonesy after Finn and Ava got together."

"I think it was the zoo's aviary and a steady diet," Emma murmured.

Jack shot her a look, and when a worried expression crossed Ava's face, Finn sought to change the subject.

"How many snowmen ended up missing, Killian?"

"Two dozen," Killian frowned. "Rusty thinks the thief is gathering them to display what he's taken.

"What do you think?"

"Someone's a bloody nutter," Killian retorted. "Other than that, I have little to go on."

"Isn't that unusual?" Jack questioned. "For a thief—or thieves—to get in and out of so many homes in Swan Harbor?"

"And no one sees anything?" Finn asked.

Killian nodded. "Liam thinks I'm trying to solve it the wrong way."

"What does that mean?"

"He said to stop trying to solve it like my other cases," Killian relayed.

"So, you're going to solve it another way?" Emma surmised.

"Ostensibly," Killian confirmed.

"Is that your way of saying you don't know what that is?" Finn laughed.

Killian shrugged. "I'm letting the evidence … germinate."

"Well, that's one way to do it." Jack sniffed and glanced toward the kitchen. "Do I smell cookies?"

"Yes." Ava hopped up and led the way. "Emma and I were practicing for the cookie exchange."

"Ahh, the cookie exchange," Jack murmured. "I've never had the pleasure, but Rose used to make these cookies called Snowflakes."

"Snowflakes?" Ava repeated. "I think I have that recipe."

"Finn, want a cookie?" Jack asked.

"No thanks, Jack."

Finn wanted to warn the older man but watched him take a couple of cookies and a napkin before returning to sit.

Jack had the cookie halfway to his mouth when his eyes caught Finn's. "What?"

"Nothing," Finn hurried to assure him.

Jack studied the cookie for an extra second before taking a bite. The way his eyes widened told Finn everything he needed to know.

"Hard?"

"As a rock." Jack hit the cookie against the table. "How can that be?"

"What?"

"Look at them." Jack held up the cookie, which looked perfectly edible on the outside. "They look good, but they won't break."

"Overzealous cooks and not enough flour," Finn murmured.

Killian snickered. "What are you talking about?"

Finn glanced into the kitchen, where Ava and Emma were gathering ingredients to make more cookies.

"Let's take Paris outside."

Killian and Jack grabbed their coats and followed him out the back door. Once Paris had bounded into the snow-covered backyard, Finn took another peek over his shoulder.

"Let's just say baking is not one of my wife's strong suits."

"Emma's either," Killian added.

"I suspect Ava wanted to make a good impression at the cookie exchange," Finn began.

"And bit off more than she could chew?" Jack suggested.

"That's one way to look at it." Finn laughed as another option drifted through his head. "Either that or she has my number and is waiting for me to take over."

"Look at them," Killian waved toward the window where they could see the women laughing. "They're concocting something."

"So, the question is," Jack posed. "Do you want cookies enough to take over?"

"I don't need cookies," Killian replied.

"Neither do I," Finn agreed.

"I'm not willing to say I don't need cookies yet," Jack grunted.

"But?" Finn hummed.

"I'll wait and see," Jack promised.

"Softy," Finn murmured.

"I didn't reach this age by being stupid," Jack winked.

Killian shrugged. "What do you say, he caves?"

"Probably so," Finn grunted.

SHU Holiday Party
December 18
8:30 p.m.

Laura plucked a cookie from the plate in the center of the table. "This is good. Harper, are you going to the cookie exchange tomorrow night?"

"I'm not sure," Harper shrugged. "But if I do, grandma has been baking for a few days."

"Mom does make the best cookies," Beverly murmured. "What kind is she making?"

Aiden turned his attention to Harper, but he could feel Captain Taylor sizing him up and had been waiting for the questions.

"I understand you're related to Killian Reade," Greg tossed him a simple question.

Sorry, Harper sent him a silent apology.

It's alright.

"Yes, sir," Aiden replied. "My father and Killian's mother were siblings."

"And you just happened to end up in Swan Harbor?" Greg commented. "That's quite a coincidence, isn't it?"

"Greg," Beverly scolded.

Greg gave her an innocent look. "I'm just making conversation."

"I'd heard of Swan Harbor before," Aiden explained.

"Oh?"

The look of expectation on Greg's face differed from what he'd anticipated. It had him wondering whether he was being led down a no-win path or was just curious.

"I was in graduate school at the University of Sheffield and became friendly with Cameron Hunter," Aiden went on.

"Clint and Mary's boy?" Greg asked.

Aiden nodded. "A year ago, when Jessie and Cam were in London, we had dinner. From the way they spoke about Swan Harbor, it felt familiar."

"To find cousins and a long-lost relative must feel a little surreal," added Harper.

Aiden smiled. "A little, yes."

Sarah jumped in with a question. Whether it was to save him or because she was curious, he wasn't sure. Especially since she'd been peppering Harper's uncle throughout dinner. And although he'd tried to quiet her a few times, she'd kept at it.

"I found mention of Ian carrying around a large ruby heart in November 1718. Do you know anything about that?"

"El corazón del Rubí," Josh murmured, a look of fierce concentration on his face. "Where was Ian supposedly seen?"

"Boston," Aiden responded. "Why? You act like you've heard of it before."

"Rumors," Josh answered. "Just as Captain Jack believes the hope of the town is tied to a swan—Jonesy. I've heard stories surrounding a ruby heart but never put much stock in them."

"But now you know the ruby is real," Sarah said. "Does that make the rumors more likely?"

"What about the name Isabelle Williams?" Aiden went in a different direction.

Josh frowned. "Why?"

"I found a poster," Aiden admitted. "It said Ian Jones was wanted for the murder of Isabelle Williams."

"Williams was the surname of one of our founding families," Josh explained. "My knowledge is rusty, but I think one of them was a doctor. I'm not sure about Isabelle."

"And the ruby heart?" Sarah pushed.

Josh took off his glasses and cleaned them with a napkin before continuing. "I've read about a rumor of a ruby that was considered Swan Harbor's heart."

"Go on," Sarah murmured.

"The color of rubies resembles blood," Josh continued. "It was believed they held the power of life."

Could that be a part of the key, Aiden wondered. Returning the El corazón del Rubí to the town?

Sarah was still peppering Harper's uncle with questions, but something had him reaching out.

Care to dance?

Harper smiled. "I'd love to dance."

She placed her hand in his while they walked to the dance floor as if it was something she did every day.

"Finally." He tugged her against his chest.

Her tinkling laughter drifted across his skin, settling him in a way he'd never expected.

"I'm sorry about all of Sarah's questions."

"It isn't your fault," Harper assured him.

"But still ..."

"Did you see my uncle's expression?" asked Harper. "He was in heaven. It's also pretty fascinating."

"It is. But," Aiden went on, "I felt bad for your aunt."

"Oh, Laura's used to Josh going off on tangents," Harper laughed. "That's why she and my mom gossip. Usually, it's my dad who's bored. Tonight though ..."

"He had me to grill."

"Was it too bad?"

"Not awful, no."

The music transitioned into another song, and a part of Aiden wished it were warmer outside. He wouldn't mind slipping away for some alone time.

"So," he eased his way in. "Are you going to the cookie exchange tomorrow?"

Harper shrugged. "I'm not sure. It's held at the mayor's home, and there are usually so many people there, it's crazy. Why? Do you want me to steal cookies for you?"

Aiden chuckled. "I hadn't thought of that. But I wouldn't mind."

"It would be easier just to bring you some of my grandmothers."

"I do like her peanut butter ones. But ..."

Her eyes met his. "What, Aiden?"

"I was wondering," he cleared his throat, "if you would ... spend the day with me tomorrow."

Harper smiled. "But don't you need to entertain Sarah?"

"If I know my sister," he murmured. "She'll want to spend the day at the library. Besides, I need to buy a few gifts for my new family."

"And you need help?"

"Yes, do you mind?"

"Not at all," she replied. "I would love to spend the day with you."

"Perfect."

As one song blended into another, he couldn't get over how good she felt in his arms. Nor could he rid himself of the image of dancing her into a corner and touching his lips to hers. Slow down, Jones, he scolded, searching for a neutral topic.

"Tell me about your mom's family," he suggested. "She's one of how many?"

"Six," Harper laughed. "Danny is the oldest and is married to Sally ..."

Ava & Finn's Cottage
December 18
9:00 p.m.

"How many dozens of cookies did Sally suggest we bring?" Ava asked, studying the recipe in front of her.

"Three," Emma replied, measuring out flour.

"Would you two like some help?" Jack strolled into the kitchen behind them.

Ava smiled, thinking it was about time, and pushed the recipe across the counter.

"That would be terrific."

He beamed and tucked a towel into the front of his belt. "I remember one time when your mom, Grace, was about eight."

"And you were twelve?" Ava guessed, knowing he'd gone to live with his sister when he was four.

"About that," Jack nodded. "Grace wanted Rose to make cookies, but she was doing something, and so she asked me to help."

"Were you annoyed by that?"

Jack stared off, and a sentimental smile crossed his face. His expression said she assumed he was remembering her mother.

"Oh, I didn't mind. I actually enjoyed cooking. But those cookies ..."

"Didn't turn out so well?"

"Hardly," Jack chuckled. "Grace put too much sugar and too little flour in the bowl."

"Oh no," Ava laughed. "I bet they were awful."

"They were," Jack nodded. "But Ray ate them as if they were amazing. It got a little dicey when Grace wanted to share the cookies with the neighbors."

"What happened?"

Before he responded, the lights flickered as the wind blew around the old home.

Ava exchanged a look with Finn. "We're not expecting another storm, are we?"

"No love," Finn assured her. "It's just the wind because we're up on a hill."

"Lights flicker all the time," Jack told her. "We should be fine."

Ava nodded, but just to be sure, lit the candles on the table and found a flashlight.

"Okay, tell me what happened when mom wanted to share her bad cookies with the neighbors."

"Rose called Terri and asked her if she had any cookies we could exchange."

"And Terri did," Ava guessed.

"Of course." The entire time Jack was talking, he was measuring, sifting, and dumping everything in the bowl, making Ava feel useless. "We lived down the street from where Terri lives now. Rose sent Grace up to change and—"

"—You ran and picked up some new cookies."

"I did," he agreed. "Barely made it back too."

"But you saved the day," Ava smiled. "Just like you're saving the day for my cookies."

Jack lowered his voice. "I saved the day, but Grace's cookies were bad because of an accident. Your bad cookies ..."

Her gaze drifted to Finn, who was sitting across the room petting Paris. He glanced up and winked, and her heart flipped.

"I have nothing to say."

"I thought as much," Jack chuckled.

The howling of the wind and the flickering of the lights cut him off, sending goosebumps racing along Ava's arms.

"I've never heard the wind make those sounds," she shivered. "It's spooky and sounds like …"

"A man crying out in pain," Jack murmured. "Today is what? The sixteenth?"

"Eighteenth," Ava replied, and then a chill ran through her body, and her gaze met Emma's. "Hope died on December 18th."

"It's Ian's cry," Finn whispered, pulling her against his chest. "The day Hope died in his arms."

SIXTEEN

Main Street Mall
December 19
2:00 p.m.

Harper stood by and watched Aiden methodically sort through some Christmas ornaments.

"Are you looking for anything specific?" she finally asked.

Aiden glanced up, his glasses askew, and before she'd even thought it through, she'd set them right.

"Thanks." He blushed. "I need to adjust them, but ..."

"You never think about it until you're out, and they slide down."

"Something like that."

Unconsciously, he pushed them back up and gave her one of his endearing, crooked smiles. Then, just like every other time, her heart flipped.

"What are you looking for?" she asked again.

"An ornament."

Harper laughed. "That, I do know."

This time when he smiled, it was sheepish. "Meet Paris, Finn and Ava's new dog." He showed her a photo on his phone.

"So," Harper guessed. "You want an ornament with a dog that looks like that?"

"Actually," he corrected. "I want one that has a male and female plus a dog that looks like that."

"That's pretty specific." She pushed aside a few of the ornaments, searching for a dog that resembled Paris. There were big dogs, little dogs, and spotted dogs. But it wasn't until she'd reached the bottom of the rack that she found a terrier.

"Will this work?" Harper held out the ornament for him to see.

Aiden grinned, and his blue eyes sparkled. "You're bloody brilliant."

"Why, thank you, kind sir."

He set the ornament in the basket he was holding before consulting something on his phone.

"And this time?"

"A male, a female and three cats."

"Do the cats have to be a certain color?"

Aiden glanced up, a panicked look on his face. "I don't know what color they are. Maybe I should ..."

"Relax," she hurried to assure him. "If you got one of these ornaments, the color wouldn't matter."

"Are you sure?"

Harper pointed to an ornament. "This one looks like my kittens, as you can see the orange and black. But this one, they have sweaters and stocking caps on. You just have to have their names added."

He nodded and, after setting that ornament in his basket, quickly chose several more.

"Wait a minute," she laughed. "What's the deal with the last few you added?"

Aiden glanced into his basket. "Those were the easy ones."

"So, you chose the harder ones first?"

"Well, sure." He frowned. "It's more rewarding when you find something you've worked for."

When their gazes clashed, Harper couldn't stop the thought, *Is that with everything?*

His, *Most definitely,* and the heat in his eyes told her more than words. That *she* was what he was working for.

While he paid and gave instructions regarding what name went to which ornament, Harper checked the time. They'd only been together for a few hours, and yet, he'd found everything he needed. Was that it for their day together? Would he take her home and join Sarah at the library?

A few seconds later, Aiden took her arm and directed her away from the Christmas store. "The saleswoman promised she'd have my ornaments done in a few hours. How shall we spend the time?"

"Oh," Harper exclaimed. "I thought. I mean. I just assumed ..."

"Just spit it out," Aiden laughed. "You thought I'd join my sister at the library?"

Her cheeks flamed. "Well, yes."

He tugged her away from the flow of shoppers. "Harper, I admit, I'm curious, but I'm where I want to be. Unless you ..."

She grinned with relief. "My time is yours."

"Good." Aiden took her hand as they resumed walking. "Then what is your pleasure? Are you hungry? Do you need to shop?"

There were a few more gifts she needed to find, but something told her Aiden would rather see Swan Harbor's hidden gem.

"Have you been to the Underground Museum?"

"The Underground Museum?" he repeated, and just the tone of his voice gave her the answer.

"Swan Harbor has a mass of tunnels underneath it that were used for bootlegging years ago," she explained. "There's a strip under Main Street that's a museum of sorts. It's like a walk through Swan Harbor's history."

"Really?" His smile reminded her of someone whose greatest wish had been granted.

Harper tugged him along. "Let's leave the gifts in the car, and then I'll show you."

"I like the way you think."

She was quickly coming to think she liked much more about him than just the way he thought. But as he'd commented when they were dancing, what had happened with Joel was still floating around in the back of her mind. Which was what kept her from falling headfirst.

"Have you ever been in here?" Harper asked, leading him into City Hall and through a nondescript set of doors.

"I've no bloody idea where we are," he murmured.

Harper giggled. "This section of City Hall used to be the original County Courthouse. But sometime in the early 1900s, it was rebuilt."

They turned a corner, and the hallway gave way to a narrower passageway, more tunnel-like than not. The farther they walked, the cooler the temperature and the danker the air.

"It smells like an old library," Aiden noticed.

"Very good, Doctor Jones. The other end of the tunnel actually ends in the library's basement."

"The stories I bet these walls could tell," she thought he muttered.

Harper tugged a five-dollar bill from her pocket and pushed it into an old postbox at the end of the tunnel.

"During the summer, the tourists go through here for a few dollars. I think the city uses the money for upkeep."

"No one works down here?"

"Community service volunteer hours." Harper stepped through another set of doors, but these were wooden.

"Bloody hell," Aiden whispered, immediately moving to the first picture.

Just seeing the look on Aiden's face as he went from picture to picture convinced Harper she'd made the right choice. There were photos of the harbor and pier and ones of the downtown area, including Sally's, City Hall, the library, and Swan's Spirits, taken in the 1990s.

As they moved from images depicting the 1900s into the 1800s, Harper realized Aiden was humming.

"Look at that." He pointed to a photo of a covered bridge on the outskirts of town. "Can you imagine crossing that in a horse-drawn carriage?"

Then, without waiting for her to answer, he moved on and resumed his humming.

"Christmas Canon," she murmured, when what he was humming finally clicked.

"What?" Aiden asked, his attention still on the photos.

"You were humming Christmas Canon," she repeated. "It took me a minute to figure out what it was."

"I was? Sorry." He shrugged. "I've been listening to it lately."

Harper touched his arm. "I wasn't complaining."

Aiden smiled, and she thought he was going to say something else. Then his attention was drawn to a large plaque hanging next to the doors leading to the library.

"Bloody hell, is that what I think it is?"

Harper glanced at the list of names she'd not paid much attention to her entire life. "If you're asking if they're Swan Harbor's founding families, then yes." She pointed to a name about two-thirds of the way down. "See, Patterson family. Laurence, Elizabeth, Denis, Henry, Faith, and Marion."

Aiden linked their fingers and tugged her against his chest. "What do you know? Your ancestor and mine could have run into each other at one time."

Harper was having a hard time thinking. He surrounded her with his heat, his smell, and with his arm locked against her back, it would be so easy to ....

The rattle of keys had her taking a step away just as the door opened. Walt Manning, the night clerk from the Sheriff's department, walked through, surprise on his face when he saw them.

"'Bout scared me to death." He placed his hand over his heart as if it were beating too quickly. "I didn't expect anyone to be here."

"Sorry, Walt," Harper smiled at the older man. "I was just showing Aiden the pictures."

"Killian's cousin." Walt nodded. "Well, carry on."

Aiden gave her a sheepish smile and took out his phone to take a picture of the plaque. "For future reference."

Asking him to resume the position didn't feel right, and after a check of the time, she directed him back to pick up his gifts.

Sally's Diner
December 19
6:00 p.m.

Aiden held the door for the ladies to enter Sally's ahead of him. He'd been happy to hear their conversation on the way from the library bounce from one topic to another. But for the past few minutes, Harper had been trying to talk his sister into going to the Gala with one of her male cousins.

"You're wasting your breath," he cautioned Harper, sliding into the booth next to her. "My sister is stubborn."

Sarah stuck her tongue out at him. "Be nice, or I'll tell Harper some of your dirty secrets."

He gave her an innocent look. "I don't have any dirty secrets."

"Everyone has dirty secrets, Big Brother," she tossed back.

"Behave." He handed her a menu and glanced sideways at Harper. "Would you like a menu, or do you have it memorized?"

Her laughter rippled across his skin. "Guilty. But sometimes Sally changes the desserts, so those, I check."

"Did you get your shopping done?" Sarah asked.

"I did," he nodded. "Do you need to go shopping?"

"No." She smiled coyly. "Mum shopped for both of us."

"That's not fair."

She shrugged. "Sue me."

"Did my Uncle Josh answer all your questions?" Harper interjected, almost as if she were heading off a tiff.

Sarah grinned at him before answering Harper's question. "He was wonderful. Talked to me about the possibility of coming to Swan Harbor University as a Ph.D. student."

"He's very passionate about his subject," Harper offered.

"It would be amazing to live in an area of someone I'm ..." Sarah's voice faded, and her attention drifted away.

Aiden exchanged glances with Harper, who shrugged, *No idea.*

She's a bit daft.

"Stop that, you two," Sarah scolded.

Aiden frowned. "Stop what?"

"That," Sarah waved her hand between him and Harper, "that thing you do."

Harper frowned. "What do we do?"

"Communicate without words," Sarah muttered. "You're not even married or anything. It's kind of freaky."

"Sorry." Harper sent him, *Others can tell?*

Sarah rolled her eyes and leaned on the table. "Did you know there are jockstraps hanging from the ceiling?"

Sally sidled up to the table, hearing the end of Sarah's question.

"Aren't they colorful? You wouldn't believe the business they've brought in."

"Really?"

"Definitely," Sally nodded. "What can I get you?"

Everyone gave their order, and after Sally left, Sarah was still staring up at the ceiling. Aiden readied himself for whatever might come out of her mouth.

"Aiden!" Her eyes grew large. "Is that your old pink one?"

"What?" he sputtered, searching for the proverbial hole to crawl into.

Like it was washed with something red?

He could hear Harper's thoughts. It made him afraid to look at her, worried she was laughing. Before he could decide how to handle the situation, Harper slid her hand into his and squeezed his fingers.

"See that purple one in the center of the room?"

"Yes," he answered hesitantly, wondering where she was going.

"I was trying to figure out why it looked so familiar," she snickered. "It belongs to my dad. My mother washed it with a purple cotton sweater and ..."

"It isn't supposed to be purple?"

"Oh, no," Harper shook her head. "It was white. You can imagine what he had to say the next time he put on his softball uniform."

"Oops," Sarah chuckled.

"Yes, indeed," Harper agreed.

Thank you.

My pleasure. She squeezed his hand again, and he couldn't stop the goofy smile he was sure graced his face.

"Stop that!" Sarah pointed at one, and then the other. "It's creepy."

Harper laughed. "Stick around Swan Harper awhile, and you'll get used to it."

Sarah gave them one of her '*Sure, I will*' looks, and Aiden couldn't keep hold back a smirk. Luckily, Sally delivered their food, or he was sure he'd be on the receiving end of another of Sarah's snarks.

"Did you find any new information today?" Harper asked once they'd started eating.

Sarah reached for the notebook she carried everywhere. "I found more information about the ruby heart."

"Really?" Harper hummed. "What?"

"I think it was brought from England," Sarah began. "Except I couldn't find out by whom or why. But it's mentioned several times in passing and was lovingly called 'The Heart of Swan Harbor.'" She glanced at her notes before continuing. "After Swan Harbor became a 'town,' someone stole it, and Geoffrey Prince offered a reward."

"No one ever returned it?"

Aiden thought back on everything he'd read about the early days of Swan Harbor and wondered why he'd never discovered the information Sarah was sharing. Was it as he'd been told by several, that things happen when they're meant to happen in the small town?

"I couldn't find anything about it being returned," Sarah admitted. "But there's always tomorrow."

It was quiet while they finished their meals, and Aiden's thoughts jumped ahead.

"What have you planned for us next?" he asked.

"Ice skating or bowling at Sonny's," Harper suggested, her dark eyes shining.

The thought of wearing ice skates caused his feet to ache. "I'll let you choose."

"What do you think, Sarah?" Harper grinned at his sister. "Should we spin circles around him on the ice skating rink or take pity on him and bowl?"

"What do you think, Big Brother?"

"I think I'm screwed."

Terri Patterson's Home
December 19
10:00 p.m.

Harper unlocked the door and led the way into her grandmother's house. "Grandma must have gone to the cookie exchange," she murmured when the lights were off, and the television wasn't blaring.

"I hate you're missing that," Aiden said, not for the first time.

"If you wanted to get rid of me—"

"You know that's not the case," he cut her off.

"I know," she assured him and then repeated the same words he'd said to her earlier. "I'm where I want to be."

"Alright." His smile had an important thought fluttering by that was gone before she could catch it.

She led them into the kitchen and pointed for him to have a seat at the table. "

"Would like some cookies?"

Aiden's eyes lit up, and he gave her a little-boy grin. "Peanut butter?"

"I knew you were going to say that." Harper placed several cookies on a plate and set it on the table. "Coffee, tea, hot chocolate …?"

She glanced up, and their gazes clashed. There was so much heat in his, her pulse skyrocketed, and whatever she was going to say faded. Since he'd pulled her into his arms while they'd been in the museum, it had been almost impossible to focus on how she'd felt. On how much she wanted to be held by him again.

"Harper."

Aiden reached for her hand and tugged her closer. Before she could get too close, the doorknob rattled, causing her to fall into a chair instead of his lap.

"Well, hello there." Harper saw Terri's gaze zero in on her fingers, still tangled with Aiden's. "You missed a humdinger of a party."

Sorry, Harper sent Aiden before turning her attention back to Terri.

Harper grinned. "I'm afraid to ask. More underwear capers?"

Terri took off her gloves and coat and settled in a chair across from them. "Oh, no. Mitzi accused Glynnis of stealing her cookie recipe, and they got into a shouting match."

"Mitzi owns show poodles," Harper told Aiden.

"And spends more money on them than her kids," Terri added.

"I see." Aiden nodded.

Harper had to bite her tongue to keep from giggling because the look on his face said he didn't see at all.

"And then what happened?" she encouraged Terri to continue.

"Mitzi took Glynnis' plate of cookies and threw them on the floor," Terri sighed. "It shocked poor Glynnis so much, I wasn't sure what she was going to do. She got the last laugh, though."

Harper groaned. "What happened?"

"When Mitzi wasn't looking, Glynnis took her fancy fur coat outside and dropped it in the snow."

"And Rene was okay with this?" Harper frowned, surprised to hear their mayor hadn't been expressing her displeasure rather loudly.

"I overheard Rene make a snide comment about Mitzi's coat." Terri shrugged. "Then the talk moved to the moaning sound the wind was making last night."

"That *was* kind of freaky," Harper agreed. "What was the consensus?"

Terri sent them a pointed look. "Apparently, Jack believes it was that poor Ian Jones crying when his Hope died in his arms. Isn't that just awful?"

"Awful." Harper's eyes met Aiden's. *Had you heard that?*

No, but the dates match.

"I should go." Aiden stood and put on his coat. "It was nice to see you again, Mrs. Patterson."

"You too." She scurried around and dumped several types of cookies into a baggie before handing it to him. "I'll see you at the dance. Jack volunteered to take me this year."

"I didn't know you were going, grandma."

"Wouldn't miss it for anything," Terri grinned.

"Be sure and save me a dance," Aiden told her with a wink.

"I definitely will," Terri preened. "Drive safely.

Aiden thanked her again, and as she walked with him outside, Harper couldn't help but wonder. Would tonight be the night?

"Thank you for spending the day with me," he whispered, almost as if he didn't want to break the spell wrapping around them.

"I enjoyed it."

"Good." He caught her hand, and she thought, this is it. His Adam's apple bobbed up ... then down when he swallowed, and his gaze landed on her lips.

"Are you ready for the dance?"

"I'm looking forward to it.

"Me too."

Aiden lifted her hand and placed a soft kiss in the center of her palm and then closed her fingers around it.

Sweet dreams, Angel, floated in the air long after he was gone.

SEVENTEEN

The Lighthouse Inn
December 21
8:00 p.m.

Aiden glanced up, surprised to see Liam ambling toward him.

"Cuz." Liam smirked and thumbed over his shoulder toward the dance floor. "I told you if you needed help with Harper to ask Killian."

"Bloody hell, Liam," Aiden frowned. "What are you talking about?"

Liam nodded toward where Harper was dancing. "It didn't take you long to lose her."

"Did you have one too many umbrella drinks while in Aruba?" Aiden laughed. "Harper and I are doing just fine."

"Then who's the bloke she's dancing with?"

Aiden looked out at the dancers, and while he couldn't see her, he could see her partner. "He's another cousin. Christian, I think. But you're the newlyweds. Did you already lose your wife?"

"Of course not," Liam exclaimed. "When we arrived, Emma and Ava were on their way to the ladies' room ..."

"What is it with that anyway?" Aiden murmured. "The thing where women go to the bathroom in packs?"

"Been like that since the dawn of time." Jack joined the conversation.

"What's been like that since the dawn of time?" Finn asked before welcoming Liam back.

"Women going to the can together," Jack explained. "And then they complain about us."

"Nothing for Elsa to complain about," Liam quipped.

"Yet anyway," Killian added. "You just got back to town."

"Wanker," Liam snickered.

"Tosser," Killian shot back.

"Boys," Finn sighed. "Must you get started?"

Killian chuckled. "We just needed to make sure we were still in sync."

Jack laughed. "Aiden, do you and your brother behave like this?"

"Quinn and I are very different," Aiden replied. "But we had our moments growing up."

"And he's flying in with Miriam on the twenty-third?" Finn confirmed.

"He is," Aiden confirmed. "I appreciate the fact that you offered mum and Sarah a place to stay. They booked a room a few months ago."

"It was our pleasure," Finn smiled. "Ava's so excited about this Christmas, she's almost like a child."

"But she's not doing the baking, is she?" Jack winced. "I'm not sure my teeth could take that."

Liam exchanged a look with Aiden. "I must have missed something."

"Same here."

"Don't worry about it," Jack replied. "It's not important."

"It's forgotten." Liam held up his glass. "I'm going to get a refill. Does anyone want anything?"

After Killian, Finn, and Liam left for the bar, Aiden could feel Jack's gaze trained on him.

"Have you found anything new about the Heart of Swan Harbor?"

"Sarah and I spent most of yesterday in the library, looking for information about the ruby," Aiden admitted.

"And by the smile on your face," Jack concluded. "I'm guessing you found something."

"There is mention of a ruby that was as big as a man's hand and as red as blood that was part of Swan Harbor's beginnings," Aiden explained. "Just as they believed the swans brought the town hope, they felt the ruby gave it life. Then sometime between 1714 - 1720, the ruby disappeared, and an illness swept through the town, killing many."

"But Sarah said Ian had the ruby in 1718," Jack murmured.

"Sarah said Ian had a ruby," Aiden clarified. "We've found nothing that leads us to believe Ian's ruby is also Swan Harbor's Heart."

"Any more on the woman Ian was to have killed?"

"Isabelle Williams?" Aiden stood as the women returned and pulled out Harper's chair.

"Did you say Ian Jones killed someone?" Elsa asked.

"He was wanted for murder," Jack told her. "I don't believe he did it."

"But he was a pirate," Emma shrugged. "Wasn't that what pirates did? Walk the plank and all that?"

"She's got you there," Killian laughed. "But why don't you think Ian killed Isabelle Williams?"

"Isabelle Williams?" Elsa repeated. "Really?"

Aiden nodded. "The Williams were one of the founding families. There were five of them: Ralph, Agnes, Thomas, Edmund, and Sybil. Most likely, that's where the county name came from."

"You think Isabelle was married to Thomas or Edmund?" Jack guessed.

"Maybe," Aiden shrugged. "But we don't know where the woman was killed or even if she was from Swan Harbor."

"Did you find any mention of an Isabelle in Swan Harbor?" Jack continued to push.

Aiden thought back on the list of individuals he'd been reading about earlier in the day. "There was mention of an Isabelle Michaels. She was the daughter of Anne Michaels, who I believe was a medicine woman, if you will."

"So, if Isabelle married Thomas or Edmund, she'd be Isabelle Williams," Jack tossed out. "But why was Ian accused of killing her?"

"It's a good thing my family isn't from Swan Harbor," Elsa replied with a nervous laugh. "Because my mother's maiden name was Williams."

Liam exchanged looks with Aiden before turning back to Elsa.

"Why would you say that love?"

"Because if your ancestor killed Isabelle Williams, who might have been my ancestor," Elsa pointed out. "That would be just as freaky as Killian and Emma's ancestors being connected."

"Bloody hell," Aiden murmured.

"Wait a minute," Ava jumped in. "Surely not."

Finn kissed Ava's fingers. "We've discussed the idea that a force bigger than any of us guided us to Swan Harbor, remember?"

"And when we were here for Emma and Killian's engagement," Liam continued. "Elsa said ..."

"That I felt as if I had walked the streets, stood on the cliffs, and looked out to sea," she murmured.

Jack lifted his glass and toasted the table. "What have I always said about Swan Harbor?"

"That things happen when they're meant to happen." Terri clinked her glass against his and turned to Aiden. "Next, you'll discover that one of the Pattersons is linked to Ian Jones. Wouldn't that be a kicker?"

Aiden's gaze drifted around the table, the others' expressions equal parts disbelief and as wigged by the possibility as he.

Think that's possible ... Angel?

That our ancestors were woven together somehow?

Yes.

At this point, I'd say, not only possible but probable. Harper's words were similar to the very ones he'd been thinking.

Killian squeezed Emma's fingers, knowing the talk about the connection of their ancestors freaked her out. Except the music changed before he could say anything. There was something about it that had him scanning the room, looking for what, though, he couldn't say.

The music swelled, and Terri straightened in her chair, peering toward the front of the room. "This is the part I've been waiting for." She grinned at Harper. "Remember when you were part of the choir?"

"The choir?" asked Ava.

Harper nodded. "There's a large stage behind that curtain, and every year a different group performs."

Aiden grinned. "And you sang?"

"My high school choir sang," she clarified. "They've had children's choirs, bands, and even groups from the university for the entertainment."

"Who's performing this year, Terri?" asked Ava.

"I'm not sure what they decided this year," Terri replied, a slight frown between her brows.

Killian readjusted in his seat, wanting a better view of the room at large. But the tables were packed too tightly together. Something was going to happen, just as Terri had been expecting, but what exactly, he didn't know.

There was a drumroll, and the curtain rose.

"Bloody hell," Killian muttered when the curtain was about a foot off the floor.

"Finn!" Ava exclaimed. "Our snowman!"

"I would guess twenty-four snowmen and snowwomen," Killian muttered.

"Well, maybe twenty-four snowmen," Terri pointed out. "But beside each snowman is a child. Aren't they cute? Look, there are Noah and Cooper."

"Cousins," Killian heard Harper reply.

As soon as the children's choir started singing, Killian let his gaze slide lazily from one snowman to the next. Each wore a piece of lingerie, his boxers, Emma's t-shirt, and a nightgown.

"See that red flannel nightgown," Terri whispered. "That's mine. Be sure and get it back for me."

"You didn't give it to them?" Killian raised a brow in question and waited, more for her reaction than a response.

"Me?" Terri's dark eyes clashed with his. "Why, I never."

But once she'd turned back to the singers, he realized she'd never given him an answer.

"Killian?" Finn began.

He met his father's look head-on and gave a subtle shake of his head, sending the message, *Trust me.*

Finn studied him for several seconds before finally tilting his chin in acknowledgment.

The children sang for twenty minutes. When they were done, they left all twenty-four snowmen behind. Then the band, who'd been providing the music, took over, and the dance floor filled.

"Come dance with me, Doc." Killian held her chair.

"Bugger that, Killian," Liam frowned.

"Liam," Killian cut him off. "Remember what you said to me about solving the underwear case?"

"Vaguely."

"You said, 'perhaps you're trying to solve it in one way when what you really need is to go another.'"

Liam laughed. "You figured out what I meant, didn't you?"

"I did," Killian acknowledged. "Now, Doc and I are going to dance."

He led her onto the dance floor and tucked her against his chest. "You have questions?"

"No, really?" Emma blew out a breath. "Your boxers with dogs are up there for everyone to see."

"As is your sleep shirt," he acknowledged. "And I'm guessing something that belongs to our parents and Liam and Elsa."

"But we're dancing?"

"Yes, we are." He brushed a kiss across her forehead. "Did I tell you how beautiful you looked tonight?"

"You did."

"And did you tell me how handsome I looked tonight?" Killian chuckled at her expression and dropped a light kiss on her lips.

"You know you look good," she tsked.

"But it's nice to hear it from the woman I love." Killian kissed her again and manipulated them into the middle of a group of people.

"Terri says the red nightgown is hers," someone claimed.

"Really?" another voice hummed. "I thought that looked like mine.

"Killian, Emma," Madge danced by with her husband, Jimmie. "Lovely night, isn't it?"

Emma murmured hello, and once again, Killian manipulated them closer to another group.

"Did you see that black nightie?" a third voice remarked. "I bet that's from *Rebecca's Fantasy.*"

"Oh, it is," a fourth voice replied. "I saw it in the newest catalog."

"I wonder how it would look on me?" voice three mused.

Rupert and Lois danced by, and Killian had just turned away from them when he heard. "I see your skivvies made another appearance, Killian."

Lois gasped. "Rupert."

Killian met Emma's questioning eyes. "That's what I was waiting for."

"What?"

"Watch."

After seating Emma, Killian went searching for his partner and the sheriff. He found them at a table in the corner with their wives and the Hunters.

"Dylan, Rusty, a moment."

Surprisingly, they said nothing before following him into the hallway, and away from the noise.

"Bloody hell, were you two in on it?"

Dylan exchanged looks with Rusty. "That depends on exactly what *it* is."

"It." Killian held up a finger for each item on the list. "The bras on the tree, the flying boxers, the panty wreaths, and the stolen snowmen."

"We didn't take those things, if that's what you're asking," Rusty hedged.

"But you know who did," Killian clarified, "and condoned it."

"Now, Killian," Dylan pointed out, "condone is a bit harsh, don't you think?"

"If it makes you feel any better," Rusty responded, "they pulled this prank on me my first Christmas in Swan Harbor."

"And that was before you were sheriff?" Killian looked at Dylan.

"Yes, Rusty and I were partners." Dylan gave a self-deprecating sigh. "They had us going too. Come on."

Killian followed Dylan and Rusty back into the ballroom and pinned his gaze on Rupert and his gang.

"For a bunch of retired secret agents, you've gotten quite sloppy."

"Hey, sugar," Madge stepped forward. "Watch who you're calling sloppy. If loose lips here hadn't opened his trap—"

"Hey, who're you calling loose lips?" Lois jumped in. "You're the one who kept going on and on."

"Ladies," Lance Diamond, the youngest of the retired agents and the current manager of Haven House, took over. "Congratulations. You won this round. Rupert ..."

Rupert stepped forward, and just as he was flanked by his friends and family, Killian felt Emma slip her hand into his on one side. While on the other, were his father, Ava, Elsa, and Liam.

"Was I right when I guessed it was an initiation of sorts?" he asked.

As they'd been talking, several individuals had been making their way around the room. A glass was shoved in his hand by one, only to be filled with champagne by another.

"Swan Harbor is and always has been," Rupert began, "a place where we weren't just friends but also family."

"And families take care of each other," Lois added. "It has been many years since Rupert and I followed Granny's advice and retired here to care for Haven's House. But when you've spent years chasing after the bad guys, and that's suddenly over, you feel—"

"—Worthless," Jimmie picked up the conversation. "And oh, sure, Jack talked about looking for the key, someone's cat went missing, or a dog was lost, but we needed to feel alive."

"And so, we pilfered undies," Madge took over. "Then challenged Swan Harbor's newest detectives to catch us. But no one could—"

"Until you," Rupert regained control. "When you blew into town, you sported quite the ego, but little by little, you found your place. Then you met the lovely Doctor Foster."

"And boy did the gossip lines have a good time," Lois laughed. "Then your union brought Elsa and Liam to town."

"Those two gave the gossip line a lot of material," Madge exclaimed. "But as always, their hearts spoke, and they listened."

"Even if he was stubborn." Jack stepped into the middle of the circle. "However, their union brought Ava and Finn to town. Who not only created excitement but made it a good news day for Sydney. Most importantly, though, I got the family I'd lost back. And because of your family, Jonesy and Swan Harbor's hope lives on."

"What the old fool is trying to say," Terri pushed Jack aside and claimed the floor, "is we're glad you've found your way back to Swan Harbor. Merry Christmas, and now, everyone, drink up."

Killian took a sip of the champagne he was holding, surprised to find a rather large lump in his throat.

"Bloody hell."

"What is it?" Emma took his glass and set it next to hers on a nearby table.

"I never thought I'd need to solve a case called The Great Underwear Caper." He pulled her into his arms and was quiet for a second, multiple thoughts bouncing in his head. "But my dog boxers, really? They're never going to be the same."

"I'll buy you some more," she promised. "What would you like? Dancing hotdogs, some that say hot lips, or ..."

The Lighthouse Inn
December 21
11:30 p.m.

Aiden twirled her across the dance floor, making Harper feel like she was floating. "You're going to make me dizzy."

"Am I?" he apologized, and the tenor of his voice had her heart melting.

"I was teasing," she assured him. "But you are quite the dancer."

"My mum made all of us take dance lessons when we were younger," he shared. "She told Quinn and me someday we'd thank her."

"And have you," Harper grinned, "thanked her, that is?"

"No. I've not had many opportunities to show off," Aiden admitted. "But when she gets to town, I'll have to remedy that."

"That's probably a good idea." Harper was quiet for several beats, allowing the music to flow around them because being in Aiden's arms was ....

"Did you know who the thieves were?" He put enough distance between them so she could see his face.

"No," she denied. "But there was one time when I asked my grandmother what she knew, and she said, 'there's nothing I can tell you about who is doing this.'"

"Nice play on words there," Aiden acknowledged.

"Wasn't it, though? Sneaky old woman," Harper grumbled. "I wonder if she's the one who donated my royal blue bra."

"I, I," he cleared his throat. "I can't help you there."

Harper leaned her forehead lightly against Aiden's chest. "I'm sorry. Open mouth ..."

"You're fine." He nuzzled her temple, and she was glad he was holding her up. "I've had my share of those moments. Although usually it's the opposite. I open my mouth, and nothing comes out."

"And you send silent *help me* messages to see who's listening," she teased.

"I'm glad you were listening that day."

The huskiness in Aiden's voice had Harper turning her head enough for her to look him in the eye. What she saw in his eyes had her wishing they were alone and not in the middle of a room with most of Swan Harbor.

"Me too. I noticed you didn't follow through on something tonight."

Aiden frowned. "What??"

"Dance with Morgan." Harper glanced across the room to where the other woman was plastered against her date. "Who is she with anyway?"

"Check the gossip line," Aiden muttered tongue-in-cheek.

"Don't remind me," Harper groaned. "Grandma told me, 'when sparks ignite, the gossip line takes flight.'"

"Are they gossiping about us?"

Harper smiled. "Why would you ask that?"

She wasn't sure how long they stood in the center of the dance floor with the music spilling around them. But she waited, wanting him to acknowledge she wasn't the only one feeling something.

He cradled her hand closer to his chest and crooned, "When sparks ignite .... I don't know about you, but I think the sparks between us are pretty bright. Do you feel them?"

Harper opened her mouth to respond, but when his lips brushed across her fingers, her breath hitched. An invisible current traveled from that place on her hand, up her arm, and wrapped around her heart. The whole once-bitten, twice-shy thought process died and spun away.

Aiden's pupils widened, and slowly, his head lowered, so close his breath blew across her lips.

Harper opened her mouth, readying for that first touch. She pushed up on her tiptoes ....

The lights flashed, and the moment passed.

"Bloody hell," Aiden snapped.

"Aiden, Harper," Liam called as he and Elsa danced by. "We're heading to Sally's. You guys coming?"

Harper linked her arm with Aiden's. There would be other times. After all, they were in Swan Harbor where things happened when they were meant to happen. Even kisses, apparently.

EIGHTEEN

Aiden's Apartment
Christmas Morning
7:30 a.m.

AIDEN HEARD HIS PHONE BUZZ, BUT HE WAS TOO BUSY KICKING himself over his failure the night before to see who was texting so early. When the phone buzzed again, he grudgingly opened one eye. The third time, though, the sound was different. That time, it was a whistle ....

Harper.

He slid his thumb across the screen.

> Harper: Merry Christmas, Aiden. Enjoy the day with your family.

"Merry Christmas, Angel."

Instead of sending the message he wanted, he aimed for neutral.

> Aiden: Merry Christmas, Harper. What time will you make your way to Sally's?

While he was waiting for her to respond, he pulled up the texts he'd missed—one from Liam.

> Liam: So? How did things go when you took
> Harper home last night?

Aiden rolled his eyes, thinking he'd felt like a teenager taking his girlfriend home from a first date. Because not only was Harper's cousin, Christian, staying with her grandmother. So were an uncle and his family.

> Aiden: There were more people there than at the
> dance.

> Liam: Did you make plans to see her today?

Yeah, right, he thought. With his mum and Sarah in town, plus everything Ava had planned for the families, he'd be lucky to get a moment to text her.

> Aiden: You're kidding, right?

> Liam: Sometimes, you have to fight for what you
> want.

> Aiden: I'll see you at the Community Center.

> Liam: Chicken.

He can go that route, Aiden thought. He caught the woman of his dreams. Whereas he and Harper ... were a work in progress.

While it wasn't exactly where he wanted them to be, it was, however, an excellent way to describe them. That thought had him moving on to his next message.

> Clark,

> Some years you're Frosty, others the Grinch, but
> this year you're feeling like Ebenezer Scrooge.
> Hmm, that makes me curious about how you're
> spending the day. Except something tells me that
> would be too personal.

> Have a wonderful Christmas!

> Rosalind

After reading Rosalind's message, Aiden pounded on his brother's door, then jumped in the shower. They were meeting the Reade family at the Community Center at 11:00 a.m., ostensibly to aid Captain Jack in playing Santa to families who weren't as fortunate as others. Which was why he was feeling a bit like the version of Ebenezer, who hadn't liked the future he'd seen during his dream.

Once dressed, Aiden left his room, surprised to find Quinn up and waiting, even though his eyes were half-mast.

"You look awful."

Quinn grunted. "Bloody jet lag is killing me. Too many time zones."

"Look at it like this." Aiden slipped on his coat and grabbed the box of gifts. "You can be Sleepy today instead of Happy."

"What?" Quinn frowned. "Did you just say I could be Sleepy?"

"Well, yes." Aiden threw Quinn his coat and checked to make sure his gloves were in his pockets. "Sleepy the elf."

Quinn snorted. "You realize Sleepy isn't an elf, right?"

"Really?" Aiden handed Quinn a few boxes, and after locking the door, they took the stairs to the car.

"He's one of the seven dwarves."

"Elves, dwarves," Aiden shrugged. "Either will do."

They put the gifts in the trunk and headed toward The Beachside Inn, where his mother and sister were staying.

"What have you done with my brother?" Quinn asked when they were halfway there.

"What?"

"Who is she?" Quinn suddenly asked.

Aiden cut a glance in Quinn's direction when he turned into the Beachside Inn's parking lot. "I told you I went to the Gala with Harper Taylor."

"Right, the police captain's daughter," Quinn smirked. "What about that research project you were a part of?"

"I'm still a part of it," Aiden sighed. "But every time I hear from Rosalind, I can't help but wish it were Harper. They're merging in my thoughts."

"Maybe that's your answer, A," Quinn pointed out. "When there are two distinct women in your life, and you can't keep them straight, maybe you need to let one go."

"That's what I was afraid you were going to say," Aiden winced. "But I don't like the idea of hurting someone, and besides, what if …?"

"Things don't work out with Harper?"

"Yes."

Quinn smirked. "Well, I would say that depends on you. How hard are you willing to work for what you want?"

"You sound like Liam," Aiden grumbled. "He said something similar."

"Appears you have some thinking to do then."

"Maybe so."

On the way up the stairs to their mother and Sarah's room, the more Aiden tried to separate Rosalind and Harper in his mind, the more they merged. That wasn't good. Not good at all.

Harper's Parents' Home
Christmas Afternoon
1:30 p.m.

"Mom, what do you want dad to do with the extra gifts under the tree?" Harper acted as the go-between with one parent in the front room and the other in the kitchen.

"Tell him to put them in that big box," Beverly called. "Then put them in the car."

But when Harper looked over at her father, he'd already collected the gifts and was in the process of putting them in a box.

"Dad, why did you want me to ask mom if you already knew what she wanted you to do?"

"Just wanted to make sure she hadn't changed her mind."

Was that it? Or had he somehow heard the words before she'd said anything? That was something she'd wanted to ask her mom for a few days, but the opportunity hadn't presented itself—yet, anyway.

Harper found her mom in the kitchen, talking to herself while she was taking a pie out of the oven. "I wonder if that's going to be enough," Beverly muttered.

"If what's going to be enough?" Harper asked.

Beverly glanced up, and her expression was blank for a few seconds. "What?" Then her thoughts cleared enough for her to continue, "Enough food."

"Mom," Harper sighed. "We always have more than enough food. You know that."

"True." Beverly pointed to a counter where a cake and several pies needed attending. "Can you put a cover on those for me? I want to make sure your father gets all the gifts."

"Mom, relax," Harper laughed. "You're scurrying around just like grandma was this morning. It will get done."

Beverly had been halfway out the door but, with the question complete, stopped and glanced over her shoulder. "I know that." She winked. "But if I didn't check on your father, he wouldn't be able to grumble that he knows what he's doing, now would he?"

Harper shook her head, the sounds of her mother lightly chiding her father for some perceived transgression reminding her of Christmases past.

"There," Beverly returned, her face alight with laughter. "I've done my job."

"I'm sure dad appreciated it."

Beverly chuckled. "After all these years, he's come to expect it."

Harper made a noncommittal sound, but her thoughts were on Aiden.

"What is it?" Her mother's question interrupted her musings.

Harper finished covering the last of the pies and put away the wrap before replying, "What is what?"

"Are you thinking about Aiden?" Beverly reworded her question. "Or is it Clark?"

"Aiden." Harper shrugged. "Clark. They're merging in my head."

"How so?"

Harper searched for a way to explain what she was thinking and feeling. "Aiden spent the morning and lunch at the Community Center."

"Where Jack plays Santa," Beverly commented, "and then helps serve Christmas lunch to many."

Harper agreed. "And Clark told me he was feeling like Ebenezer Scrooge this Christmas as opposed to Frosty or the Grinch."

"So, giving back," Beverly murmured.

"Yes."

"Well, just a few more days, and you'll know."

"Will I?"

"What is it, Harper?"

"My gift."

"Yours." Beverly hesitated, then her eyes grew wide. "Oh, no, Harper. We'll just have to change the dates. I'm sure it won't be a problem."

"Let me think about it," Harper murmured. "Maybe I'll just have him meet me there. Or maybe Aiden."

"I knew you wanted to see the sunsets in Key West, and when your dad showed me the package he'd found, I jumped on it," Beverly explained. "But that was in September before …"

"I was involved in the project or with Aiden.

"Yes," Beverly sighed. "How are things going with Aiden? At the party the other night, you seemed out of sorts. But then …"

Harper sighed, knowing she needed to give her mother a bit more information about her breakup with Joel.

"I was out of sorts," she admitted. "I'd seen Aiden hugging Sarah and thought—"

"—He was stepping out on you." Beverly surmised.

"Yes."

"But why, Harper? That doesn't sound like you."

"Joel."

Beverly's brows arched in surprise. "The boy you liked in Gainesville?"

"It was on its way to more than liking," Harper confessed. "I thought he loved me, was going to propose, and then we'd …"

"Sail off into the sunset," Beverly concluded.

"Something like that."

"I'm sorry, honey," Beverly consoled her. "I didn't realize it had gotten so serious."

"Well, apparently, it was only that way in my mind," Harper admitted. "Because when I came back to the apartment one day, he was in bed with my roommate."

Beverly hissed. "Ouch. But it makes sense that you would be hesitant about jumping into anything right away."

"That's why I was excited about the secret match project. I thought it would help me ease into something."

"And then, Aiden came along."

"Yes." Harper grabbed a cookie, noting that it was peanut butter, Aiden's favorite, bringing everything full circle. "I'd seen him around campus before. It was different the night of the tree lighting, though."

"Something happened, didn't it?"

"He winked," Harper smiled. "And a few other times I heard his thoughts. It was freaky."

"Oh, honey," Beverly smiled. "That's your heart's way of communicating with its match. Listen to it."

"Because it knows," Harper finished the saying she'd heard more times than she could count.

"Exactly. Now, get those pies. We're going to be late."

Listen to my heart, Harper sighed. *I'm trying.*

Ava & Finn's Cottage
Christmas Evening
8:00 p.m.

Christmas Day had been a day unlike any other Christmas Day in Aiden's life. Had they been in England, the day would have been quiet. His mum would have cooked, and it would have been the four of them. Then, maybe late in the day, his father would have shown up bearing gifts.

But his first Christmas in the States had been much different. He'd played elf and served lunch at the Community Center. Then everyone had returned to Ava and Finn's for gifts and a dinner that was noisier than Thanksgiving had been. More family than he'd ever experienced at once. Plus, with all the Reades paired off, he couldn't help but wonder if it was time for the Joneses to follow suit.

What was Harper doing? Why hadn't he ...?

"Look what I found." Liam held the wishbone from the turkey aloft. "How could someone have just set this aside? It's magical."

"The wishbone is magical?" Aiden scoffed. "Right."

"No, really," Liam insisted. "You just make a wish, and if you get the longer portion, your wish will come true."

"Haven't all your wishes come true?" Aiden sent a pointed look toward where Elsa was sitting next to her mother.

"Well, yeah," Liam conceded. "But, I thought I'd be magnanimous and share with you."

"Why do you think I need a wish?" Aiden asked. "Everything is going well in my life."

Liam lowered his chin and glanced up from under his brow. His look said, '*Really, that's how you're going to play this*'? Should he admit he wished he'd made plans to see Harper? However, the look on his cousin's face said no ... he'd needed to play along.

"Bloody hell." Aiden reached for the bone. "It can't hurt."

Liam grinned. "See, that wasn't so bad, was it?"

Aiden rolled his eyes. "Just give me the bloody thing."

"Nah nah nah," Liam snickered. "I need to come up with my wish."

"You might as well have a piece of pie." Finn walked by with a plate in each hand. "Liam can ponder for hours."

"For days," Killian corrected. "Remember that one Christmas he kept it in his room for three or four days?"

"It was five," Liam corrected. "And it was a good thing, too. That was when ..." His voice faded when Elsa and her mother entered the kitchen.

"When what, Liam?" Elsa put him on the spot.

"When I got to spend time with you at the New Year's dance." Liam tugged her into his arms for a quick kiss.

Elsa laughed and smoothed her hand over his cheek. "Nice save." Then, she helped her mother choose some cookies before they headed back into the living room.

'*See*,' Liam's grin said. '*You too could have that.*'

"If you're going to ponder your wish, I'm getting pie." Aiden stepped around his cousin to examine the assortment on the counter.

"You can't go wrong with one of those." Jack nodded toward the pies on one side of the counter. "Terri made them. And if you thought her cookies were tasty ..."

"What do you suggest, Jack?"

"Well," Jack hummed. "The apple is good, especially if you have some vanilla ice cream to put on it. As for the blueberry. It's also good. Not too sweet and not too tart. Then there's the pecan pie ..."

"So, what you're saying is you'd like a sliver of each?" chuckled Aiden.

Jack grinned. "Marvelous idea. Would you like one too?"

"Sure, Jack," Aiden agreed. "That sounds good."

"Alright, I'm ready." Liam held out the bone before Aiden had even cut the pies.

"But I was going to eat ..."

"You don't want me to offer it to someone else, do you?"

Aiden sighed. "Has anyone ever mentioned you're a pain in the arse?"

"More than once," Liam laughed. "Now, are you ready?"

Aiden reached for the bone, but Liam pulled it back before he could touch it. "Pinkie finger, cuz."

"Bloody hell." Aiden looped his little finger through one side of the bone.

"Did you make your wish?" Liam asked.

"I've made my wish," Aiden assured him.

"What is it?"

"I'm not going to tell you what my bloody wish is," Aiden retorted.

"Fine," Liam smirked. "Pull."

Aiden tightened his little finger and pulled, feeling the bone bending until finally, it snapped.

"Bugger that," Liam barked, holding his piece of the bone aloft. "Looks like my wish won't be coming true tonight."

Aiden glanced at the longer piece of the wishbone in his hand. He'd 'won,' but what had he won?

"Here's your pie." Jack handed him a plate. "Congratulations. Eat your pie and then send Harper a text to meet you in the gazebo next to the town tree. There's always plenty of mistletoe—if you know what I mean?" He winked, and before Aiden could regain his equilibrium, the older man started toward the living room.

"Are you going to eat that?" Liam pointed at the plate in his hands.

"Yes," Aiden grumbled. "Get your own."

But when he took the first bite, his attention wasn't on the sugar and spices on his plate. They were sorting through what Jack had said and how to make it happen.

"Have you sent her a text?" Liam asked when he'd returned with his own dessert.

"No," Aiden admitted. "There's my mum, Sarah, and Quinn. I don't want to be rude."

Liam grunted. "Don't worry about them. We'll get them where they need to be. Go."

Aiden glanced at his mum, Sarah, and Quinn and thought about the gift he had for Harper in his car. With that thought, it wasn't too hard to decide. He put his plate away and pulled out his phone. But before he'd sent the text, he spotted his piece of the wishbone, still on the table.

"For luck." He shoved it into his pocket.

Sally's Diner
Christmas Evening
9:00 p.m.

Harper stepped outside of Sally's, and as soon as the door shut, closing off the noise, her heart raced. Aiden was waiting for her, and somehow, she knew their time together was going to be momentous.

She double-checked she had the right gift, and with slow, measured steps, started toward the square. The large Christmas tree still stood in the center of the town square. But the gazebo, usually inhabited by Santa, was empty ... except for one man.

Once she was close enough, Harper noticed he was pacing, almost as if he were nervous. A line from an earlier message floated through her head. *He was just a normal, average guy who was a touch awkward.*

"Just like Clark," she murmured, stopping a few feet from the gazebo, and the implication of her thought processes took her breath.

When he looked up and their eyes met, Harper took several more steps in his direction and stopped just inside the gazebo. Her heart pounded so hard, she ended up grabbing the side for support.

"Hi."

Aiden's voice was low, hesitant, and so sweet, she gripped the wood tighter to keep her hand from shaking.

"Hi yourself." Harper's gaze drifted around his face, memorizing his features as if it had been days since she'd seen him.

"How was your Christmas?"

"Good." She thumbed over her shoulder toward Sally's. "Noisy. Crowded. Did you get everything you wanted for Christmas?"

He swallowed, and the V of his jacket where he'd forgotten to fasten the top button caught her attention. She could see his red sweater peeking out, and it looked so soft, she couldn't wait to bury her nose there.

"Did I get everything I wanted for Christmas?" he repeated.

Harper nodded, afraid that if she said anything, the bubble surrounding them would burst.

"I'm working on it," Aiden murmured so softly that if she hadn't been watching him closely, she might have missed it.

You are?

His nod was subtle, and then his gaze locked on something just over her head. He reached into his pocket, and when he pulled his hand free, it was closed into a fist, almost as if he were protecting something.

I am.

"What?"

Aiden took a deep breath and slowly, methodically removed his glasses, then slipped them into his pocket.

"This," he uttered seconds before one hand cupped her head, the other folded behind her back, and as he tugged her forward, his mouth covered hers. The kiss was assertive, consuming her, and threatened to send her thoughts spinning out of control.

The transformation is complete, whipped through her head seconds before Aiden switched the angle of his mouth. Harper grabbed handfuls of his coat, and the longer his mouth was on hers, the weaker her knees grew.

Aiden groaned—the sexy sound pulled from deep inside. "I've got you."

A kiss whispered across one of her eyelids, then grazed along her cheekbone. "I've got you, Angel."

Harper's breath stuttered, and just as she'd expected, hearing him call her Angel sent her over the edge. His kisses consumed her, and no matter how tightly he held her, it wasn't close enough.

Aiden cupped her face, and every time his lips landed, Harper fought to lift her eyelids. But her emotions were so overwhelming, all she wanted to do was feel.

"I hope this is alright?" he murmured against her mouth.

She chuckled. "I've been waiting."

His breath hitched, and he lifted his mouth. "Open your eyes, Angel."

She was powerless to his command, barely able to drag her eyes open.

"Look," he pointed up. "My favorite flower."

Harper tilted her chin to see several sprigs of mistletoe attached above her. "I don't think I'd call it a flower."

"Mistletoe produces flowers." Aiden dropped a quick kiss on her mouth. "And from now on, it's my favorite."

She reached to brush her fingers across his bottom lip and realized the red bag she'd brought with her still hung from her wrist.

"Merry Christmas, Aiden."

"For me?" His eyes lit up with anticipation. "It just so happens I have something for you as well."

They moved farther inside the gazebo, where each dug into their gifts.

"You went back and bought it." Harper pulled the ornament with the orange and black kittens on it from the bag.

"Guilty," he grinned. "And you …"

He lifted the ornament she'd bought him, which was a man sitting in a chair reading *As You Like It*.

Orlando and Rosalind, she heard before aloud, he questioned, "How did you know it's one of my favorites?"

"Remember when we ran into each other in the copy center?"

"When I ran into you," he corrected.

"A page from your test ended up attached to one of mine."

His gaze locked with hers, and for a second, the look in them was almost too big—almost too much.

Her ornament disappeared, and the next thing she knew, Aiden's mouth was on hers. She knew she needed to tell him about her gift, but just like Scarlett, she decided there was always tomorrow.

NINETEEN

Swan Harbor Library
December 30
9:00 a.m.

AIDEN HUNCHED OVER THE TABLE AT THE LIBRARY AND TRIED TO focus on Ian Jones and not Harper Taylor. When he'd kissed her, he'd not expected the rush of feelings that had spread throughout. With every kiss since, his emotions had grown until she was always at the forefront of his mind. Those were not feelings he'd expected to have about a woman, especially one he'd been involved with for less than a month. But his heart didn't seem to care about the time frame, and neither did his body. The more time he spent with her, the more he wanted her.

There! He'd admitted it. He wanted her, but ...

He'd promised her they could take things as slowly as she needed. If he had to take a cold shower or two, he could handle it. After all, he wasn't a young kid who didn't know how to be patient.

The click-clack of heels alerted him that the ever-efficient librarian, Amanda, was on her way to his corner hiding place. Chances were, she'd found the book he'd requested about pirates in the 17th and 18th centuries.

"Aiden?" she whispered, setting the book on the table. "Is this what you were looking for?"

"Yes, thank you." Aiden slid the book closer and flipped through several pages. And suddenly, a thought popped into his head.

"What do you need?" Amanda asked before what he'd been thinking had even completely formed.

Aiden grabbed a piece of paper and wrote two names on it. "The Williams and Pattersons were among the original settlers in Swan Harbor. Can you see if you can find anything about any of the family members between 1700 and 1720?"

Amanda picked up the paper, and her pencil-thin brows drew together as she studied the names he'd written.

"I think I might have seen a diary or journal that belonged to one of these families. Let me see what I can find."

"Thank you, Amanda. You've been a tremendous help."

"Well, you know our motto," she laughed. "I like to be helpful."

"And you are very helpful," he assured her.

"I'm glad," Amanda replied. "And besides, my son loves pirates, and well …"

"Makes for a good bedtime story, huh?"

"It does," she agreed. "I'll let you know."

Aiden flipped open the book, bypassing the preface and the first few chapters. Then he turned a page, and the words *El corazón del Rubí* stood out.

"Bloody hell." He noted the chapter focused on pirates seen along the Maine coast during the timeframe Ian Jones would have been there.

From the early 17th century to the early 18th century, several notable pirates sailed along the Maine coast.

Dixie Bull was an Englishman who turned to piracy after his ship was robbed. He became known as The Dread Pirate because he plundered small settlements along the Maine coast.

Black Sam Bellamy captured 53 ships in just a year. And because of his success, he was considered the wealthiest pirate recorded in history. He earned the nickname of Prince of Pirates, and compared himself to Robin Hood because of his generous behavior. In April 1717, he was on his way to Richmond Island off the coast of southern Maine. Why … no one knows, but the ship diverted toward Cape Cod, where it was caught in a nor'easter and lost.

In the same month, a pirate known only as the Professor and his crew hobbled into the dock in Swan Harbor. His ship, the El corazón del Rubí, remained docked while it was repaired. No one ever discovered the professor's real name.

"Bloody hell," Aiden murmured. "Ian Jones sailed into Swan Harbor in April 1717, and by December 1718 he had met and impregnated Hope Prince.

He pulled his pad of paper close and wrote a few questions he'd like to have answered.

When did Ian and Hope meet?

How did Ian and Hope meet?

What repairs needed to be done to the ship? And who had done them?

How long did it take?

Did Ian sail in and out of Swan Harbor often?

Why did Ian leave Hope behind?

Why was Ian known as the Professor?

It seemed the more he found out about his ancestor, the more questions he had. And with his new knowledge, Aiden drew out a timeline.

Ian Jones was born in May 1690.

In July 1715, a hurricane hit Florida, and the Nuestra Señora de Concepcion was thought to have sunk.

In the fall of 1715, the Nuestra Señora de Concepcion possibly hobbled into The Carolinas.

Fall 1715, El corazón del Rubí was seen sailing between Delaware and Boston.

In April 1717, El corazón del Rubí arrived in Swan Harbor.

In November 1718, Ian Jones was seen in Boston carrying around a large ruby.

On December 18, 1718, Ian Jones arrived in Swan Harbor, and Hope died in his arms.

On December 1719, Ian Jones was in Boston and had pieces of eight melted into jewelry. One was a heart with a lighthouse.

On January 10, 1720, Ian Jones was pictured on a wanted poster for the murder of Isabelle Williams.

On February 14, 1720, Ian Jones left the ship that had first been Nuestra Señora de Concepción, then El corazón del Rubí, and then Hope's Haven, docked in Swan Harbor with no name and silver.

In July 1722, Ian Jones died in England.

But Aiden still wondered how they knew the ship and silver were for Ian Swan?

The clicking of Amanda's heels had Aiden glancing up. "You've found something," he guessed when she smiled, and her dark eyes sparkled.

"I did." Amanda laid what looked like a journal on the table with a caduceus on the front of it. "I think you'll enjoy this."

Aiden flipped open the cover to see the name, Doctor Thomas Williams.

He turned the page, and then another. With every turn, the more excited he grew.

"It's a list of patients he treated."

Amanda hummed. "Keep looking. It's about ten pages in."

Aiden studied her for several seconds before turning to the suggested page.

July 1717

I arrived at my clinic after supper to find the door wide open and Henry Patterson waiting for me in the front room. He had brought me a patient who'd been beaten and stabbed multiple times. The following is Henry's story.

Henry had ...

Sheriff's Department

December 30

10:00 a.m.

Killian set the cup of coffee on his desk and opened the box from Paula's Pastries. Then, before helping himself, he waved the box around, ensuring the smell covered all corners of the office he shared with Rusty. He'd just helped himself to a donut when his partner strolled in, and his gaze immediately went to the sweets.

"For me?" His hand hovered over the box.

"Did you give me anything when I was chasing after the underwear thief?" Killian shot back.

Rusty frowned. "Oh, come on, Killian. You can't possibly still be mad about that. Can you?"

Killian blew out a breath. "Mad, hmm, that doesn't quite fit ..."

"So, I can have one?"

"But annoyed," Killian went on as if Rusty had said nothing. "Now that one fits."

Rusty grinned, and without waiting, grabbed his favorite, pulled out his chair, and took a bite. "Just look at it like this," he mumbled. "At least you didn't have to go around interviewing everyone."

"I did too," Killian sputtered. "I interviewed all the women whose bras were hanging on the tree."

Rusty waved his hand as if that were no big deal. "But that was it. When Dylan and I were investigating, whenever something new came along, we interviewed everyone."

Killian winced. "Sounds slippery."

"You can stop with those," Rusty groaned. He opened his top drawer, took out a file, and tossed it on Killian's desk. "Here are all the notes on Ernie Luka's case."

"Then, there were actual notes." Killian flipped open the file and looked at the signature and start date.

"Of course, there were notes. Dylan is supposed to be looking for the ones we wrote."

"And when it happened to you?" Killian hummed. "How did Dylan not remember a case involving underwear thieves?"

"How did I not remember what?" Dylan asked, having entered the office to hear the end of the question.

"That there had been an underwear thief case before."

Dylan pulled up a chair and helped himself to a donut before answering, "I was in high school."

"Meaning if it didn't affect you," Killian laughed. "It wasn't important."

"Something like that," Dylan agreed.

Killian glanced at Ernie's notes.

December 1, 2000

When the Christmas tree in the town square was lit up, multiple bras were dangling from the branches. The bras ranged from size 34B to 44DD and included a variety of colors. Only five of the thirty garments on the tree were unclaimed.

Below that, there was a list of the names of the women who had claimed bras. And among those names were Lois Duncan, Madge Tanner, Terri Patterson, and Dorothy Mann.

He then read.

Sally Patterson called on the morning of December 4 to report that someone had broken into her diner. However, nothing was stolen. Instead, someone left dozens of jockstraps hanging from the ceiling tiles.

She was interviewed but refused to have the jocks removed and placed in the evidence room. Sally insisted they were good for business, and she would write names and numbers if someone claimed them.

"Bloody hell," Killian grunted. "Even in 2000, Sally was using the same excuse for not removing them."

"Well, it's all about that bottom line," Dylan pointed out. "You just want to make sure it's covered."

Killian shook his head and turned to the next report.

On the morning of December 12, calls came in from multiple places, reporting that someone had removed their flags and skivvies were flying high over their places of business.

The Beachside Inn - White boxers with fish.

Black-and-white striped boxers flew about the sheriff's department.

Swan Harbor General - White boxers with red crosses.

And on and on the list continued. Killian flipped through the next few pages, discovering that instead of stealing snowmen to display at the Gala, the snowmen all over town were sporting underwear.

And on the last page,

On December 26, the culprits were discovered when I was called to Sally's. I arrived expecting to find a different 'decoration.' Instead, Rupert and Lois Duncan, Madge and Jimmie Tanner, and others greeted me and explained why they did it.

Charges weren't filed. Case closed.

"No wonder Ernie told me the case was for me," Killian muttered. "I thought there was something odd about his comment."

Dylan laughed. "That sounds like Ernie. But how did you figure out who it was?"

"Liam suggested I try solving it differently," Killian explained. "I listened, watched, and realized Rupert and his gang were always in the middle of it."

"Maybe if I deputize them," Dylan murmured. "It would stop their shenanigans."

"Perhaps," Killian agreed. "Or maybe we see if we can figure out a way to make them feel useful."

"Like you had them helping when planning Emma's engagement?" Rusty suggested.

"Maybe," Killian nodded.

"Well, they're all heading to Florida to visit Ernie," Dylan stated. "So, we have a few months." Then, on his way out, he snatched another pastry.

Killian pushed back and propped his feet on the desk. "Think things will slow down for a few weeks?"

Rusty laughed. "This is Swan Harbor. What do you think?"

Terri Patterson's Home
December 30
12:00 p.m.

Harper was listening to Rachel talk about her business proposal while she tossed clothes into her suitcase. She'd just laid her favorite sleep shirt on the pile when Rachel was suddenly quiet.

"What?" Harper glanced from Eden back to Rachel. "Did you ask me a question I missed?"

"No," Rachel grumbled and removed the shirt. "I was horrified when you threw that old rag into your suitcase. Take it out."

Harper grabbed the shirt and held it in front of her. "What's wrong with it?"

"It's old," Eden replied.

"And has holes." Rachel pointed along the hem that was fraying.

"Plus," Eden tugged it away and threw it toward the trashcan. "It's not sexy."

"Why do I need sexy?" Then she noticed the expectant expressions on her friends' faces. "I'm not doing this so I can have sexy times with Aiden."

Eden communicated with only a raised brow.

"Really," Harper reiterated. "I'm an adult. Besides, if I wanted to spend the night, I wouldn't need permission."

"Okay." Rachel pushed the suitcase over and settled against the headboard. "Then explain what's going through your mind."

Harper searched for how to explain where her thoughts were coming from.

"You know I've told you, Aiden and I have this ability to communicate without words, right?"

"Yes," Eden nodded. "And that your mother and grandmother claim it's because your hearts are connected."

"Do you love Aiden?" asked Rachel quietly.

"Maybe?" Harper gave up trying to pack. "I thought I loved Joel, and look what happened. But when I kept 'hearing but not hearing' Aiden call me Angel, it touched something inside. I knew that if he ever said it out loud, it would shatter the bricks around my heart."

"But?" Eden pushed.

"It shattered ... most of them," Harper admitted. "Except every time he looks at me as if he's going to tell me he loves me, I freak. It feels like it's too much. And then I think about Clark."

Rachel frowned. "But isn't Clark, Aiden?"

"I believe so, yes."

"Then what's the problem?"

"Because if I think Aiden and Clark are the same person," Harper explained. "I'm giving my heart to only one man."

"And if Aiden is seeing you," Rachel guessed. "But in writing to someone else, he's not completely committed."

"Yes."

"Why don't you say something to him?" Eden suggested.

Harper groaned. "I've thought about it, but what do I say?"

"Well, that's easy," Eden pointed out. "You ask him if he's Clark."

"And if he's not?" Harper prompted.

"He's going to think you're nuts," added Rachel.

"Look," Harper grabbed her phone and pulled up the 'secret match' app. "Here's what I wrote.

> Clark,
>
> I'm heading to the place I've always wanted to visit. You can watch the sunrise over the Atlantic Ocean in the early morning. And in the evening, watch it sink into the Gulf. Meet me at sunset on December 31 at the southernmost point. We'll watch the sun fade and let it signify our new beginning.
>
> P.S. I'll be holding your favorite flower.
>
> Rosalind

Harper finished reading the note she'd sent and held her breath, waiting to hear her friends' responses.

"That's not bad," Eden said. "But how do you know Aiden will understand?"

"I don't know for sure," Harper admitted. "But I told him my parents had given me a trip to Key West for Christmas. Then I said I wanted to watch the sun come up on one side of the island and see it set on the other. I'm just hoping he'll remember that."

"What did he say when you told him you were going to be gone for New Year's Eve?" asked Eden.

Harper winced. "I kind of led him to believe the trip was for my family."

"Harper!" Eden exclaimed. "How could you?"

"I didn't want him to wonder why I wasn't inviting him."

"But you're inviting him," Rachel pointed out. "Just the Clark side of him."

Harper resumed her packing. "I want to know that Aiden has chosen me and that I'm the only woman on his mind."

"After my major faux pas with Cameron." Eden shuddered at the memory. "I can see that. But how do you know his favorite flower?"

Harper grinned and plucked her kitten out of the suitcase. "It's Mistletoe." She pointed to the sprig she'd tossed onto the dresser. "He told me the other night."

"Well, aren't you clever?" grinned Eden.

"I hope so." Harper pushed her suitcase aside. "Now, let's talk about something else. What was it Ava wanted you to do regarding your business?"

Rachel smiled. "She wants me to cut costs by finding a place to hold the classes without having a lease hanging over my head."

"How does she expect you to do that?" Eden questioned.

"She wanted me to talk to Tyler." Rachel grinned, and the smile on her face was one Harper hadn't seen in a while.

"About having the classes at his club?" Harper guessed.

"Yes!" Rachel exclaimed. "And so, I did…"

Sally's Diner
December 30
1:30 p.m.

Liam followed Killian into Sally's and got his first glimpse of the jocks hanging from the ceiling.

"How much longer do you think Sally's going to leave her decorations hanging?"

"Until Danny needs one," Killian quipped.

"Until they're all claimed," Sally corrected. "And none of them belongs to my husband."

Killian winced. "You don't think staring at them is a bit off-putting?"

Sally laughed. "No one notices them but you. Want a table?"

"We'll join Aiden." Liam nodded to the back of the diner.

"Do you need menus?"

"The usual," Liam replied, never taking his attention off Aiden.

"What's going on with Aiden?" Killian murmured.

"Woman trouble," Liam whispered. "I'd bet on it."

Aiden didn't look up until they pulled out chairs. "Liam, Killian, have a seat."

"We will, thanks," Liam smirked. "Looks like I arrived just in time."

"What?" Aiden gave him a blank stare.

"Come on, cuz." Liam tilted his head in disbelief. "Spill. You look like you've lost your best friend. What did Harper do?"

Aiden frowned. "She did nothing."

"Is that the problem?"

"Liam!" Killian exclaimed. "You don't just say …"

"If I'm going to help," Liam stated. "I need to know what's going on."

"Things are fine with Harper," Aiden explained. "Her parents bought her a trip to Key West, is all."

"And she didn't invite you?"

"No." Aiden flipped his phone around. "But Harper's not the problem. It's Rosalind."

It took Liam a second to remember he hadn't told Aiden that Rosalind was, in fact, Harper.

"You're still writing to Rosalind?"

"Tomorrow is supposed to be the end of the project," Aiden shared. "But for the past few days, when I hear from Rosalind, I wish it was from Harper."

"Then why are you still writing to her?" Liam asked conversationally.

Aiden glanced up, wearing a shocked expression. "I don't want to hurt her."

"He's right," Killian pointed out. "We told Hayden to break up with Peyton before asking out Katrina."

"And look how that ended up," Liam muttered. "So, does Rosalind want to meet you tomorrow?"

"She does." Aiden pushed his phone across the table. "I'm supposed to meet her somewhere at sunset. But bloody hell, I have no clue where she's suggesting we meet."

Liam pulled the phone close enough to read it. "You can watch the sunrise from the Atlantic Ocean in the early morning. And in the evening, watch it sink into the Gulf. Meet me at sunset on December 31 at the southernmost point. We'll watch the sun fade and let it signify our new beginning."

"It's certainly not in Swan Harbor," Killian retorted.

"There are very few places you can watch the sun rise out of the ocean," Liam replied. "Then watch it sink back into the Gulf."

"An island," Aiden tossed out. "But bloody hell, how am I to know which island?"

Liam thought about what Aiden had told him about Harper's trip. But how did he lead Aiden to come up with Key West as the answer to the riddle?

"Where does the sun sink into the Gulf?" Liam mused aloud.

"Sunsets?" Aiden repeated, and then as if something occurred to him, a pucker developed between his brows, and he grabbed his phone.

"What are you looking up?"

"The Gulf," Aiden muttered before suddenly proclaiming, "Bloody hell."

"What?" Liam waited, hoping all the pieces had clicked into place.

"Harper is Rosalind." Aiden grinned. "And by telling me, as Harper, where she was going, she knows I'm Clark."

"'Bout time you figured that out," Liam laughed. "So, what are you going to do?"

"What do you mean?" Aiden shrugged. "I'll just tell her I'm Clark, and I'll be waiting for her when she gets back."

"I have a better idea." Liam smiled. "One guaranteed to assure you catch the girl."

"Haven't I already caught the girl?"

"But my way will be so much more fun," Liam promised. "Here's what you're going to do."

TWENTY

The Florida Keys
December 31
12:00 p.m.

AFTER AN EARLY MORNING FLIGHT, HARPER LANDED AT MIAMI Airport, upgraded her rental car to a convertible, and jumped on the US-1. As she drove through Key Largo, Islamorada, and Marathon, the variety of colors had her fighting the desire to stop and sightsee. But time was of the essence, and if all went as planned, Aiden would meet her in Key West.

That he might not have understood the riddle wasn't something she wanted to focus on. Neither did she want to consider the possibility that Aiden wasn't Clark. Instead, she pushed any doubts away and concentrated on their meeting at sunset. Concentrated on their reunion growing closer with every mile.

When she drove onto the seven-mile bridge, the blue water stretched as far as the eye could see. Its beauty took her breath and her worries. And with each mile closer to Key West, a sense of peace seemed to settle over her. So much so she imagined hearing Aiden saying,

I'm on my way, Angel.

Once on Key West, Harper followed the US-1 around the island. She drove past the yacht club, a park, a cemetery and then took several side streets through the downtown area. On the one hand, that sense of peace remained, but on the other, as soon as she parked, the butterflies swarmed. *He's coming, he's coming*, she kept telling herself.

She was staying at Casa de la Esperanza, a Bed & Breakfast, in a beautiful three-story Victorian. Swaying palms and colorful gardens surrounded it. The southern-style porch sported several oversized rocking chairs and a hammock —a peaceful oasis.

"You must be Harper Taylor," a woman who appeared ageless greeted her. "I'm Vivi."

"I am," Harper laughed. "But how did you know?"

"That's an advantage of owning a small place," Vivi smiled. "I can get to know my guests. Besides, you're the only single woman checking in today."

"Your place is beautiful."

"Thank you." Vivi handed her several forms and the key to her room. "Do you need help with your luggage?"

Harper shook her head. "I'm good. Just point me to my room. I want to change and then go to the Hemingway House."

"Your room is right up those stairs." Vivi opened a map of Key West and showed her where they were. Then marked several spots on it. "Enjoy."

"Thanks, Vivi."

But as she carried her suitcase up to her room and changed into cooler clothes, the butterflies returned. This time, friends joined them.

Don't go there, she scolded herself. Just focus on the first time you see him at sunset and know you're the one he's chosen. And then imagine what you will say.

Could she do that, she wondered, stepping out onto the wide porch. Could she keep the negative thoughts at bay and focus only on the positive ones?

He's coming, he's coming, she kept thinking as she headed toward the Hemingway House.

Key West, Florida

December 31
2:00 p.m.

Aiden stared out the cab's window at the passing scenery as they drove away from the Key West airport. Buildings that were pink, blue, yellow, and green intermixed with glimpses of the water beyond. And more greenery than he'd seen in months.

"Here you are." The driver stopped in front of a pink Victorian home.

"Thanks, mate." Aiden handed the driver several bills and stepped out into a tropical oasis.

"Enjoy yourself." The driver beeped his horn as he drove off.

"Bloody hell." The heat had Aiden taking off his coat and folding up his shirt sleeves.

"Are you Aiden Jones?" A pleasant-looking woman called from the porch.

"Yes, ma'am." Aiden gave her a sheepish smile and ran up the stairs. "I was just admiring your home."

"She's a beauty, alright." The woman smiled. "I'm Vivi. Let's get you checked in as I'm sure you'd like to change into cooler clothing."

Aiden glanced down at his wool dress pants. "It is warmer down here than where I came from."

"Come in, come in." She waved him inside and, within a few minutes, handed him the key. "If there's anything you need, just let me know."

Aiden thought about asking her if Harper had checked in, but since she didn't know he was coming, he'd honor her wishes. Sunset was only a few hours away.

His room was on the second floor, and as he climbed the stairs, he imagined he could smell her perfume. Had she passed this way recently? Or was he just being fanciful?

Once he'd exchanged his cold-weather clothes for jeans and an old T-shirt, Aiden put on his sunglasses and started walking.

He strolled down Duval Street past a beautiful old church before crossing over to Whitehead Street. Then something had him buying a ticket and jumping on the Conch Train Tour. It would take him around downtown Key West and help him pass the time.

The train drove past the Key West Aquarium, where several people got off and others got on. The driver pointed out Mallory Square, which he recommended for watching sunsets, and then turned onto Whitehead Street.

"You'll see the Hemingway House up ahead," their driver announced.

Key West, Florida
December 31
3:30 p.m.

The Hemingway House, a historical landmark, was full of beautiful furniture, interesting architecture, and cats. The grounds were lush and peaceful, but each time Harper passed a couple, she wished Aiden were with her. Every time she saw something that excited her, she wanted to tell Aiden. When she caught herself taking a picture to send him, she finally gave up. If all went as planned, they would return—together.

Harper left the Hemingway House just in time to see the Conch Train Tour pass by. Goosebumps raced across her skin, her heart rate kicked up a few beats, and the word *Angel* floated in the air.

Her breath caught, and her gaze followed the train as it disappeared. With time to waste, she meandered along Whitehead Street, then crossed back onto Duval. Before she'd gotten far, an outdoor market captured her attention.

Duval Village boasted an assortment of vendors, each proclaiming they had what she wanted. She'd only taken a step into the entryway when suddenly the air changed.

Angel.

The word sent a chill running down her back. Harper stopped and glanced over her shoulder. But other than the Conch Train and several tourists, she saw nothing out of the ordinary.

Aiden?

When he didn't answer, she put the words, *He's coming* back on silent repeat, and walked into the marketplace.

A floppy straw hat captured her attention in one place. A few colorful T-shirts in another.

I love you, Angel.

She closed her eyes and allowed the words to wash over her.

"Miss, are you okay?"

Harper opened her eyes to find an older gentleman watching her, a concerned look on his face. "I'm fine. I just …"

"Was taking in the island's essence?"

"Something like that," Harper agreed.

The older man held out a small figure made of seashells. "Here's a gift for you."

Harper looked into his eyes, and the kindness staring back at her had her reaching for the figure. "It's an angel."

"Yes." He smiled. "It fits you."

"Let me pay—" she began before he held up his hand.

"It's yours." He took it back, carefully wrapped it, and placed it into a bag. "A gift."

"Thank you. The island is beautiful."

"It is." He nodded. "Enjoy your stay."

Harper smiled and wandered away, but the feeling of being watched followed her from place to place. Was she being paranoid? She stopped to admire some seashell jewelry and casually glanced around.

You're my Angel.

Aiden jumped back and almost knocked over a display.

"Whoa, young fella."

He looked over his shoulder into the unlined face of a woman who could have been forty or eighty. "I'm sorry, ma'am. I was …"

"Trying to stay hidden from your girl," she stated matter-of-factly.

"How?"

"I've been watching you," she chuckled. "Nice touch to buy that figurine for her, but to have George give it to her as a gift."

Aiden glanced toward George's booth. "How?"

"I've been around a long time." She shrugged. "Plus, there are some things I just know."

He thought about pushing for more but was afraid he was going to lose

Harper. "It was nice meeting you." Aiden had taken a couple of steps when the woman hooked her arm through his and halted his progress.

"You're going to meet her at sunset," she proclaimed, rendering him speechless. "While you love her, you're not sure she's ready for the next step."

Aiden opened his mouth to respond, but couldn't come up with anything to say.

She led him to a booth, and after waving her hand over a tray of rings, placed a pinkish one in his palm. "Coral is much like love. It takes time and work to form. But once created, if cared for, can last forever. Place this ring on your girl as your promise to her. Be happy." Then she closed his fingers around the ring and kissed it.

While she held his hand the whole time, Aiden kept feeling the need to say something, but it seemed like his lips and tongue were frozen.

When she let go, he glanced up to say thank you. Except she was gone. Slowly, he opened his palm, and there lay the ring. A promise, he couldn't help but think, tucking it into his pocket.

By the time he'd gathered his wits, Harper was gone. He knew there were several souvenirs he needed to buy, but waited. They would come back later ... together.

Key West, Florida
December 31
4:30 p.m.

With a little over an hour until sunset, Harper started toward her destination. The southernmost point of the continental United States is where Whitehead Street meets South Street. With every step she took, taking her closer to her meeting place, the bigger the crowds. It had her wondering if she'd even be able to see him.

But if not, won't you be able to hear him?

Would she, though?

Harper stopped in the doorway of a store to get her emotions under control. She took several fortifying breaths, then peered around the door and searched for the man who'd somehow come to hold her heart. Was she ready to tell him? But more importantly, was what she'd seen in his eyes—love?

Angel.

She heard his call before she saw him on the opposite side of the street. He'd changed, just as she had. He stood straighter and looked her in the eye, letting her see what he was thinking ... and feeling. Aiden had become much more of a Superman than a Clark.

When he stopped and looked in the window of a store, she had to wonder what he saw. He was wearing jeans, an old t-shirt, and sunglasses, something she couldn't ever imagine him wearing at home. Then he brushed back his hair and angled toward the buoy, wearing a crooked smile. And just like always, her heart flipped.

Aiden.

His smile grew, her pulse raced, and pulling the sprig of mistletoe from her bag, she stepped away from her hiding place.

Harper crossed the street, her steps confident, and while a part of her wanted to jump into his arms, she hesitated.

"You came," she murmured, stopping in front of him. Then, he smiled at her in such a way the spit dried in her mouth.

"Did you doubt for even a minute I wouldn't?"

Harper dropped her gaze to the center of his chest. "I wanted—"

"—To make sure I would choose you," he replied.

"How?"

"I don't know. I just do."

"Did you always know it was me?"

Aiden laughed. "Not at all. But many times, Rosalind and Harper merged in my head."

"That was exactly what happened to me," Harper admitted. "Suddenly, when I read a note from Clark, I heard *you* saying the words. Or when *you* said or did something, I imagined Clark saying or doing it. Is that why you wouldn't play the piano for me?"

Aiden blushed. "No. I've always felt self-conscious when I play for people." He cupped her face. "But maybe you can persuade me to play something for you."

"Oh, really?"

"Yes, really." His smile grew. "But it might cost you."

Harper's gaze dropped to his lips, and the mistletoe in her hand begged to be used. Just not yet.

"Is the price negotiable?"

Aiden's eyes flared. "I'm pretty sure we can work something out."

"I hope so." Harper swallowed and then brought up a previously unmentioned topic. "How long do you plan to stay?"

He frowned, she was sure, trying to read where she was taking the conversation. "In Key West ... or in Maine?

"Maine."

Her question had temporarily taken him aback, but then he figured out what she was asking. Which meant he mattered to her, causing him to relax and let go of the tension he'd been carrying.

"Are you asking if I plan to go back to England?"

"Yes," she murmured, refusing to meet his gaze.

"Would it matter?"

"I," then she hesitated, and slowly lifted her gaze. "Maybe."

Aiden brushed his thumb over her bottom lip. "Well, that all depends on a few things."

"Such as?"

He forced his gaze off her bottom lip, and back up to meet hers. "A job for one. After all, my position is a visiting line."

"I sense a but ..."

"But I was just informed it was being turned into a permanent one, and they want me to apply."

"What, what will help you determine whether to do so?"

"I think you know."

"Maybe I do." Harper paused, and he couldn't help but wonder what she was going to say. "You said it depended on a few things. What else?"

Aiden's stomach tied itself into knots as he jumped to an area he hoped she was ready for.

"In Swan Harbor, I've found a mystery surrounding an ancestor of mine," he began. "I've also found family. And just like Finn reminded Ava the other night, sometimes it feels that a force more powerful than any of us is leading us to something."

"Why do you think that?"

"Think about it," he responded. "What were the chances that Elsa and Liam would meet, get married, and end up in Swan Harbor? Or Emma and Killian? Or us."

Harper's eyes flared and dropped again, and he wanted nothing more than to kiss the fear off her face. He gently tilted up her chin. "Angel, remember that night you told me you were interested in my research?"

"Yes."

"That was the first time any woman I'd dated cared about my interests."

She gave him an impish smile. "Well, obviously, you've been dating the wrong women."

"Obviously," he went on. "And then your grandmother said, 'wouldn't it be a kicker if—?'"

"—You found something connecting my family to Ian Jones," she finished.

"I did." Aiden pulled out his phone and offered it to her. "Would you like to read it?"

She rolled her eyes. "You know the answer to that question."

"The librarian found a journal that belonged to a doctor, Thomas Williams," he explained. "Thomas arrived at his office in July 1717 and found one of your ancestors, Henry Patterson, waiting for him. This is what Henry told the doctor."

I first met the Professor in April 1717, when his ship, El corazón del Rubí, hobbled into the dock. The ship had hit some bad weather and needed several repairs. For weeks, I worked on the vessel, expecting the Captain to be elsewhere. But day after day, he worked by my side, and we became friends. Yet, I knew him only as the Professor or the Captain. All that summer, the Captain and his crew would come and go. Most of the time, I didn't know when he'd return, but when he did, we'd meet at the tavern for a drink or two.

And then yesterday, I was at the docks, and his ship was there, which surprised me. Not thinking anything of it, I boarded the ship and saw drops of blood, and found the Captain in his cabin. I'm not sure how long he'd been there, but I asked him what had happened. He told me he'd been taking a walk and had rescued a damsel in distress.

He'd become my friend, and I didn't want him to die, so I patched him up as best I could. And then brought him here. He barely made it before he passed out. But his last words to me were, "Ian. My name is Ian."

⁂

The entire time he'd been reading, the lump in Harper's throat had grown until she felt a tear run down her cheek.

Aiden cupped her face and swept the tears away. "Where did those come from?"

"I'm not sure. But you're right about feeling as if we're being guided by a force stronger than any of us." She brushed her hand down the front of his shirt. "And it all started with a wink."

He chuckled. "A wink?"

"Yes." Harper nodded. "The night of the Christmas tree lighting, you winked, and something inside of me changed."

"We've both changed." Aiden whispered a kiss across her cheek. "Which is why wherever the future leads me, I hope you're by my side."

"I ..." Before she could say anything, Aiden kissed her. It was a kiss that shut her up, but just wasn't long enough for her to take part.

"Let me finish."

"Okay."

"I love you."

Harper's breath hitched, and she wanted nothing more than to jump into his arms. Except, the look on his face said he wasn't done.

He pulled a ring from his pocket, and her heart raced. "I'm not proposing,

Angel. But the woman who gave me this said coral is like love. That it takes work to create and work for it to last. This is my promise, that I will be patient and wait for you."

"Oh, Aiden," Harper sighed. "I do love you. I'm just not ready ..."

"I can be patient."

But the question was, could she?

"May I?"

Aiden slipped the ring onto her finger and gently kissed her hand. Then, he tugged her against his side, so they both were looking out at the sunset.

"Wow."

Slowly, the sun turned orange as it lowered into the water and painted everything around it gold.

"I feel like I'm being given a gift."

"You, Angel," Aiden murmured. "You're my gift."

"Oh, Aiden." Harper lifted the mistletoe and held it above her head. "Kiss me."

"My pleasure."

When their lips touched, her heart was finally whole.

EPILOGUE

Swan Harbor Vet Hospital
January 14
2:00 p.m.

EMMA TOOK OUT THE PB&J SHE'D THROWN TOGETHER AT THE last minute and looked over the assignment her mother had given her. With only four weeks until the wedding, her daily tasks had become more time-consuming.

She took a bite, and while she chewed, contemplated the first thing on the list.

1) Decide on colors!

February 14 was Valentine's Day, and nothing said love more than red. However, her phone rang before she could text her mother her choice.

"Good afternoon, Jack," Emma answered. "Is everything okay with Bandit?"

"Bandit is fine," Jack's concerned voice came across the line. "It's Jonesy."

Of course, it was, she thought. "You know my stipulations regarding Jonesy."

"But this is different, Emma," Jack told her quietly. "He's losing all hope."

Emma looked at her sandwich and suddenly couldn't stomach another bite.

"I don't know what you want me to do. Finn and my mom are married. So are Elsa and Liam. Aiden and Harper are a couple, and Killian and I are getting married in a month."

"I'm not sure Jonesy is going to last a month," Jack cried. "But I think I found a place where he can be free ... and safe."

"Oh, really? Where?"

"I'll send you a picture and the directions," Jack said cryptically. "Can you meet me there?"

"Okay, Jack," Emma sighed. "Send me the directions."

The picture of Jonesy came through, and Emma had to agree. He didn't look well. Then the text arrived with Jack's solution, and she had to wonder what he was thinking.

She threw away her sandwich and put in a call to the wild bird organization. If needed, they could help capture Jonesy and either care for or transfer the swan. With that done, she readied to face the elements.

"Sadie," Emma addressed her office manager on her way out. "Can you reschedule the rest of today's appointments?"

"Sure," Sadie frowned, "but what's going on?"

"Jonesy," Emma sighed. "He's not doing well, and Jack thinks if we '*free*' him, that will make a difference."

"But the tone of your voice says you don't agree."

"Who knows?" Emma pulled up the picture and showed Sadie. "He doesn't look good, does he?"

"No," Sadie agreed. "Poor Jonesy."

"Poor Jack," Emma added. "He's been caring for that swan for fifty years. If something happened to him ..."

Sadie winced. "Is that your way of saying Jonesy might die?"

"Swans rarely live as long as Jonesy has," Emma admitted. "I worry."

"If Jonesy dies, what happens to Swan Harbor?"

Emma shrugged, the weight of caring for Jonesy suddenly feeling heavier than usual. "I'm going to take the van to meet Jack. It's better in this weather."

"Good luck." Sadie glanced out the window. "Remember, we're under a heavy snow warning."

Emma looked up at the gray sky as she climbed into the van and waited for it to warm up. If she were lucky, the trip would be quick, and she'd be home before the snow started.

She was meeting Jack at Lover's Cove, a grouping of rocks and a shallow cave, close to her clinic. The legend surrounding the cove always brought a smile to her face. It stated that if a couple made love there, they would be engaged before the end of the year. Worked for her, she thought, pulling into the parking lot.

"You made excellent time, Emma." Jack smiled as soon as she climbed from the van.

"That's because it's supposed to snow, and people have been told to stay in," she pointed out.

"Pfft," Jack laughed. "It's not here yet, is it? But come. Let me show you what I found."

He led her across the parking lot, down a path, and around a set of boulders that protected the cove. Behind them was the shallow cave where recently her mother and Finn had found Paris and her puppies.

"What did you say I needed to find before setting Jonesy free?" Jack asked as soon as they were in the cave.

"That you needed to find shelter with warm water for Jonesy," she repeated what she'd said several weeks previously.

"You found Hope's journal in this cave," Jack reminded her. "It should provide plenty of shelter for Jonesy."

"Okay," Emma agreed. "But the water in the cove is shallow and freezes. How would he be able to find food?"

"You're right. Usually, the water does freeze." Jack directed her to follow him to the other corner of the cave. "But look."

Emma stepped to the front of the cave and had to blink several times. "What happened?"

Beyond the mouth of the cave, a pool had formed, perfect for Jonesy to swim and feed in. And with the boulders in front, and the cave behind, they would protect him from the weather.

"Why isn't the water frozen, Jack?" Emma asked. "It is on the other side of the rocks."

"Feel it."

Emma studied him before pulling off her glove to feel the water. "It's cold but not too cold."

"I checked it earlier today," Jack answered, wearing a satisfied smile. "It was 60 degrees."

"But how?"

"There are hot springs up in the hills that surround Swan Harbor." Jack shrugged. "If I had to guess, I'd say our little explosion caused a crack."

"Oh, wow," Emma laughed. "Mom asked if I thought you would find a place, and I told her it wouldn't happen without a little help."

"You know how Swan Harbor is," Jack pointed to the little pond. "We get what we need when it's time. When can we move him?"

"I called the organization that helped last time. Once this storm passes, we'll bring them in."

He said nothing more on the way back to their cars.

"Emma," Jack called before she'd climbed into her van. "Have you and Killian read Hope and Ian's journals?"

"We looked at them," she hedged. "But with the holidays and all ..."

"Read them," Jack implored. "I don't want to lose you too."

Emma nodded, and as she pulled out of the parking lot, she had to keep blinking back tears. While Jack had said little, he'd still made her feel guilty.

When she returned to the clinic, Killian was waiting. "What are you doing home?"

"Dylan sent me home early in case I'm needed to help after the storm." He tugged her down onto the old sofa and nuzzled her cheek. "You're cold. Where have you been?"

"Lover's Cove."

"Should I be jealous?"

She laughed and quickly shared why she'd been there. "Jack found a section of the water that's warm enough for Jonesy."

"I'll tell Gray to have the engineers check the stability in the area."

"Probably a good idea," she agreed.

"What is it, Doc?"

"Jack wants us to read the journals. He said he doesn't want to lose me."

"I don't want to lose you either." Killian hugged her. "Where are the journals?"

Emma pointed to a filing cabinet where she'd laid them, thinking they'd look at them someday.

"You don't want to read Hope's, do you?" He crossed the room to get Ian's.

"It makes me sad," Emma admitted. "Before I only knew about my grandmother ..."

"And now, it's Grace, Rose, Margaret, and Ruth Prince," he finished.

"And so many more."

Killian sat down, opened the journal, and flipped through several pages. "Bloody hell."

"What is it?"

"The date is May 1717."

As I exited the tavern, a vision crossed my path. Her coppery tresses hung halfway down her back, and she was wearing a gown as yellow as the sun on a spring morning ...

Ancient secrets. Star-crossed lovers. The future of Swan Harbor at stake. Download a copy of **Hope, Hearts & Forever,** *and see if Swan Harbor's can be saved.*
https://books2read.com/HopeHeartsForever

Quick Author's Note:

Sometimes a story idea pops into my head, and I have zero idea where it will go. This story was just there, and so far, it's makes me smile every time I read it. I hope that it made you smile at least once or twice.

Harper & Aiden were a fun couple, and you haven't seen the last of them. Eden's Book is #9 - *The Forgiveness of Love* and Rachel's is #11 *A Christmas Love Song.* I loved how both turned out.

The Key West B&B first showed up in From Darkness into Love, and will show up again - in fact, it turns out the Vivi and her husband are related to some of Swan Harbor's residents. I think you'll be surprised.

Next up is the Hope story's conclusion. It's a balance between the past and present.

I think you'll find that Aiden and Harper's song is appropriate. It is *Can You Read My Mind* by **Maureen McGovern.**

Swan Harbor's Hope Playlist.

https://sophiebartow.com/swan-harbors-hope-story-playlist/

Moving right along ...

If you are new to the Swan Harbor series and enjoyed my writing style, sign up for my newsletter. Keep an eye out for a bonus scene to this book. Any specific scene you would like to see?

My newsletters have news about free books and what's coming to Swan Harbor. I've even been known to toss in one or two of my favorite recipes, pet pictures and opinions.

If you are already a member of my newsletter, you should have the secret link to download all the bonus material. If not, just click below, and enjoy reading Aiden & Harper's Sleigh Ride.

The Sleigh Ride.

https://www.subscribepage.com/swan-harbor_bonus_scenes

Thanks for hanging with me this long.
Until next time,
Sophie

P.S.

In Book 6, **Hope, Hearts & Forever,** you finally get to see where the hope story is leading. This book is told in a dual timeline. In the present day, Emma, Killian, and the rest of their families have to put together the clues to save hope. And in the past, 1717-1720, Hope and Ian's story is told. Plus, you find out 'why' the Swan and Prince women die before age 45.

Look for **Hope, Hearts & Forever at your favorite bookstore today.**

HOPE, HEARTS & FOREVER
SWAN HARBOR'S HOPE STORY BOOK 5

Can the Past Save the Present?
Or is Hope Doomed?

Emma Foster and Killian Reade have finally set a date for their wedding. But as their special day draws near and the fate of Jonesy and his hope rests in their hands, will they really be able to say, "I do"?

For generations, a Spanish galleon has been the centerpiece in Swan Harbor. It belonged to a pirate who had loved and lost Hope Prince. With their journals revealed and Jonesy fading, it becomes a race against time to reunite the star-crossed lovers and keep hope alive.

Join Emma, Killian, Captain Jack, and the rest of their families as they learn the love story of Ian Jones and Hope Prince. As they follow in the lovers' footsteps, will they find the answers they're searching for?

Can Jonesy, the embodiment of Swan Harbor's hope, be saved? Or is the town's hope destined to fade away?

*A pirate's vow. A swan's song. A town's destiny on the line. Start reading **Hope, Hearts & Forever** now—because some promises can't be broken, and some destinies can't be denied.*

Hope & Hearts Series
Without hope, there would be no happy endings.

FROM DARKNESS INTO LOVE

KITTENS, PUPPIES & LOVE

BROTHERS, HOPE & HEARTS

KISSES, FAMILY & HOPE

A TREE, MISTLETOE & A SUNSET

HOPE, HEARTS & FOREVER

THE MEMORY OF LOVE

THE INNOCENCE OF LOVE

THE FORGIVENESS OF LOVE

THE POWER OF LOVE

THE CHRISTMAS LOVE SONG

THE KISS OF LOVE

THE LESSONS OF LOVE

THE HEART OF LOVE

THE JOURNEY TO LOVE

Bonus Hope & Hearts

CYGNETS & DREAMS

Hope & Hearts Historical Novellas

GUIDED BY LIGHT - 1952

GUIDED BY HEART - 1964

GUIDED BY LOVE - 1969

WELCOME TO SWAN HARBOR- 1979

FINDING HER LOST HEART- 1983/1990

GUIDED BY A KISS - 1995

Mystical Waters Canyon
Where hearts can be heard.

WHISPERS OF LUCK

WHISPERS OF THE PAST

October 31, 2025

WHISPERS OF A MIRACLE

December 2025

WHISPERS OF LOVE

February 2026

Love's Promises Series
A Swan Harbor Spinoff

THE PROMISE OF HOME - Magnet

THE PROMISE OF TOMORROW

THE PROMISE TO DANCE

coming in summer 2026

ABOUT THE AUTHOR

Sophie crafts small-town mystery romances that weave intricate plots with richly developed characters. Her female leads are intelligent, resourceful, and resilient, while her male characters, often stubborn, exude sexiness, wit, and a protective nature. She delights in building slow-burn romances, savoring the tension and delaying that first kiss for as long as possible. No matter the trope, every story she writes has a happy ending.

After a fulfilling 30-plus-year career as a speech-language pathologist, working with adult post-stroke and Parkinson's patients, she is enjoying her new journey. With their four children spread out, Sophie and her husband live in South Florida. They share their home with a pampered cat named Irma.

You can find her on her website: **https://sophiebartow.com/***Sophiexo*

facebook.com/SmallTownAuthorSophieBartow

x.com/SophieBartow

instagram.com/sophiebartow

goodreads.com/sophiebartow

bookbub.com/profile/sophie-bartow

pinterest.com/SophieBartow